SAM MILLAR

THE BESPOKE HITMAN

BRANDON

First published 2018 by Brandon
An imprint of The O'Brien Press Ltd
12 Terenure Road East, Rathgar,
Dublin 6, D06 HD27, Ireland.
Tel: +353 1 4923333; Fax: +353 1 4922777
E-mail: books@obrien.ie.
Website: www.obrien.ie
The O'Brien Press is a member of Publishing Ireland.

ISBN: 978-1-78849-006-1

1 3 5 7 6 4 2
18 20 22 21 19

Printed and bound by CPI Group (UK) Ltd, Croydon, CR0 4YY
The paper used in this book is produced using pulp from managed forests.

Published in:
DUBLIN
UNESCO
City of Literature

LOTTERY FUNDED

THE
BESPOKE
HITMAN

'A complex crime noir story balanced with
Millar's legendary dark humor and fast-paced plotting.'
Jon Land, *New York Times* best-selling author

'Hold on to your seats. You're in for
the ride of your life with The Bespoke Hitman.'
Michael Lipkin, *Noir Journal*, USA

Winner of many awards, including the Brian Moore Award for Short Stories, and the Aisling Award for Art and Culture, Sam Millar is the author of highly acclaimed crime novels, several of which have sold internationally. He has also written a bestselling memoir, *On the Brinks*.

'Millar's words will mesmerize you. He is like a poet of darkness ...'

Village Voice, New York

Also by Sam Millar

Fiction
The Darkness of Bones
Dark Souls
The Redemption Factory
Black's Creek

Karl Kane novels
Bloodstorm
The Dark Place
Dead of Winter
Past Darkness

Memoir
On the Brinks

Play
Brothers in Arms

Recipient *Golden Balais d'or* for Best Crime Book of 2013–14
Recipient *Trophées 813, du meilleur roman*
Le Monde's prestigious Top Twenty Thrillers for 2013-2014
    for *Bloodstorm: A Karl Kane Novel*

www.millarcrime.com

DEDICATION

For My Best Russian Friend, Olga Mamonova

ACKNOWLEDGEMENTS

Sincere thanks to the hardworking team at O'Brien Press, for all the belief and encouragement.

Prologue

The gods envy us. They envy us because we're mortal,
because any moment might be our last.
Everything is more beautiful because we're doomed.

Homer, *The Iliad*

Night. When gods slumber and demons plot. Stephen Garland opened his eyes in the bedroom of his north Belfast home. Something had interrupted his sleep, but he wasn't quite sure what. Turning onto his back, he fine-tuned his eyes to the darkness, searching for some unknown entity lurking there. Shadows were gathering, *like puddles of boneless skin.*

'Stephen …? What … what's wrong?' His wife's voice was slightly slurred with tiredness and lingering Havana Club rum.

'Oh … nothing, Grace. Can't sleep. I'm just going to grab a cig.'

'I really wish you wouldn't smoke in bed. It's dangerous.'

'So is being a cop.' He laughed softly.

'Don't be sarcastic.'

'Go back to sleep, love.' He tenderly kissed the top of her head. 'I'll make it quick – *and* safe.'

A small time later, her soft snoring started up again, like an asthmatic cat.

Reaching over to the bedside table, Stephen craned his Ronson lighter and a packet of Park Drive. Apprehending a cig from the packet, he balanced it on the ledge of his lips. Got comfortable. Fired up the lighter's miniature inferno and granted life to the tobacco.

Releasing a prayer of smoke from his nostrils, he sighed with satisfaction.

'Ah ... nice ...'

About to click the flame dead, Stephen saw him standing there in the godless gloom, face expressionless, splintered off from normality like Francis Bacon's 'Head of a Man, No.1'.

'What the ... you scared the hell out of –' Stephen's voice suddenly became a whisper. '*What ... what're you doing with my service revolver, son?*'

The eleven-year-old stood there in the dark, pointing the gun straight at Stephen's face. The gun looked ridiculously large and vulgar in the two half-curled fists.

'*Please ... son, put the gun down before an accident happens ... someone gets hurt. You ... you don't want to upset your mother, do you ... seeing you playing with a gun?*'

The boy's small thumbs began awkwardly pulling back on the weapon's reluctant hammer, the sound filling the room like a bleached bone being snapped.

Stephen flinched visibly, squirming like a trapped rat.

The boy began to squeeze the trigger, eyes filled with concentration and purpose.

'Please, son ... don't do –'

The bullet hit hard, slicing off a good portion of Stephen's face, slamming him violently against the headboard. The boy fired again, this time hitting his mother smack in the philtrum, just above the upper lip. She moaned something incoherent, then went quiet. Deadly quiet.

The stench of burnt gunpowder began engulfing the room, expunging the remnants of his mother's expensive perfume from this evening's dinner-dance at the police social club.

Originally, he had planned to kill them earlier that afternoon, when they were naked, fucking and howling like filthy animals in heat, on top of the bed. That was when he had tiptoed to the slit in the bedroom door, watching her sucking greedily on him.

The sight made him seethe with anger and disgust, but also caused a strange stirring in his groin. Something forbidden and dangerous had occurred, and it perplexed him, his heart beating jaggedly in his ears. Eventually, he backed away from the door. A clearer mind, a shift in the time frame, would make for a better opportunity.

Tonight.

Tonight, waiting for them as they returned home in the dark, drunkenly giggling and snorting like Victorian villains, hiding a sinister secret.

A very sinister secret, indeed.

Unfortunately for them, he had known their sinister secret for a very long time.

A very long time, indeed.

Outside the charming detached house, the night was an army of soulless old men in rags. Filthy rain drummed hard against the windows, like nails being hammered into a coffin. *Or two.* It was the only sound now, in a moment where boundaries had been torn and discarded, where power dynamics had been run through a mincer.

For a long time, he stood in this bedroom of carnage, simply listening as the drumbeat of the rain and the echo of his heart fused into one. He stared at the gun in his hand, as if seeing it for the first time, a look of awe awakening on his young face.

At length, he walked over to the parental bed, gazing down with wonderment and delight upon his newly formed creation of destruction and murder.

A shocking crimson was quickly pooling on the cloud-white duvet. Above him, the pillows' bloody goose feathers floated in slow motion. It resembled a Christmas snow-globe, all snow and spreading poinsettias – or discarded entrails on a butcher's slaughter-block of pre-feast.

The impacts had been catastrophic, the faces now no more than a spongy mush of blood and bones. More akin to *papier-mâché* than flesh. It was a bigger mess than he had anticipated, but that didn't diminish the euphoria tingling the stepping-stones of his spine.

Wanting to preserve the detail in his memory, he bent into the scene, exploring with eager eyes. Grace's face – what remained of it – appeared peaceful. In contrast, Stephen's had a grimace of horror etched in his left eye, the right eye no longer existing.

A bloody air bubble protruded from Stephen's left nostril, and the boy now watched in fascination as the bubble ballooned in and out, a life of its own born from a dead man's breath. He could see his own face captured in the bloody sphere, distorted beyond anything human.

Smiling, he reached and popped the bloody bubble with the gun's barrel. Then, disentangling his fingers from the trigger-guard, the gun fell with a dull thud on the plush carpet. The heavenly release of heavy metal made his hands and soul feel light, cleansed of all earthly burdens and guilt.

Bizarrely, Stephen's smothering cigarette remained jammed between victory-salute fingers, releasing tiny plumes of vapour into the air. The boy eased the cigarette out from the dead fingers, careful not to tear its tobacco-filled belly. He studied its thin, pale body – speckled with a gathering of blood-splatter – as an entomologist would study a newly discovered insect.

Bringing the cigarette to his mouth, he sucked hard, listening to the paper and tobacco crackle and hiss. Allowed the smoke to snake inside his mouth for a few seconds, before placing the cigarette back between the 'V' in Stephen's fingers.

He'd been wrong: the blood didn't alter the taste of the tobacco in the slightest.

Content with the nightmare he had orchestrated, he returned to his room, sprawling out on the bed, arms outstretched in nail-less crucifixion.

He listened to his heart. Its rhythm now normal. A metronome of calmness. Everything in the world was good again. The way it was meant to be from the beginning. Before darkness had come, suffocating the light out of him.

From beneath the pillow, he removed the comic book he had abandoned for the last hour, as he carried out the plan of a lifetime. Or deathtime.

He smiled at his own pun, then turned back to re-reading *Fantastic Fabulous Fables #1*, the seminal issue featuring the first appearance of the Dark Avenger and his winged steed, Mercury.

He touched the comic tenderly. It had become a sacred icon, a talisman, keeping the demons at bay on this most unholy of devilish nights.

'I told you I'd do it, didn't I?' he whispered reverently, voice filled with admiration. The Dark Avenger smiled out at him from a splash page.

The Devil may well have been at play tonight in this house of Hell, but the boy was smiling like a Heavenly Seraph touched by the hand of a miscreant God. Not only did he have the smile of an Angel, he looked like one:

Lucifer.

Chapter One

Halloween. Spooky night-lights flickering inside Belfast City Hall, like melting candles of great expectations on Miss Havisham's decayed wedding cake of betrayal.

The oppressive, heavy rain – having commenced with a vengeance in the early morning – was still going strong, cascading off the majestic roof and onto the impressive building's saturated lawn. People attired in every conceivable fancy-dress costume were flooding the streets along with the rain.

Directly facing City Hall, a nondescript, rust-speckled van was parked in a side street, sandwiched between two burly construction lorries and four over-stuffed rubbish skips.

Three associates – Charlie Madden, Jim McCabe and Brian Ross – waited patiently in the van, semi-attired in wolf costumes, for what they hoped would be the biggest payday of their lives: tax-free money. Bags of it.

'Never stops pissing down in this god-awful place, and those thieving bastards in Stormont have the brass neck to try and charge us for water!' Charlie, the oldest of the three, was grumbling, glancing up at the filthy sky from the back window of the van. A Colt Anaconda .44 Magnum rested on his lap, like a beloved, peacefully snoozing pet reptile. 'They'd tax a fart, if they'd get away with it. Fucking politicians and fucking rain, I fucking hate them both.'

'Stop whingeing about the rain. This is perfect weather,' Brian, the youngest, enthused. A Beretta Px4 Storm semi-automatic pistol lurked to the right of him. He touched the gun tenderly, like an extension of himself. 'The rain's a good friend on a night like this – especially when you've a Storm on your side.'

Leader of the motley crew, Jim McCabe, lit another cigar – his third in the last hour. Glanced at his watch. Puffed on the cigar, before popping two heavy-duty black-market painkillers in his mouth, dry-swallowing them.

He had to be careful of overdosing – it could cause drowsiness, which was the last thing he needed tonight – but this merciless bastard of a toothache was killing him. He would just have to brace himself, and go to see a dentist. Jim shuddered at the thought. He'd rather rob a bank any day of the week than face one of those drill-wielding sadists.

'Do you have to smoke so many of those filthy things in the van?' Charlie grumbled, waving away the cigar smoke curling about his face. 'I can hardly breathe.'

Ignoring Charlie, Jim continued massaging the side of his mouth, all the while puffing away at the cigar.

'No need to be nervous, Charlie.' Brian grinned. 'This'll all be over soon.'

'Nervous? Me? Ha!' Charlie harrumphed. 'I was doing banks when you were still doing your nappies.'

'That is abso-fucking-lutely the most philosophical thing you've ever said, Mister Master Villain.'

'And you did what? Six months in prison for stealing comics! Big-time crook, you are not.'

'Considering the rare comics in question were worth over ninety thousand quid, and I was out in six weeks for good behaviour, I think I did all right. Now, your last job, in comparison, netted you what?'

'Drop it.' Charlie bristled. His voice now had the needle.

'Oh, that's right, a whopping eight hundred quid, *and* three years in prison for your troubles!'

'Damn cigars.' Charlie did another fly-swat into the air.

'Have a bit of sympathy for Jim,' Brian cut in. 'Can't you see he's in pain with a rotten tooth the size of a Rolo?'

'He'll get no sympathy from me. Should look after his teeth, like I do.' Charlie smiled a set of discoloured dentures.

'You know he's terrified of the dentist, poor wee thing. Isn't that right, Jim?'

Ignoring the wind-up, Jim continued rubbing the offending area.

'Did you know, Charlie, that Jim's favourite film of all time is *Marathon Man*.'

'Here we go again,' Charlie sighed. 'More bloody movie quotes.'

'Remember sadistic Doctor Szell, played brilliantly by Laurence Olivier, that scene where he tortures Dustin Hoffman by drilling his teeth? *I'm not going into that cavity. That nerve's already dying. A live, freshly-cut nerve is infinitely more sensitive. So, I'll just drill into a healthy tooth until I reach the pulp.*"

Charlie shuddered, then nodded. 'Jesus, I hated watching that part. I had to turn the volume down on the TV and look away.'

'*Zzzzzzzzzzzzzzzzzhhhhhssssssssssssssssssssssss.*' Brian made a drilling sound through clenched teeth.

'Hit it on the head,' Jim commanded coldly. 'I'm not in the mood right now.'

'Is it time, Jim?' Charlie glanced out the window, again. 'All this waiting is beginning to melt my head. It's sweltering inside this bloody costume.'

'We're *all* sweltering. Timing has to be perfect. Another fifteen minutes or so should do it.'

'How about a quick movie quiz, Charlie, before we go visiting for trick-or-treats?' Brian said. 'Kill a bit of time, if nothing else.'

'Okay. Hit me with something.'

'Name all of *The Magnificent Seven.*'

'Ha! Easy. Steve McQueen and Charley Bronson. Then there's James Coburn, Yul Brynner and Robert Vaughn. And the hard one nobody ever gets, Brad Dexter as Harry Luck.' Charlie smiled triumphantly.

'They weren't called *The Magnificent Six.*'

'What?'

'You only named six, not seven. You left out the *real* hard one, the one nobody ever gets.'

'Bollocks. I named all seven.' Charlie removed the hairy wolf gloves from his hands. Began counting on fingers. 'Oh … the wee Mexican. I forgot about him. What the hell was his name?'

'You give up?'

Charlie thought for a long moment. 'Yes, fuck it. Otherwise it'll do my head in, trying to remember.'

'Horst Buchholz as Chico, and for your information he was German. He just played a Mexican in the movie.'

'Don't talk shite. How the hell could he be German? You only had to look at his skin to see he was Mexican.'

'Now, Charlie, that's practically borderline racist.' Brian was grinning.

'I'm not a bloody racist. Just saying, the guy's Mexican, and proud of it he should be. They've a great history in Mexico. I was reading about the revolutionary José Doroteo Arango Arámbula.'

'Who the fuck's that? Never heard of him.'

'Also known as Pancho Villa.'

'Marlon Brando, you mean. Great film.'

'Brando didn't play Villa. He played Zapata, you big eejit.'

'Anyway, you're wrong. Horst Buchholz was German.'

'I'm telling you, he was Mexican, and – '

'Put the gloves back on, Charlie.' Jim said it in such a way as not to have to say it twice.

'What? Oh, sorry, mate, wasn't thinking.'

Brian grinned wickedly, winking at Charlie's chastised face.

'Time to hit the road. Check your weapons,' Jim finally said, expertly loading a lethal-looking sawed-off shotgun with the ease of a veteran. 'Remember, we've no more than five, possibly six minutes to get in and out. Tops. When I say time to pack up, we pack up. No ifs, ands or buts. Do *not* get greedy.'

'Like *Darby O'Gill*, eh, Jim? I've got that wee movie on DVD,' Brian said, turning to Charlie and checking his weapon. 'The ballsy Darby, trying to steal King Brian's leprechaun gold. A classic. My granny Ross loves Sean Connery in that show. Actually, truth be told, she loves Connery in *anything*, especially those blue bathing shorts in *Casino Royale*.'

'Connery was the best Bond,' Charlie said. 'Brosnan comes a close second, though.'

Jim glanced at his watch. 'Get your masks on.'

As Brian and Charlie began pulling on their wolf masks, Jim reached into a bag, removing a family of home-made incendiary devices created from floor-wax and Demerara sugar, and thick bootlaces with the aglets cut off for wicks.

'These'll go off approximately five minutes after we enter the bank. They should set the van ablaze, causing an excellent diversion and hopefully some chaos once the petrol tank explodes.'

Jim put the devices in position, small gaps apart. Lit them. Cranked down the driver's widow slightly, to the level calculated to maximise the explosion. Pulled on his mask.

'Okay, let's do it.'

The three big bad wolves hopped out, heading towards the doors of the Bank of New Republic on Donegall Place. They planned to do more than just huff and puff at the little piggy bank on the corner.

* * *

Security guard Andy Grazier stood inside the revolving door of the Bank of New Republic, glancing constantly at his watch. Three customers to be served. Two long minutes to go. One great occasion coming up. He couldn't wait to get home. Man City versus Man U, live on Sky, and the entire house to himself. Margaret, the wife, would be going out with a few friends to darts, and the fridge was well stocked with bottles of his favourite beer, Harp.

Happy Harpy Hours, Andy mused, hoping and praying there'd be no late stragglers coming with deposits. Stragglers were the worse. Always flustered and out of breath, always with lengthy, boring tales about why they almost missed the bank before it closed. By the time they'd given their excuses, a long five minutes would have elapsed.

'Andy?' the manager Dana Robinson said, emerging from her office. 'I think we can close now.'

Andy nodded, trying not to smile with relief, and turned to lock the doors. Just as he could almost taste the Harp on his parched tongue, his biggest nightmare stood before him.

Actually, it sat, in the form of a wheelchair-bound customer, trying to squeeze through the revolving door by slamming against it.

God, why tonight, of all nights? Andy squinted, looking out at the customer, but the black rain beating against the opaque glass and the bad street-lighting made visibility practically zero.

The wheelchair continued slamming relentlessly against the door, like some sort of medieval battering ram.

Bloody hell! Andy quickly held his hand up.

'Hold on! You're going to have to wait a second, until I get the accessible door open.' He reached down and pushed the blue button, opening the sliding doors. 'You almost got here too late to make a –'

Andy's voice stopped mid-sentence, as a sawed-off shotgun was pushed against his balls by a wolf, while two further wolves rushed into the bank, howling and screaming.

'Everything's gonna be okay,' Jim said, quickly exiting the wheelchair, elevating the shotgun from balls to the nose on Andy's petrified face. 'Say it!'

'Every … everything … okay …' Andy looked on the verge of fainting.

'No heroics. Say it.'

'No … heroics …'

Quickly pushing Andy to the ground, Jim hit the blue button. The accessible doors closed without a sound. The wheelchair was instantly folded up, and stashed behind a desk.

'Put your hands behind your back,' Jim instructed.

Andy quickly complied. Jim cuffed both wrists with plastic security cables, then dragged Andy across the polished-marble floor, parking his body behind a large table, out of sight of any nosey passer-by.

'Everyone! Get behind that table, and down on the ground!' Charlie shouted, waving his Magnum menacingly in the air.

The customers eagerly scurried behind the shelter of the table, stone-dropping onto the floor. Closing their eyes, they became instant statues. They had seen enough movies to know what could happen in situations like this – especially in cheap movies where everyone ends up shot to pieces. They earnestly hoped this wasn't a cheap one, especially by Belfast's cheap standards.

While Charlie kept watch on the customers, Brian ran to the nearby office. Dana Robinson had been talking to a male customer, but was now midway through rising from her chair at the sound of the commotion.

'Don't go pushing any buttons, Mrs Robinson. Little buttons create big problems,' Brian said, pointing the gun at Dana's face. '*Comprende*? *Lo entiendes*?

Vous me comprenez? In other words, do you fucking understand?'

Dana's mouth opened. No words came out. She nodded.

'Good. Now sit back down, and place your hands on top of the desk, *nice and easy*.'

Dana quickly complied.

'You.' Brian pointed the gun at the male customer. 'Get on the floor. Don't make a sound.'

The man, completely bald, face expressionless, stared back at Brian. Casually dressed, he gripped an expensive Samsonite Pro-DLX3, a large, expandable briefcase. Puzzlingly, he did not move.

'You deaf, Lex Luther? Get on the floor. *Now!*'

Instead of dropping to the floor, the man stood. He towered a good four inches over Brian's height of five-eleven, and had a smug air of defiance about him, bordering on menacing.

'I think you should leave. Now, while you have the chance,' the man said, voice calm as floating ice. 'You really don't want to fuck with me.'

Brian glanced left and right, before eyeballing the man. Then, channelling his inner Robert De Niro, '*You talkin' to me?*'

'I'm talking to you.'

'Let me get this straight. I'm the one with the gun in my hand, and you're the one with his dick in his, but *I* should leave while *I* have the chance?'

'Correct.'

'You think you're *Kwai Chang Caine?*'

'What?'

'Not what. Who. You know – David Carradine *in Kung Fu.* Think you can kill ten men with a chopstick?'

'I don't know what drug is melting your brain, but you better leave, while the chance is offered.'

'Offered? Ever watch *The Shawshank Redemption?*'

'Once.'

'Good, perhaps you remember this wee classic line from it: *"I'm not gonna count to three. I'm not even gonna count to one. You will shut the fuck up or I'll sing you a lullaby!"*'

Brian hit him on the side of the head with the gun so hard, it could be heard outside the office. The man collapsed like wet posters on a wooden fence, banging his already battered head against the edge of the desk, causing blood to appear.

Dana let out a soft scream.

'What the hell's going on in there?' Jim shouted.

'Everything's under control. Nothing to lose your fur about.'

'Hurry the hell up!'

'You heard the man, Mrs Robinson. I need you to hit the combo on the vault.'

'I … I don't know the –'

'You don't know the combo. Right?'

'Only the –'

'Only the night manager knows the combo?'

'Yes …'

'You wouldn't lie to me, would you, Mrs Robinson?'

'No.'

Suddenly, an explosion could be heard in the background, somewhere out in the streets.

'Did you hear that, Mrs Robinson?'

Dana nodded nervously. 'Yes …'

'That was God. He's angry at you for telling fibs. Okay, here's the score. I didn't even have to look at your badge to know your name.

Doesn't that tell you something? You have a child, a young girl named Sheila.'

'How … how do you know my daughter's name?'

'That's irrelevant. What *is* relevant is that you do as I say, and no more fucking about. Wee Sheila's fine – at the moment. She's staying with a friend of ours.'

'Oh my God! Don't hurt her!' Dana tried to stand. Her knees wobbled. She slumped back down. 'Please … please don't hurt her. She's only three.'

'Sheila's not three until next week, so that's more fibbing. As soon as we're out of here, she'll be released. We'll even throw in a birthday cake and a nice wee present for her.'

'I swear there's … there's no money in the vault.'

'Your definition of "no money" is probably a lot different to mine – and you're still wasting valuable time. This is not going to end right, if you do what's wrong.'

'I'll … need to type in numbers, on the computer. That's … that's how it works.'

From his wolf pouch, Brian removed a small, black device, no larger than a mobile phone.

'Ever see one of these?'

'No …'

Brian connected it to the side of the computer via a USB socket.

'It's a bullshit detector. Actually, it's a number cruncher, able to calculate numbers at the equivalent of the warp speed of the Starship Enterprise. Impressed?'

'I –'

'Good. Well, you start fucking about with the combo, and this little lady will buzz, letting me know *you're* not a lady. Understood?'

Dana nodded slowly. 'Yes …'

'Excellent. Now, do whatever magic you need to do to open Aladdin's Cave. And don't get smart. Only stupid people get smart. You really want us to get out of here, nice and safe, right? You want to be there for wee Sheila's third?'

Dana nodded, quickly typing numbers into the computer.

'What's happening in there?' Jim was leaning into the office. 'Four minutes left. Hurry the fuck up.'

'Taking an awful long time, Mrs Robinson. My boss is getting irritated. He rarely curses, except when running out of patience while doing bank robberies.'

'I'm working as fast as I can.' Dana's fingers danced deftly over the keyboard. 'It's complicated. And it's trickier when your hands are sweating and slipping.'

Brian did his best Dustin Hoffman: *'Mrs Robinson, if you don't mind my saying so, this conversation is getting a little strange.'*

'A few more seconds, please … There! That's it. The vault's open.'

'Abracadabra!' Brian shouted. 'Heaven's Gate is now open, by invitation only!'

Jim produced three large gripbags from the wheelchair's stomach. The bags were designed to look like slaughtered sheep, to go with the wolf costumes. He returned to the office. Tossed a bag to Brian.

'Mrs Robinson?' Brian said, catching the bag. 'Get down beside Lex Luther. While I'm gone, I expect you to behave. Do I have your word?'

'Yes … yes …' Dana said, kneeling down behind the desk.

'You lied to me before. Don't make the same mistake twice.'

Brian ran the small distance to where the vault's door gaped invitingly, an enormous metal wound in the wall.

'Show me the money, honey!' he shouted triumphantly, turning backwards to do a Michael Jackson moonwalk into the vault. The moment he stepped inside, however, triumph turned to despair. 'Houston, we have a problem.'

'What?' Jim said, rushing in behind him. 'What the hell's wrong?'

'It's a vault, Jim, but not as we would like it. It's empty.'

The vault was gleaming, all spick-and-span, as if it had been entered into the Cleanest Vault in the World competition.

'Fuck!'

'I think you were being a bit over-optimistic with three great big bags, Jim.'

'Come on. Get the hell out of here. We can lick our wounds elsewhere.'

'*Mrs Robinsonnnnnnnnnnnnnnnnnnnnnnnnnnnnnnnnn!*' Brian shouted, running back towards the office. He kneeled down before the trembling manager, and brandished the gun in her face. 'You lied to me. No money makes me an unhappy bunny.'

'I … I didn't lie. I told you there was no money. It's a new security procedure, new regulations. They remove all the money an hour before closing. You just missed the Brinks security van by a few minutes. There's … there's some money in the tills, but not a lot.'

'C'mon! Out!' Jim shouted, rushing for the exit.

'What we've got here, Mrs Robinson, is a failure to communicate,' continued Brian. 'You should've told me all this before the fan got covered in shit. I don't like it when people try to –'

The bald male customer began to stir. He groaned. 'What … what hit me?'

'This.' Brian smacked him on the head again, and the big man went silent. 'See, Mrs Robinson? Now I'm really pissed off.'

'Please don't hurt me. Don't hurt my baby.'

'Don't be stupid. No one's hurting you or your child. I've never hurt anyone in my life.' He glanced down at the crumpled figure on the floor. 'Well, almost never …'

'Out!' Charlie said, rushing into the office, grabbing Brian under the left arm. '*Now!*'

* * *

Musgrave Police Station, a Belfast stone's-throw away from the bank. Sergeant Colin Lindsay was taking his twentieth call of the night. He shouldn't even have been on desk duty, but three of the staff had called in sick, forcing him to cover everyone's job at once.

Just when Lindsay thought his night couldn't get any crazier, the phone buzzed again.

'Musgrave Police Station. Sergeant Lindsay speaking. How can I help?'

'I think there's a robbery going on across the road,' a badly slurred male voice said.

'And what makes you think that, sir?'

'I spotted them going in. That's what makes me think it, smart arse. They thought I didn't see them, but you've got to get up early to catch Jaunty McCambridge – ah fuck! Did I just give my name? I don't want my name being known, in case someone comes after me.'

Lindsay suspected the man had been drinking, and not just a small amount. 'It's okay, sir. I can assure you that anything you say is strictly confidential.'

'Bollocks! You people always say it's confidential. Next thing you know, everyone and their granny knows, and I'm found dead in some godforsaken place, two in the back of my nut for being a tout. Snitches always end up in ditches.'

Lindsay coughed impatience from his throat. 'Where exactly do you think this robbery is taking place, sir?'

'Can't really see the building's name, without my glasses. And all this rain bucketing down isn't helping. I think it's a bank. It's directly facing Burger God – hey, have you tried the Big Devil Special?'

'What?' Lindsay's patience was shortening.

'Big Devil Special. A Halloween one-off for less than a quid, but you've got to buy the chips – or French Fries, as they call them nowadays. Still, not a bad deal when you think of it. The sauce would burn the arse off Satan himself, so be careful. You'll be farting flames for days. I don't like their coffee, though. Too bitter. I prefer McDingle's. What about yourself? McDingle's or Burger God coffee?'

'Yes, look … the robbery? What details can you give?'

'Details? Well … there were three wolves. One of them was in a wheelchair.'

'Three wolves in a wheelchair …?'

'Have you been drinking or something? I said there were three wolves, and *one* was in the wheelchair. They were all grinning. Actually, come to think of it, they looked more like werewolves than your ordinary wolf, like from one of them there David Attenborough documentaries.'

Not another one, thought Lindsay. In the last thirty minutes, he had received reports of five drunken witches on broomsticks hovering over City Hall, casting spells on unsuspecting tourists; a colony of vampires chasing after an ambulance, looking for blood; and a gang of mummies demanding more bandages in the Royal Victoria Hospital.

'Have *you* been drinking, sir?'

'Well …' Jaunty's voice became hesitant. 'Just a few beers and brandies. That's why I'm beating this coffee into me, before I go home. Maggie – my lovely wife – would murder me in this state. Oh fuck, there I go again naming bloody names!'

'If you can't tell me anything else about this robbery that

you *think* you witnessed, and where exactly it's taking place, then you really need to stop wasting police time and get off the phone.'

'If that's your attitude, let them rob the place. Hold on a sec – just gonna ask this wee woman the name of the building.'

Lindsay was about to end the call when Jaunty's excited voice came back.

'Bank of New Republic, that wee woman says it's called.'

'Bank of New Republic? Donegall Place?'

'If that's where Burger God is.'

'Okay, sir. I'll send officers over to investigate. Thank you for calling.'

'Hold the hell on. Not so fast. Do you think will there be a reward?'

'A reward?'

'For stopping the robbers.'

'If you'd like to give me your name and address, sir, I'll see the bank gets it,' Lindsay grinned.

'Balls to that! You're not getting my address. No reward's worth that!'

The phone went dead and, for a few seconds, Lindsay debated with himself about the quality of the caller's information. It didn't sound too reliable. Still, he'd be in the shit if a robbery *was* taking place, and the brass discovered later he'd refused to respond.

'I hate Halloween duty,' Lindsay mumbled, putting out the call for a silent and rapid response to a possible robbery in progress. 'Werewolves my hairy arse …'

* * *

The anxious trio emerged from the bank, just as flashing police lights beamed through the city's drenched darkness. As they neared a corner, a police car came to a halt outside the bank, spewing out four carbon-copy cops, all overweight, young and nervous-looking.

'Walk calmly. Don't panic,' Jim whispered.

As the three wolves reached the end of Donegall Place, a group of slightly intoxicated young women in witches' garb appeared out of nowhere, and commenced walking beside them.

'Where's the party, Mister Wolf?' a pretty, green-faced witch asked, ruffling Charlie's hairy face.

Despite the fierce coldness of the night, inside the mask, beads of sweat were spotting Charlie's face, stinging his eyes.

In the near distance, two police cars, sirens blasting, chopped through the heavy night traffic, causing cars to part like Moses working the Red Sea trick.

'Cat got your tongue, Mister Wolf?' Pretty Witch gave Charlie's arse a playful squeeze.

A third police car swerved into view, slowing down to a crawl. A cagey-looking cop stared out at the posse of wolves and witches.

'Fuck sake.' Charlie tightened his finger on the trigger of the concealed Cobra.

'Easy … easy …' Jim said. *'Don't do anything foolish. Wait until I give the word.'*

'C'mon, Mister Wolf. Don't be like that. Where's the party?' Pretty Witch said, this time aggressively fondling Jim's balls.

'How about you opening a tin of shut-the-fuck-up, and slug it down your bucket mouth,' Brian said, no longer able to control nerves or patience.

'*What?* What the fuck did you say?' Pretty Witch manoeuvred menacingly towards Brian.

The police car came to a sudden halt. The passenger door opened. Cagey-Looking Cop stepped out, hand on gun holster. 'All of you, stop right there!'

Jim spun around, aiming the concealed sawed-off directly at Cagey's stomach.

'Is this girl pestering you?' Cagey said, looking directly at Jim.

'What? Oh! Well, we could do with her and her mates heading in the other direction, officer. She seems slightly intoxicated, to be honest with you.'

Cagey nodded, then pointed directly at Pretty Witch.

'Okay, you. Take a detour, along with your friends.'

'We were just having a bit of fun and –'

'*Now*, before I change my mind and arrest you for sexual harassment.'

'Sexual harassment …?'

'You want to spent the rest of Halloween in a urine-covered cell?'

'No …' Pretty Witch mumbled, turning and glaring at Jim. 'Some wolf you turned out to be, you wimpy bastard. I ought to put a spell on your fluffy arse.'

'I won't tell you again, young lady. Either move now, or I'll arrest you.'

Pretty Witch made a hissing sound with her mouth, before slowly walking off in the opposite direction, accompanied by her friends.

'Young women nowadays think they can get away with that sort of thing; they think it's acceptable,' Cagey said, shaking his head. 'Men do it, and there's bloody murder being screamed. Anyway, stay safe and enjoy the rest of the night, lads.'

'We will. Thank you, officer,' Jim said, leading the wolf pack out of harm's way.

'Women,' Cagey muttered, watching the coven of witches sauntering down the street. 'Nothing but troublemakers.'

Chapter Two

In the city there's a thousand men in uniforms,
and I've heard they now have the right to kill a man.
The Jam, 'In The City'

Antrim Road Police Station in north Belfast is a monstrosity of concrete blocks and metal, a lingering remnant of the Thatcher era, with her legacy of suicides, desolation and endemic poverty. The building is cocooned claustrophobically in supposedly bombproof metal shields, each pointed skyward and painted sporadically in bright colours, as if to add gaiety and warmth to the daily danger and dread.

The problem with the 'bombproof' label is that nothing in Belfast is *ever* bombproof, with the exception of the numerous dole offices dotted throughout the city.

Dozens of motion-detection security cameras nod nervously at visitors – the brave few who dare set foot in this intimidating place. They find themselves in a surreal world of suffocating silence and greyness, as if locked in some god-awful tomb. Political suspects brought in for questioning can find 'tomb' to be a most appropriate word.

To be fair to it, during the war, it had more than its share of bombs and bullets. But all of that was before the Good Friday

Agreement came along and put a partial halt to the bloody carnage. The Irish Republican Army and the British Army agreed to stop shooting each other, but some people were finding peace a very troubling concept.

However, Detective Inspector Harry Thompson of the Serious Crime Branch was not one of these. A Bob Hoskins lookalike, and built like a bull on steroids, Harry's face was more menacing than most of the villains he put behind bars; a face only a mother or wife could love. An air of intimidation hovered around him, and when he spoke, depending on his mood swings, it was either with a snarl or a growl.

Despite having a thumb and index finger blown off his left hand many years earlier when a loyalist bomb exploded outside a city-centre cafe, he continued as a cop, working his way up the ranks. The near-fatal explosion, and the countless excruciating skin grafts on his hand and upper torso that followed, only seemed to make him more cynical, more aware of other people's vulnerability and mortality, not his own.

But now, with barely a month left to retirement, he was more than content to sit it out quietly in the confines of the station. Then he would sail into the sunset with his beloved wife, Elaine.

Looking about the room, he watched three of his detectives alternate from television watching to newspaper reading. Bill McCauseland, long-time friend with over twenty years of service; Robert Boyd, a maverick sent to Harry two years ago for some much-needed rehabilitation; and Jeffrey Kerr, the youngest and most recent member of the team, barely off his ma's tits, as Harry liked to say.

Formerly, there had been eight detectives in Harry's team, but cutbacks and the Patten Report had ruthlessly decimated the numbers. The building itself, at one time, had been run by a staff of over fifty, from cops and dispatchers to cleaners and canteen staff, but that number had also been chopped drastically. Now there was only a skeleton crew, with no more than five or six people in the enormous building on any shift. With cleaners and canteen staff made redundant, cops were expected to do the cleaning themselves, and to bring a packed lunch if they wanted to eat. Harry often lamented that it was only a matter of time before they were all consigned to window-cleaning duty, as well.

'Another exciting evening at the High Chaparral, eh, Harry?' McCauseland said.

'Touch wood and hope it stays that way, Bill. Anything of note in the 'paper?'

'Nothing much, but here's an interesting statistic: This year in Belfast, almost eight thousand baseball bats were purchased. And here's the kicker, or actually, the swinger: only twenty-four baseballs were bought.' McCauseland grinned. 'Time to make people produce some sort of licence, just to prove they're not breaking the law.'

'And legs,' Harry added.

'Would you like me to get you a coffee, sir?' Kerr said, appearing out of nowhere, smiling like a clergyman at a nudist camp for boy scouts. Harry had Kerr confined to kitchen and office, coffeepot and stapler, all that Harry was willing to trust the rookie with for the moment.

Harry stared at Kerr for a few seconds, considering the offer. He had to take it easy with his intake of liquids, thanks to interstitial cystitis, an ailment that made him want to piss all day long. Or, as Harry would say, it liked taking the piss out of him. On top of that – actually *behind* that – he suffered from irritable bowel syndrome. There were days he felt like poor suffering Job, both ends burning, not knowing if it was a shit or a piss he needed.

'No … thanks, Kerr. I'll wait until later.'

Kerr was affable and always bubbling with enthusiasm, but Harry suspected the youngster was nothing more than a Trojan horse, one of the new breed of stallion poster boys created by the powers-that-be to bring about the demise of old workhorses like Harry and what remained of his dwindling crew. There was little doubt in Harry's mind that the old gang would all be put out to pasture, sooner rather than later, before ending up in the knacker's yard, just like Boxer from *Animal Farm*.

'Sir?' a voice said directly behind, breaking his thoughts. Harry turned. Officer Trevor Andrews, another recent recruit to the Force, though not officially part of Harry's crew. Harry had his suspicions about Andrews being a Trojan, also. Though he had to admit there were times he thought paranoia was simply stalking him.

'Yes? What is it, Andrews?'

'Reports coming in of an attempted robbery, sir.'

'Where?'

'Bank of New Republic, Donegall Place. Initial reports suggest three heavily armed raiders involved, sir.'

Heavily armed? Shit! Two words Harry didn't want to hear at this late stage in his career.

'Anyone hurt?'

'Initial reports say no casualties, sir.'

'Well, that's something. Did they get any money?'

'Initial reports suggest they fled empty-handed.'

'Initial reports! Initial reports! For God's sake, man! Can't you speak without sounding like a sound bite?'

'Sorry, sir. That's … that's how I was trained to make reports.'

'Yes, well … it gets a bit bloody tiring. Try and talk normal, instead. This isn't a TV show.'

'Would it be possible to attend, sir?' Kerr cut in. 'This could be my first real test as an officer.'

'Attend?'

'The scene of the crime, sir? It would be good experience for me.'

Attend? Bloody attend.

'This isn't a gospel meeting. We don't *attend* a crime scene.' Harry looked at the young and eager face, beaming with enthusiasm. A disaster waiting to happen. He had a sudden vision of Kerr tripping over himself, arms flailing wildly, gun clattering to the ground, shooting some unfortunate bystander, possibly Harry. 'Not this time. We're short-staffed, with only Andrews and a female dispatcher on duty. Next time, perhaps.'

'Thank you, sir! Very much appreciated, sir.'

Harry nodded to McCauseland and Boyd. 'Let's go. I want no –'

Before he could finish speaking, Harry became light-headed. He was forced to sit down. It was a long time since he had felt like this. A weariness so spine-crushingly powerful, he almost choked on its strength. He didn't like the taste it left in his mouth, or the tightness squeezing against his ribcage. A premonition of something bad about to happen?

His fingers instinctively searched his pocket. A medal. A Saint Christopher, rubbed almost beyond recognition. A present from the intended victim of the bombing, slipped into his hand as he lay there in the bloody street. A Papist payment in a Presbyterian pocket.

Keep it safe, and it'll keep you safe.

Making sure no one was watching, he rubbed it, slightly self-conscious but nevertheless feeling a bit more at ease.

'You okay, Harry?' McCauseland said, concern on his face.

'Yes, Bill, fine. Get the car ready. I'll be out in a minute. Tell the rest of the squad I want no heroics. We all come back here safe and sound.'

One more month. You can do it.

Chapter Three

'It's like fuckin' Belfast on a bad night.'
Harold Shand, *The Long Good Friday*

Elsewhere, less than a mile from Hopeful Harry's Headquarters, the spreading of joyous hopefulness was less evident.

'I don't believe this.' Charlie was staring at the empty glass held in his shaking hand. 'We risked our lives for sweet-fuck-all.'

'Stop whingeing.' Jim poured another shot of Bushmills into Charlie's glass before wetting his own. The toothache was still driving him crazy. He quickly captured a mouthful of the liquid, swirling it around the offending tooth, hoping to dull the pain. 'We weren't to know of the security changes.'

'*We*? Where the hell has this *we* suddenly come from? It was all *your* planning, if you remember. Me and Brian? We had nothing to do with it. You claimed to have inside info, someone who knew all the arrangements. Now you're telling me it was a cleaner in the bank. A *seventy*-year-old cleaner! No wonder you were so cautious about telling us, you bastard.'

Charlie downed the whiskey in one gulp. Held out his glass. Jim topped it up, before walking to the window.

Jim was certain he could still hear sirens, even though the trio were now a good two miles away from the fucked-up farce, tucked up in a safe-house. He instinctively touched the tattoo on his neck: a full rosary wrap-around with a tortured Christ, crucified and perturbed, as if he had also been in on the failed bank raid.

'Look, no point in arguing among ourselves, Charlie. What's done is done. All we can do is sit tight. I'll think of something else.'

'What the hell? Have you become an overnight comedian now? *You'll* think of something? Well, you can do all the thinking you like, as long as *I'm* not part of it.'

'One screw-up, and you want to run for the hills?'

'It's the *size* of the screw-up. We could've all been killed, and for what? Empty pockets and full prison cells.'

Jim walked over to the far corner and turned on the TV. The local news would be coming on shortly. Just then, the door opened, and in walked Brian from the toilet, grinning like a Great Dane at a balls-weighing tournament.

'*Gentlemen, you can't fight in here! This is the War Room!*'

'Drop the movie-quoting nonsense, Brian. Okay? This is serious.'

'Everything in life is serious to you, Charlie. You're gonna give yourself a heart attack if you're not careful. Lighten up.'

'Lighten up? While you were in the shitter, getting a load off your mind, our mastermind here was putting a load onto mine. He's just finished telling me where he got the info about the bank: a *seventy*-year-old cleaner. Can you believe that?'

'So?'

'So? It gets worse. She left the bank about six months ago. You can imagine how up-to-date the info was. A fucking spinster spinning tales. It's all fucked up here.'

'Nothing is fucked here, Dude.' Brian sat down at a table centred in the room. *'Come on, you're being very un-Dude.'*

'I swear to God.' Charlie glared threateningly at Brian. 'You quote one more fucking movie, and I'll not be held responsible for my actions or –'

'We have to be philosophical, Charlie. We got away without being shot or caught. That's a big plus.'

'That's a load of shite, and you know it. We risked everything for nothing.'

'Who said it was for nothing?' Brian began grinning.

Jim and Charlie watched Brian placing a slaughtered-sheep gripbag on top of the table.

'What's that?' Charlie said.

'Isn't it obvious? One of our specially designed slaughtered-sheep gripbags.' Brian placed his hand inside. Made loud grunting and farting sounds as if pulling out intestines. Produced a large briefcase instead.

'Where the hell did *that* come from?'

'The sheep's arse.'

'Can you be serious for one second?'

'If you must know, while you two big girls were running out of the bank screaming with your knickers down to your ankles,

Brave Big Balls Brian had other ideas. I grabbed Lex Luther's rather large and expensive-looking briefcase, in the hope he had something of value inside.'

'And? Had he?'

Brian opened the briefcase.

'Well, there was a little bit of money in it …'

Charlie and Jim came closer. Stared at the briefcase's contents. Their eyes began widening. Kids on Christmas morning.

'Dear God …' Charlie said in a hushed tone. 'That's crazy …'

'In Belfast, you have to be crazy to stay sane!' Brian laughed.

Jim had yet to say anything. He just stood, as if hypnotised.

'How … how much … how much is there?' Charlie muttered, staring at the bricks of money.

Brian lifted the briefcase, as if weighing it. 'I'd say half a million. Actually, half a million is exactly what it is.'

'Half a … million? You shitting?' Jim finally said.

'No, done all the shitting I needed a few minutes ago, Jim lad. I guess you could say I was doing my numbers while doing my numbers.'

'Can you really get half a million into a briefcase?'

'Duh! This is a briefcase. Inside is half a million. Question answered?'

'I don't even care if you didn't wash your hands!' Charlie grinned, reaching over and kissing Brian repeatedly on each cheek. 'You're a darling little bastard, Brian Ross.'

As God is my witness,' Brian sang in a Scarlett O'Hara voice, *'I'll never be hungry again!'*

Charlie and Jim laughed out loud, giving each other high-fives.

'This calls for a celebration,' Jim said, making his way over to the fridge, removing three bottles of Harp and three chilled Guinness glasses.

'That's alcohol abuse,' Charlie complained, watching Jim pouring the first beer.

'What the hell are you on about?' Jim handed the beer to Charlie.

'Harp in a Guinness glass. That's blasphemy.'

All three laughed. Half-a-million laughs.

Just then the news came on the television. Rioting over in Britain was the big story. Youths were hurling petrol bombs, beer kegs and pieces of paving slabs at cowering riot cops.

'They have a cheek to call *that* rioting,' Brian said. 'That looks like a good night out.'

More laughter.

A few minutes later, the local news came on.

'Hold on.' Jim grabbed the remote, increasing the volume. 'Let's have a listen.'

'Police say an attempted armed robbery was foiled at the Bank of New Republic, *Donegall Place, earlier this evening. Robbers, dressed as wolves, fled from the bank, and narrowly missed being apprehended by officers alerted to the scene. Police say no one was hurt, and no money was taken, thanks to the bank's new stringent security measures. Detectives are studying CCTV footage, hoping it will offer some clues as to the identities of the would-be robbers.'*

'A fat lot of good that'll do them, studying CCTV,' Charlie said. 'What? What's wrong, Jim?'

'No one hurt. No money taken.'

'Your point?'

'Is this a mirage in front of us?'

'What the hell're you on about?'

'We're sitting here with half a million in our laps. *That's* what I'm on about. Why didn't they mention that on the news?'

Charlie shrugged his shoulders. 'Who the hell cares? It's ours now.'

'Why didn't they mention the customer Brian slapped about?'

'What're you getting at?'

'Whoever the hell he was, he didn't want the cops or the public knowing about the money, or being assaulted. Why would he keep quiet about half a million being stolen from him?'

'Must be drug money, or some other sort of illegal shit. Right? That's why he didn't declare it. Probably got out of there as quickly as we did, in case the cops wanted a few words with him.'

Jim nodded. 'Possibly, plus the bank must've known who he was, what they were dealing with. Otherwise they'd have told the cops and the press about our little nest-egg on the table. The bank must be laundering drug money. Cert.'

'Fucking drug dealers. I hate the bastards as much as I hate thieving bankers and lying politicians,' Brain said, filled with righteous anger.

Charlie grinned. 'I'm gonna enjoy spending this money even more now.'

'We have to be careful about spending any of this – at least for now.' Jim looked directly at Charlie. 'The guy Brian smacked looked like he had Irish Alzheimer's.'

'Huh?'

'Forgets everything except grudges.'

'I'm not stupid. I'm not gonna go out and buy a new car to replace the rust-bucket I'm driving, or hand my Rosie the keys to a new house. I can be subtle when it's needed.'

'Subtle? You?' Brian laughed out loud. 'As subtle as Kathy Bates with a sledgehammer in *Misery*.'

'It's no laughing matter, Brian.' Jim began rubbing the side of his mouth again. 'This drug dealer, whoever the hell he was, is probably part of a gang. They'll not be too happy about us taking their money. They're not the cops. They won't just throw us behind bars, if they catch us.'

'How're they ever gonna catch us?' Charlie cut in.

'I'm just saying we have to be extra careful about how we spend the money.'

'You better tell *him* that.' Charlie pointed at Brian. 'The first thing he'll do is buy more of those comics and toys he likes to collect.'

'I've told you before, Charlie, they're *not* toys,' Brian responded. 'Those are investments as well as enjoyment. Better than your collection of beaten dockets from the bookies. One thing's for certain, though: I sure as hell won't be putting my share in any bank. Too many thieving bastards about.'

Charlie laughed, but Jim remained deadly serious.

'Will you promise me, Charlie? Promise you'll keep a tight rein on it.'

For a few seconds, Charlie studied the seriousness on Jim's face, knowing now that it wasn't a request.

'Okay. I heard you twice the first time. I promise. Cross my heart and hope to die.'

Chapter Four

'Well, it's a fine soft night, so I think I'll go and join
me comrades and talk a little treason.'
Michaleen Oge Flynn, *The Quiet Man*

I n a spacious private room above a well-known city-centre restaurant, a third group of concerned citizens – Conor O'Neill, George Magee, Barney Dennison and Seamus Nolan – had been gathering, just as Harry and his crew were making their way speedily down the Antrim Road in an unmarked police car.

Just like Harry and Jim's gang – perhaps more so – this cadre were keenly interested in the events of the previous two hours. However, unlike Harry's squad, filled with on-the-edge adrenalin, or Jim's crew, filled with the joy of newly acquired and unexpected riches, this group looked rather gloomy and battered.

The leader of the group, Conor O'Neill, stood smoking a Caminetto pipe, despite the 'No Smoking' sign on the door.

O'Neill had a charismatic air about him, and was renowned for his sharp intellect and keen sense of justice. An unassuming and soft-spoken man, he was feared and respected by friend and foe alike. When situations dictated, he could be as ruthless and unforgiving as a hungry lion; at other times magnanimous.

A founding member of the Brotherhood for Irish Freedom, he never missed morning Mass. Even in the bad old days of war, when he found himself on the run from the British Army and cops, he managed to receive the sacred body of Christ upon his eager tongue, disguising himself convincingly enough to fool even some of his closest friends. Widowed in his mid-thirties when wife Bridget was shot dead by terrorists, friends nicknamed him De Gaulle because of the many unsuccessful assassination attempts on his own life over the years.

Conor removed the pipe, and finally addressed the room. 'We've had some unmitigated disasters in our time, but I have no words to describe this charade.'

'At least Seamus was able to get out of there before the media and cops arrived,' George Magee put in uneasily.

Magee, a Beethoven lookalike, had been the Finance Officer for the Brotherhood in Belfast. With the onset of the peace process, this militaristic title had, of course, become unpalatable to unionists. And so, hey presto, he was now recycled to Fund Raiser in Residence.

Magee had earned the nickname Ghoulish George because of his penchant for attending funerals – even of people he didn't know or have a modicum of fondness for – as well as his bizarre behaviour of hanging around graveyards, pilfering the dead's dead flowers. These he would press into books, of which he had by now accumulated many volumes.

'I should take comfort in that, George?' Conor said. 'A bit like a doctor diagnosing a person with cancer, saying it's only devouring *half* the body?'

'Just saying, Conor.'

'Don't just say. Explain – explain how we just had a half a million stolen from under our noses by amateurs who couldn't even rob a bank without tripping over themselves.'

'I've already explained that they were armed to the teeth.' Nolan's bald head was turning crimson. 'I could've been shot, killed.'

'But you *weren't*, were you? You got a slap on the head, instead of a bullet in it. That was the limit of the damage done to you – unlike this mess you've created.'

'*I* didn't create the mess.' Nolan bristled.

'Seamus, calm down,' Dennison said.

Dennison was Public Relations Officer for the organisation. Structurally, he was a diminutive character, with an uncanny resemblance to – though without the wit, wonder or wisdom of – Truman Capote. He was nicknamed the Poison Pen Dwarf, for his notorious backstabbing of opponents, while hiding behind a *nom de plume*, in a weekly column he wrote for a local rag. 'We need to get to the bottom of this, before sending a report down to Dublin. They're not too happy about what's happened.'

'And I fucking am!' Nolan snapped back.

'You were supposed to be in the bank two hours *prior* to when you finally arrived,' Conor cut in. 'Had you not deviated from what you were instructed to do, the money would've been safely taken away by Brinks, instead of by the Three Stooges.'

'I've already told you, I believed I was being followed, and had to do a few detours to cover my tracks.'

'Believed? I wish I could say I was a believer in your story.'

Nolan's eyes tightened. 'And what's that supposed to mean? Calling me a liar?'

Conor walked slowly over to where Nolan stood, eyeballing him like an experienced knife fighter weighing up his opponent's expertise with a blade. For ten tense seconds, the men competed in a Belfast standoff, until Magee finally shoehorned himself between the two.

'Seamus, have you gone mad or what? Conor could have you up on a court of inquiry, before being court-marshalled for insubordination. Is that what you're looking?'

Nolan's chest was heaving. Teeth extended over lower lip. Features morphing into something animalistic.

'Did you hear a word I just said, Seamus?' Magee's voice began rising.

Nolan's blinked a few times, as if emerging from a trance. He looked about the room, before focusing his attention on Magee.

'Yes … I heard you …'

'Apologise to Conor, right now.'

Nolan sucked his breath in, then exhaled slowly. 'I'm sorry for my outburst. I got carried away with myself.'

Conor sucked on the pipe. Exhaled the smoke, then, calmly but with a hint of menace: 'Make sure that's the last time you get carried away with yourself, otherwise you *will* be carried away. Clear?'

A couple of tense seconds faded before Nolan answered. 'Yes.'

'Okay. Here's what we do,' Conor said to the room, as if nothing had happened. 'I'll contact an outside agency to deal with this mess, and then we –'

'An *outside* agency?' Nolan looked like he'd just had his head battered again. 'You're joking?'

'Do you see me laughing?'

'Some cowardly scumbag sticks a gun to my face, before whacking me across the head, and you want to bring in someone from outside to deal with it? *I'm* the one to put manners on them, not someone from outside.'

'This is more important than your injured pride or head. We need a proxy to sort this mess out. We have to send a clear message, but without the finger of blame being pointed directly at us.'

'Fuck that. You think I'm going to let some clown boast of what he did to me? No one humiliates me and gets away with it.'

Conor looked at Nolan for a few seconds, before turning his attention to Magee and Dennison.

'George? Barney? I need a word in private with Seamus.'

Both men nodded, and walked to the door, accompanied by Conor. At the door, Conor said to Magee:

'I need a wee word with Barney, George. See you tonight, after seven.'

'Okay, Conor.'

When Magee had left, Conor whispered to Dennison: *'Contact Doc Holliday. Find out what he's discovered about the robbery. Get back to me, ASAP.'*

Dennison nodded and left, and Conor turned his attention back to Nolan.

'You know I despise you; always have. I'm sure you believe you're quite cunning, but to me you're an open book, and not a very intellectual one at that.'

'Now that we're alone, it's good to see we can talk frankly without your little altar boys listening. You don't like me and I don't like you. What's new, eh?'

'I watched you growing up as a little thug, a sadistic bully. The only thing to change over the years is your size. Now you're a bigger thug and sadistic bully. I detest what you do; you and your nutting squad, and the fact you get away with it because of your uncle's position in the movement.'

'You really think I give a flying fuck about your preaching? You detest the fact that I hunt out informers and execute them. I do the dirty jobs, so that people like you can hold your pious noses high in the air. People like me are the backbone of the movement.'

'Backbone? You're a psychopath, plain and simple, a rabid dog, and one that should have been put down a long time ago.'

'If I didn't know better, I could misinterpret that as a threat.'

'Interpret it as you wish.'

'Know what really sickens me? All that sanctimonious holier-than-thou shit. It's all a bit rich coming from you, with the people you killed when you were one of the most feared snipers in the North. You'd no qualms about that, I bet?'

'I killed out of necessity and the circumstances of the time. All of those killed were military personnel. Never civilians.'

'Want to know an uncomfortable truth? We're the same, you and me. We just go about our business in different ways. Now you pray, but I still slay.'

A look of disdain crawled over Conor's face. 'You and I are cut from entirely different pieces of cloth. I know all about your gallant stories, how you tell those about to be executed not to worry, that they'll be going home soon, back to their loved ones, their wives, husbands, children.'

'Always keep them calm, until you no longer need their calmness. That's my motto. I treat them charitably, even handing out cigs and bars of chocolates to some.'

'How do you sleep at night?'

'As soundly as you. Unlike your long-distance shooting, I have to look into the eyes of those about to be killed. How easy it must be to look down the scope of a rifle, never to see the faces of those you kill. They're only silhouettes, and then you judge others who have to get up close and personal.'

'But you never do look into their eyes, do you?'

'What the hell would you know about it?'

'Oh, I know alright. I know you only shoot people in the back.'

Nolan looked as if he had just been sucker-punched in the gut. He moved closer, within an inch of Conor's face.

'You really need to be careful of what you say about me, old man. You *really* do.'

'Get out of my sight. Maybe this time, even your uncle's influence won't save you.'

Nolan turned, sauntered to the door. Opened it, then turned to look directly over at Conor. 'Just remember what I said: no one humiliates me, and gets away with it. *No one.*'

He exited, slamming the door behind him so hard, dishes rattled on a nearby table.

Chapter Five

There's a man goin' 'round takin' names. An' he decides who to free and who to blame. Everybody won't be treated all the same …
When the man comes around.

Johnny Cash, 'When the Man Comes Around'

The Brighton Building in Belfast's Alfred Street is a prestigious, five-storey affair, comprising forty high-quality, much-sought-after apartments, which rarely ever appear on the market. The BB, as it's known locally, is located right smack in the city centre, within easy walking distance of City Hall, and other landmark buildings sought out by tourists from all over the world.

Residents of the building include two best-selling authors, two professors from Queen's University and five well-known local celebrities from television and radio.

One resident, Rasharkin, apartment 4F, has been an avid art collector for many years, avidly hunting down anything to do with original pages from American comic books, but predominantly those of Harmenszoon, mononymous god-like visionary creator of numerous superheroes, villains and deities for the comics' cosmic universes. To date, Rasharkin's collection has grown to almost four thousand pages, one of the world's largest private compilations.

To pay for this ever-accumulating and expensive collection, he works beyond the normal curriculum boundaries of nine to five, rarely taking a weekend off or having paid holidays. Being self-employed has other disadvantages also, such as being on standby twenty-four-seven, every day of the year, including Christmas and New Year's Eve.

Clients can be quite inconsiderate with their demands upon him, even if they do pay extremely well. Still, he can't really complain. This is the lifestyle he has elected to pursue. No one put a gun to his head to do it. Truth be told, he's the one putting guns to heads, killing for a living.

Post workout in his private gym, Rasharkin was stripped to the waist, drying the beads of sweat from his skin. His body was built like a god's angry fist: lean and intimidating, powerfully gnarled, and scarred with hashtags – the afterburners of knife-marks and long-healed bullet wounds. A man's man. The sort of man you wanted by your side if you had a body to bury secretly and quickly; the sort of man you hoped would never put you on his to-do list.

Finished drying, he adorned himself in a bathrobe, then walked to the living room window, glancing out at the darkening streets below.

Streetlamps were pouring their golden light on lonely commuters heading home from work. The evening rain diluted their shadows, transforming them into inky stick figures from a Lowry scene.

The rain. Lovely rain. A pluviophile, he could watch it for hours, if given the luxury of time.

He glanced at his watch just as the UPS van came into view at the top of the street, making its way towards the side of the building.

Despite the calmness on his face, his stomach was giving little kicks of anticipation. It always did when the famous brown van came visiting. To Rasharkin, the van was Santa, coming down the chimney on Christmas Eve, though he had to acknowledge that in all probability he would only ever make it on to Santa's extremely naughty list.

Leaving the window, he picked up ten quid from an assortment of paper money on top of a side table and walked to the front door. Opening it, he looked down the corridor at the lights of the lift, ascending painstakingly slowly. The lift door finally opened with a soft *ping!*, and the van's driver stepped out.

'A package from New York, Mister Rasharkin,' Tony the driver said cheerfully, as he walked down the corridor. 'I stopped here first, so as to get it to you as quickly as possible.'

'Thank you, Tony. Very much appreciated.' He handed Tony the tenner with one hand while the other scribbled a signature into a hand-held postal tracking device.

'Thank *you*, Mister Rasharkin.' Tony smiled, handing the package over. Slipping the ten into his pocket, he headed down the corridor towards the lift.

Back in the apartment, Rasharkin went straight to his climate-controlled art room, turning on the lights while closing the door. The room was a shrine to Harmenszoon.

An old art desk, once belonging to the legendary artist, took centre stage in the room. Numerous props decorated the top of the desk, all from the master: a pipe, faded erasers, pens and pencils. There were some wood shavings from one of Harmenszoon's pencils, kept in a tiny plastic bag. The desk itself had ineligible scrawls embedded in its skin, alongside faded names and places, as if it had been used as a wooden notepad.

Placing the package on the desk, Rasharkin removed a pair of nitrile surgical gloves from a drawer. Slid them on like a surgeon about to perform major surgery.

Satisfied with their snugness, from another drawer he retrieved a Fällkniven NL1 Thor hunting knife. He rarely ever used the deadly piece of metal any more in a professional capacity, preferring to keep it for more mundane domestic duties.

Still, there were occasions when the blade unfortunately needed to be reintroduced. Silent and deadly, the hunting knife's legendary blade was capable of slicing through muscle and bone like other knives cutting string. He had always loved this knife, of course because of its perfect balance, but more importantly because it had no moving parts capable of slipping at the most delicate moment, when trying to prise a pearl of information from the oyster shell of an unwilling tongue.

Slicing the heavy-duty tape with one touch of the blade,

he freed the package from its restraints. Uncovered the contents. Gingerly. Delicately. Lovingly.

It was a drawing, encased in a protective, museum-quality Mylar sheath. An original sketch of the anti-hero known as the Black Avenger, warp-speeding in and out of the cosmos on his winged stallion, Mercury. It had cost a small fortune, but he would have paid double the asking price. He eased the drawing out with extreme care.

'Beautiful …'

Sitting down at the desk, he was overcome with emotion. Tiny bolts of electricity began massaging his body. It never failed to happen, each time he presented himself at the desk. He pictured Harmenszoon, sitting right there, creating wonderful new worlds of dark deities and demons.

Bringing the drawing to his face, he closed his eyes, inhaling the paper's vellichor, the opium-like smell of yesteryear and childhood. In an instant, paradoxical happiness and tranquillity swept over him, mixing with sadness and anger.

From another drawer, he removed a small box made of pure gold. Squeezed off the lid. Inside, tiny stamp-sized strips of potent, unadulterated LSD, enriched with BBC – Bad Boy Coke – slept like nursing babies. Normally, one strip would suffice, but this was a rather special occasion, and special occasions called for just that little bit of over-indulgence.

Removing two strips, he placed them on top of the desk. With the knife, he delicately scraped off particles of dust and fibre from a corner of the drawing, careful not to go too deep in case of wounding. Minuscule particles floated downwards onto the strips.

Just then, the blue phone began ringing on an antique table in the corner.

Brrrrllllllllll … Brrrrllllllllll … Brrrrllllllllll …

He watched the little trail of dotted silver lights leapfrogging to the red security descrambler, journeying all the way to the cordless white phone.

Brrrrllllllllll … Brrrrllllllllll … Brrrrllllllllll …

I should answer that. My lifeline.

He resisted, focusing rather on his cocktail of drugs, bringing the two strips to his mouth. Instead of the normal procedure of sublingually disposing of them, he swallowed the contents whole. Heading back to the living room, he chased them with a glass of sixteen-year-old Lagavulin single malt.

He walked over to a CD player resting against the wall and pressed the small orange button, bringing the machine to life. Charlotte Church's heavenly voice began singing 'The Flower Duet' from Léo Delibes' opera *Lakmé*.

Satisfied, he turned all lights off, sitting down and stretching out on an impressive Raft Manhattan corner sofa.

The entire room was now bathed in funereal darkness, with the exception of the little line of silver dots snaking back and forth from phone to phone like a mercury rosary.

Brrrrllllllllll … Brrrrllllllllll … Brrrrllllllllll …

I should answer that …

Brrrrlllllllll … Brrrrlllllllll … Brrrrlllllllll …

I … really … should …

He smiled. Closed his eyes. Head began spinning. Felt a *déjà vu* momentum sweeping over him in retro reflected images of monochrome silvery greyness.

The sofa began moving. A small aperture appeared in the middle, gradually expanding outwards like a black hole in space, its gravitational pull urging his body towards it.

He fell right into it, and was gobbled up, into a universe of dark secrets and sorrows.

***

Rasharkin stood on the wobbly edge of the world – or *worlds* – looking out beyond swirling black holes and curved twilight zones of then-and-now, all painted beautiful hues of reds, greens and blues. Meteorites and space debris zipped by at incredible speed, narrowly missing his head. But instead of being frightened, he giggled, like a child being tickled. He wanted to reach out and grab a meteorite, bring it back with him, add it to his collection of all things great and magnificent.

In God's honest truth, he didn't want to go back. He wanted to remain here forever in this kingdom of peaceful chaos; to escape from all the pain and horror of his life, the bloodline of suffering he endured as well as inflicted on countless victims and enemies.

'Where are you?' he shouted into the vast nothingness of outer space.

Where … are … you …? His voice echoed back, bouncing off planets and dying stars.

'Please … I need to see you. I've waited so long … Don't torment me like this.'

Like … this … this … this …

Then he saw it. The dot of recognition, a million light years away, hurtling towards him, gaining momentum, getting closer and closer. The Dark Avenger on his winged-steed, Mercury. His god. The one true god. Had to be. No one else could dodge through space-obstacles so gracefully.

'I knew you would come for me. I never gave up my belief in you,' he said, face lit in enraptured ecstasy, like an apostle in the splendid revelation of his god's holy presence for the first time.

The Dark Avenger came nearer and nearer, and then, just as quickly, became just another dot among a trillion others.

'*Nooooooooooooooooooooooooooooooooooooooo!*' he screamed. 'Please, don't leave me … please … not like *thissssssssssssssssssssssss sssssssssssssssssss!*'

* * *

Brrrrlllllllll … Brrrrlllllllll … Brrrrlllllllll …

'Huh …?' Feeling as if his head had been cleaved in two by an Asgardian mystic axe, he wiped away the wetness from his eyes.

Good trip? Bad trip? This had been an in-between trip. Tantalisingly close, yet without conclusion. For now.

Brrrrlllllllll … Brrrrlllllllll … Brrrrlllllllll …

Pushing himself up from the sofa, he stood unsteadily, forcing his body towards the phone. Checked the number. Instantly recognised it, despite the passage of time. Problems and pain for someone. Profits and pleasure for him. Picked the receiver up.

'Hello?'

'I've been calling for quite some time,' Conor O'Neill's voice said curtly.

'Sorry, I've just got back from … a … trip.'

'I've a little problem needs sorting. Actually, it's more than little, and more than one. Three, in fact. Two days ago, someone had the audacity to take something that didn't belong to them. A lot of something. This needs handling discreetly, but not too discreetly, if you get my meaning.'

Rasharkin thought for a few seconds. 'I understand your situation. You can't afford come-backs to your door, but you need a message sent to others who may be contemplating the same sort of foolishness.'

'Precisely. Things are a bit sketchy at the moment, but we hope to have a clearer picture very soon.'

'Send me the details the usual way. In the meantime, I'll start making preparations.'

'Twenty-five percent recovery fee still the going rate?'

'Only for you. Everyone else, thirty. It's good to be working with you again.'

He clicked the phone off and opened a drawer in the desk. Removed a plastic bottle containing a gathering of Pristiq antidepressant tablets. Popped two in his mouth. Used the remainder of the whisky to wash them down before making his way into the bedroom.

At the foot of the bed, an old 8mm film projector waited in silence.

He hit a small button, and the machine came to life in a series of soft mechanical click-clicks, beaming images onto a bleached-white screen. A hazy number countdown appeared, followed by a close-up of a woman's face.

The film was grainy, but it failed to diminish the woman's beauty. She resembled a movie star from the past. A Jane Russell lookalike, smiling coyly but oozing sex.

The camera began zooming out. She was wearing a bra and lace panties. A man's voice in the background was telling her to remove them. She complied. Slowly. Teasingly. Now naked, all pretence of shyness was gone. She began moving her body seductively for the camera.

'Now play with yourself …' Rasharkin said, voice becoming low, hoarse.

Now play with yourself, the voice on the film said, a split-second later.

The woman closed her eyes, letting her fingers do all the work down below.

'That's it. Get those fingers working, like little naughty tongues nibbling your juicy clit.'

That's it. Get those fingers working, like little naughty tongues nibbling your juicy clit.

'Harder …'

Harder.

'Harder! Fuck yourself harder!'

Harder! Fuck yourself harder!

The woman went into a state of ecstasy, thrusting harder and harder, beads of sweat forming on her upper lip. She opened her mouth wide, and her tongue began licking the beads seductively away.

'I … want you to … to fuck me.'

The woman stared directly into the camera. Close up. Lips pouting. *I … want you to … to fuck me*, she said, a moment later, speaking for the first time, voice trembling.

'Then … then in the ass. Hard in my ass … with … with that big cock of yours.'

Then … then in the ass. Hard in my ass … with … with that big cock of yours.

With a press of a button, the machine went dead, leaving a dull hum buzzing in Rasharkin's head.

He fell back on the bed. Tears began forming.

Chapter Six

O the bricks they will bleed and the rain it will weep
And the damp Lagan fog lull the city to sleep
It's to hell with the future and live on the past
May the Lord in His mercy be kind to Belfast.
Maurice James Craig, 'Ballad to a Traditional Refrain'

Mary Ross was preparing some vegetable soup for herself when Brian appeared unannounced at the open kitchen door. She was small, in her early seventies, her once golden hair now completely silver. She had her back to him and had yet to feel his presence.

He was carrying a large brown package under his arm. He tilted the package against the door, before tiptoeing over and kissing the top of her head.

'Holy Mother of God!' She turned, startled, then slapped him on the arm. 'Brian! Don't sneak up on me like that. Are you trying to give me a heart attack?'

'You're too healthy to have a –' Brian suddenly became vexed. 'What's wrong, Granny? You've been crying.'

'Crying? Onions. That's all. All these years and the onions still get to me.' She kissed him on each cheek, hugging him tightly before releasing him. 'Where've you been? I was so worried. I haven't heard from you in weeks.'

'Weeks? I called you two days ago. Remember?'

'Two days ago …? Are you sure?' Mary looked confused. 'I … I'm almost certain it was weeks ago.'

A sadness appeared on Brian's face. He quickly banished it. 'You know what, Granny? You're right. It *was* weeks ago. I'm sorry for fibbing, but I just didn't want you to be angry with me.'

She ruffled his hair. 'Don't be silly. I could never be angry with my favourite grandson. Now, sit yourself down. I can see you haven't been looking after yourself, living on your own. I'm going to make you something to eat, put some fat on those skinny bones.'

'Sounds great. But first, I brought a little something for you.' He walked to the door, retrieved the package and handed it to her.

'You shouldn't have done this, Brian. I keep telling you to save your money, don't go wasting it on an old woman like me.'

'You're *not* old. And anyway, who else would I spend it on?'

'Some pretty girl.'

'Pretty girls keep costing me a fortune!'

She smiled, then delicately peeled away the paper, revealing a framed photograph of Sean Connery.

'Oh, my goodness! My Sean! Now I really am going to take a heart attack!'

'And it's signed.'

'No!'

'Yes!' Brian laughed, pointing at the signature on the picture. 'In bold black for all the world to see.'

'This … this must have cost you a fortune. You really shouldn't have done this. I'm annoyed with you for buying something so expensive.'

'Annoyed enough to want me to send it back?'

'Not *that* annoyed.' She laughed, then kissed him. 'Besides, I don't want to hurt your feelings.'

'After eating, I'll put it up for you in the parlour, between Kennedy and the Pope. That'll be your Holy Trinity.'

'Wait until Lilly Larkin sees it. She'll be cabbage-green with envy. Now, sit down, and I'll get started on some food for you.'

'Also, I've ordered you a new shed.'

'A new shed? But I don't need a shed. I already have one.'

'That monstrosity in the garden? It's ready to collapse. I keep waiting to hear something terrible has happened to you, every time you do your gardening. Besides, wait until you see this shed. You'll not believe your eyes. You'll be able to have friends over for tea, during the summer.'

'But –'

'I can never repay you for looking after me, all these years, so just let me do these wee things for you. *Please?*'

Mary sighed. Smiled. 'Okay.'

'Good. Now how about that food?'

'Sit yourself down. I won't be a minute.'

Brian seated his bulk at the table, eyeing the *Irish News*, opened at the obituary and anniversary pages. Mary had obviously been reading them. He suspected that was the real reason for the tears.

A chill came over him. He wished he hadn't seen the newspaper. Today was the anniversary of their murders, but for years he had tried wiping it from his memory, as if erasing it meant it never happened.

He could see it all again in bloody *déjà vu*. The flash from the gun's muzzle. Smell the stench of singed hair and skin. Burning gunpowder in the heavy air. Warm blood in his mouth. His parents pulped to nothingness by bullets of madness.

'Are you okay, dear?' Mary was looking at him, concerned. 'What … what's wrong?'

Rage travelled from his stomach to his throat. He captured it in his mouth, holding it there like a caged creature until it weakened, until he could control it, until he could talk again.

'I'm fine, Granny …' *As fine as I'll ever be.*

Chapter Seven

'My, my, my! Such a lot of guns around town and so few brains.'
Philip Marlowe, *The Big Sleep*

Harry seated himself in the briefing room, drinking a morning coffee, though he knew he would pay dearly for it with many trips to the loo. He was reading the early edition of the *Belfast Telegraph*, while his team milled around, chatting.

Last night's robbery had made the front page, though not as the main story. A well-known Belfast actor had stolen that particular piece of thunder, visiting the city to make his latest movie. Pictures of the actor smiling and doing a walkabout with the crowds covered most of the front page.

'Can't stand him,' Harry said, more to himself than anyone in the room. 'Hasn't made a decent movie in years. Can't act the fool.'

Secretly, Harry was hoping his picture would've been on the front page as investigative officer, a final hooray and swansong. In the bad old days of war and madness, he'd been a regular in the pages, talking to eager journalists on the latest victory against the paramilitaries on both sides of the political divide. The media couldn't get enough of good old Harry, back in the bad days, filling him with Johnny Walker Black, backslappings and handshakes.

He was always in demand in those days. Now? Ha! They didn't even call that time he was hospitalised after breaking a toe running after a suspect down a flight of stairs. Not even a bunch of grapes from the miserable bastards.

'Okay, enough chit-chat.' Harry threw the newspaper into a waste bin. 'Kerr? What've we got so far?'

Kerr stood. Read from a report pad. 'The abandoned van found partially burned out at the building site had been stolen three days ago, from a city-centre car park, sir. It belonged to a wastepaper removal company and –'

'Wastepaper removal? At least they've a sense of humour,' Boyd said.

Small laughter rippled in the room.

Kerr continued. 'Some amateurish incendiaries had been prepared in the van to cause a diversion. Most had been blown out by the wind, because the windows had been opened too much. Despite that, one of the devices managed to ignite and set off the petrol tank. Thankfully, not a great deal of damage was done. After the robbery, the suspects' movements were captured on CCTV, walking as far as Corn Market, where they boarded a double-decker full of tourists and people in fancy dress. The cameras only go that far.'

'Have you checked out the local fancy-dress outlets, to see if anyone remembers the costumes being purchased or rented?' Harry asked.

'Nothing so far, sir. I went to Jackson's Fancy Dress, first thing this morning. They don't stock wolf costumes. I've phoned a couple of smaller vendors in Smithfield. No luck yet.'

'What about the wheelchair?'

'Went missing from the Mater Hospital, two weeks ago.'

'Any fingerprints found on it?'

'Not a mark, sir. Wiped clean.'

'What about paw prints?' Boyd said.

'Enough of the bloody wise cracks.' Harry glared at Boyd. 'Forensics?'

Chastened, Boyd quickly glanced at his notepad. 'So far, nothing worthwhile found at the bank, sir. However, numerous cigar stubs were discovered in the partially burnt-out van. We're hoping they belong to one or two of the suspects. Saliva tests are being carried out for DNA.'

'Bill? Have you got word out on the street to our nearest-and-dearest?'

'The usual suspects are being grilled, Harry. A couple of our informants have their ears to the ground for any titbits of info floating about. Told them to get back to me with anything, no matter how trivial it may sound, ASAP.'

'Watch out for that made-up shit they come out with when they want one of their competitors out of business.' Harry's mobile rang. He glanced at the number, then back at the gathering. 'I'll be back in a sec. This is a very important call.'

He quickly exited the room, and went into the toilet at the end of the corridor.

'Murray? Tell me you got them, mate.'

'No luck yet, Harry, but don't worry. I'm hopeful of capturing them tonight.'

'You're sure?'

'As sure as I can be.'

'You know the hell I'll face if you can't find them?'

'Of course I know. But everyone wants to see Tom Jones at the Waterfront. The tickets are bloody gold dust.'

'Elaine'll skin me alive if I don't get them.'

'Well, I just called to tell you not to be panicking. I know what Elaine's like when it comes to her Tom. Listen, I've got to go. Someone's on the other end. I'll call you later if I get them.'

Harry clicked off the phone, and went to the urinal.

'Bloody coffee … like acid.' Unzipping, he began urinating, easing the pressure on his overworked bladder.

A full minute later, he re-zipped, washed his hands, farted twice, then headed back down the corridor into the briefing room.

'Okay, this is what we have so far. The manager, Dana Robinson, says one of the robbers stuck a gun to her head, saying they were holding her young daughter hostage. We now know that was untrue. They hadn't got the child, and were bluffing to put pressure on her to make her panic.'

'More than likely an inside job, sir,' Kerr suggested.

'If that's the case, the information wasn't up to scratch. They didn't know about the extra security precautions.'

'Perhaps whoever had given the gang the info, left the bank before the new policy came into force? That's why it was useless to them?'

'Get a list of employees who left in the last six months.'

'I already did that, sir,' Boyd cut in. 'There's only been one. A cleaner. Seventy-year-old Ms Maggie Johnson. I spoke to her on the phone. In all honesty, the poor woman didn't even know what day it was. Thought I was her son from Australia. Kept calling me Peter.'

'One of the robbers could've known the manager personally,' Kerr suggested.

'You think Dana Robinson was in on it?'

'It's a strong possibility. Rule nothing out until you've ruled everything in.'

Boyd glared over at Kerr. 'Dana Robinson was in a state of shock when I interviewed her. If not, she's one hell of an actress. She was shaking like a leaf.'

'Okay, Boyd, don't go all personal on us,' Harry said. 'Someone dim the lights. I want you all to look at this CCTV footage from outside the bank. We'll be getting to the bank's own footage, later.'

Kerr turned off the lights, and Harry pressed the remote control. The screen came to life, showing the robbers entering the bank. Harry froze the picture, before zooming in.

'Weapons of choice for these gentlemen are a sawed-off, a Magnum and a Beretta. Kerr, I want you to find out if we know of any criminals with these particular weapons preferences.'

'Yes, sir.'

Harry fast-forwarded the scene. Robbers leaving in a hurry. Police arriving just as the robbers depart.

'Jammy bastards,' Boyd said. 'We almost caught them by the balls and –'

'Quiet!' Harry snapped. 'Keep watching.'

Shortly after the cops arrive, a man is seen leaving the side entrance of the bank in a hurry.

Harry paused the tape.

'Anyone recognise this gentleman?'

A silence filled the room for all of three seconds.

'I'd bet my retirement money, that's Nutty Nolan,' McCauseland said. 'I'd recognise that big baldy bastard anywhere.'

'You're right, Bill,' Boyd said. 'It's him. No doubt about it. A psychiatrist's wet dream.'

'I think we're all of one mind on that,' Harry said. 'Now, the question is: what the hell was Mister Seamus Nolan, formerly of the allegedly now-defunct Brotherhood, doing in the bank? Of equal importance: why was he in such a hurry not to be seen *leaving* it?'

'Why's he holding his head, sir?' Kerr asked, coming closer to the screen, pointing. 'That looks like a wound. Was any blood found at the scene?'

'Boyd?' Harry said.

'No one was told to look for blood,' Boyd said defensively. 'We'd no reports of anyone hurt. Why the hell would I be looking for blood?'

'Don't get testy. This isn't a pissing contest. Was there blood, yes or no?'

'I didn't see any … but … there was a distinct smell of bleach when I entered the office. To be honest, I never thought anything of it, at the time.'

'Bleach? *Hmm*. I think we need to have another word with Dana Robinson. Find out why she's so concerned about keeping her office sparklingly clean after such a *horrifying experience*. Whatever's behind this sudden rush to clean, could end up being very dirty.'

Chapter Eight

'He'll regret it till his dying day, if ever he lives that long.'
Squire Danaher, *The Quiet Man*

Charlie Madden was feeling rather pleased with himself, and with life in general, which was a double rarity in his precarious life. For the first time in a very long time, the good days were now starting to outnumber the bad ones.

He was in his pigeon coop, talking to his beloved birds in a hushed, secretive tone.

'I'm trusting you not to say a word to anyone. Understood? No stool pigeon allowed into my gang.'

The birds began making strange coo roo-c'too-coo sounds in response to his voice, while he continued emptying seeds from cloth sacks into plastic bins. When the sacks were half-empty, he dropped bricks of money into them, before re-topping up with the seeds.

'Charlie!' a voice shouted from the house. 'Dinner's ready.'

'Coming, love! Just finishing!'

He quickly completed the task and headed back into the house. A film of white dust seemed to cover every inch of the ageing place. He washed his hands, then made his way to the small kitchen, where his wife Rosie had prepared his favourite meal – mince pie, roast spuds, peas and OXO gravy.

'This dust is getting worse, Rosie. Can't even sit down without being covered in it.'

'And whose bright idea was it to go along with troublemaker Tommy Norton's madness of "Let's stand our ground against the wrecking ball"?'

'Would you rather we were shoved into one of those high-rise flats, never seeing a soul again?'

'Never seeing a soul again? Are you on your funny half-hour? We haven't seen a soul in six weeks, except nuisance Norton at the other end of the street.'

Rosie joined him at the table. Unlike Charlie, who would eat a scab from a dead man's nose, she was a finicky eater, and rarely had large meals of any description.

'What? What're you gawking at, Charlie?'

'You, you beautiful sexy woman.' Charlie winked. 'Is there a law against that?'

'You're up to something, Charlie Madden. If you're looking to borrow money from me, you've no hope.'

'How long's it been since we've had a holiday, darling?'

'Well, seeing you've been in prison on and off for the last fifteen years, I'd add another five to that. Why? Thinking of taking me to Bangor again, like on our honeymoon? A fish supper and dipping our toes in the Pickie Pool?'

'What've we always wished for, if we won the Lotto?'

'You're a genie now?'

'Go on. Humour an old dog.'

'A barge to float away in, leave all our worries behind. Happy now?'

'I'm only happy when you're happy, darling.' Charlie leaned over, kissing her full on the lips, before placing a magazine atop the table.

'What's this?' Rose reached out and took the magazine. '*Canal Boats and Barges*. What're you doing with this?'

'I'm buying. You're picking.'

Rosie laughed. 'Where on earth would we get the money for a rowing boat, never mind one of these beauties?'

'If I told you the horses, would you believe me?'

'Probably not.'

'Well, that's what happened. I finally hit the big one. *Really* big.'

A look of concern came over Rosie's face. 'What's going on, Charlie? Have you been up to something, after telling me those days were behind you? I don't want to see you going to prison any more. I'm getting too old for all that nonsense starting again – and so are you.'

'For God's sake, stop working yourself into a lather. There's nothing to be concerned about. We're going to start enjoying ourselves, after all these years of struggling just to survive. I promise you.'

'I'd rather you'd just promise me that you'll never go back to prison. That would mean more to me than any fancy boat.'

Charlie smiled, reached over and held Rosie's hand, kissing it tenderly.

'You've no need to worry, my darling. Things are finally looking up for us. You'll see. I'm never going back to prison. *Never*. That's a promise. Now, Hurry and get ready.'

'Ready for what?'

'We're booked into the Merchant for a dirty weekend.'

'The Merchant …? Where all them singers and actors go? I'm not going there.'

A horn beeped.

'Too late. There's the taxi.'

'But I've nothing to wear for such a posh place.'

'You will in the morning. We'll go shopping at Victoria Square. C'mon! Grab some stuff and stick it in a bag.'

Twenty minutes later, away they went, rushing out the door, laughing like two teenagers on a first date, not a care in the world.

Not a care in this bloody world.

Chapter Nine

Comics are a gateway drug to literacy.
Art Spiegelman, Maus, *A Survivor's Tale*

Heroes and Villains comic book shop in Belfast's Cornmarket may not be the biggest place. It has rivals dotted throughout the city. But no other shop has the killer ace up its sleeve, namely Kieran 'King of Klassic Komics' Kelly.

Kieran is the walking Stephen Hawking on all things science fiction, fantasy, horror and comic-related in the whole of Ireland, though he likes to substitute 'Ireland' with 'world', depending on his surroundings and company. He's also the creator of his very own registered onomatopoeia: Kieranzapuma – though he has never divulged its true meaning to anyone.

A graduate of Queen's University, he is in all probability the only person on the planet to have a degree on the life and times of Harmenszoon, legendary creator of some of the biggest super-heroes and villains flying about the skies and universes. In fact, Kieran's knowledge has become as legendary as the great Harmenszoon's creations, with only one other mortal on the planet brave enough to verbally joust with Kieran, proclaiming himself heir to the Throne of Asgard and Knowledge: Brian Ross.

'All right, Kieran?' Brian said, exiting a taxi as Kieran finished pushing up the rusted and graffiti-covered shutters of his shop.

'Dude! What the hell's got you up so early? Don't tell me you pissed the bed again?' Kieran began knotting his shoulder-length hair with a Spiderman webbed red ribbon. The ageing flower-child resembled Willie Nelson on a very rough day, which is a very rough look indeed.

'Had an early appointment with my tattooist. Can't wait to show you the finished business.'

'Still wasting money on taxis, I see. I keep telling you to get yourself a wee run-around. All those taxis must be costing you a fortune.'

'I've no interest in cars. I can't drive and have no intention of ever learning. Anyway, cars are destroying the planet.'

'And that taxi you arrived in isn't?'

Kieran walked through the shop into the storage room, Brian following close behind.

'Wait until you see this tat, Kieran. You're going to love it.'

'First things first, dude. Morning isn't morning until I have my tea.' Kieran struck a match, and give flame to a ring on an old gas stove. Placed a kettle on the flaming ring, and dropped a teabag into a Batman cup. 'Need to get these old bones working with the help of some caffeine.'

Brian waited patiently until the kettle whistled, and Kieran filled his cup.

'Okay, dude. Let's see this Michelangelo.'

Brian removed his leather jacket and Doctor Strange T-shirt, quickly stripping to the waist, exposing a body mapped in tattoos, mainly superheroes and sexy heroines with ridiculously exaggerated body forms.

'Well? What do you think?' Brain angled his upper torso and stretched out his arms so Kieran could see the intimidating scale of Mercury, flying its way through the cosmos at incredible speed, mounted by the Dark Avenger, his flaming sword slicing and dicing invisible foes. Mercury's wings spanned both of Brian's arms, making him look like the Fallen Archangel of Darkness.

'Oh ... my ... God, *duuuuuuuuude*! That is *beautiful*. It looks so fucking real, like you could mount it and fly skywards into the heavens. Harmenszoon would've loved it.'

'Two weeks to complete, cost me a fortune and still hurts like hell, but well worth it.'

'You didn't come here this early in the day just to show me the tattoo, impressive as it is. What's up?'

'The cape. You still have it?'

Kieran nodded. 'It's not going anywhere. Owned it for five years. Probably end up owning it for another five.'

'I'm here to buy it.'

'Of course you are. You've been saying *that* for the last five years. Lucky for you, I'm in a good mood this morning. You can see it, but no touching. I'll be back in a sec.'

Kieran walked into an adjacent room. A large, intimidating Chubbsafes Duoguard 300 security safe stood silently in the corner.

Opening the safe, Kieran sorted through a series of large steel drawers, each controlled by a pneumatic tube system. Finally selecting the drawer in question, he removed it and walked back to where Brian waited.

'Remember: no touching.' Kieran placed the locked drawer on top of the counter, opening it seductively slowly.

'*Ohhhhhhhhhhhh* …' Brian whispered, watching as the box revealed its secret. 'You're sure this is one of the originals?'

'Dude, if I didn't love you like a son and respect you so much, I'd be shoving you out the door with an insult like that. Have I ever owned anything but the genuine article? This Superman cape is one of only five signed by the original Man of Steel himself, George Reeves, before he shot himself – or was murdered, as most of us die-hard fans suspect.'

'Hard to believe the cape's over sixty years old. Looks pristine.'

'Doubting Thomas, this is our Shroud of Turin, the likes of which will never be seen again. It has powers beyond your wildest dreams. Now, if you don't mind, it's time to put it away. I don't like rotten air, such as your breath, gnawing at it.'

'The price?'

'You ask me that very same question every month, and the answer is still the very same: twenty thousand quid. Not a penny less. Not a penny more.'

Brian reached into the Eason's plastic bag he had been gripping since his arrival, and removed a large brown envelope. Opened it. Began counting out lines of fifties and hundreds from the envelope.

'What the … where the … how the …?' Kieran's voice trailed off. His mouth closed. Opened. Closed.

'Count it.'

Kieran, hands shaking, began separating the fifties and hundreds into two camps, before fanning each pile with his thumb. 'Ouch!'

'What?'

'This money's so hot, burnt the fingers off me. I think I'd better let it cool down for a few days in my secure fridge, don't you think?'

'I think your thinking is right on the money.'

Brian reached over and delicately removed the cape from its metal enclosure. Brought it to his face. Inhaled its yesteryear aroma. Kissed the cloth tenderly. 'My *preciousssssssssssssssssssssss!*

'That's creepy, dude. You're actually starting to morph into Gollum. Just don't open up the cape indoors.'

'Why?'

'Because it's bad luck, that's why. A curse after Reeves' murder. Give me a second to put this money away. This calls for a celebration.'

'Hope it's more than tea?'

'A lot more. Pull down the "Closed" sign, and lock the door. Work has ceased for the day.'

* * *

'*Oh, mannnnnnnnnnnnnnnnn!*' Brian said, deeply inhaling a king-size joint, relaxing in the back of the store, curled-up on an old rocking chair. 'What the hell *is* this stuff?'

'*Mountainusk Thunderfuck*, dude. The best marijuana this side of a Taliban's turban.' Kieran stretched out on the floor, eyes shut tight, a fat joint smouldering at the side of his mouth. A smile of sheer pleasure inked his face. 'A friend smuggled it in yesterday from Amsterdam, up his arse. That's why it's still warm.'

'Thank you for sharing that appetising piece of information. All the time I've known you, I never once saw you doing coke. Why's that?'

'That's the Devil's dandruff, dude. Those white lines will guide you straight over the cliff to Hell. I had a good friend who died of a heart attack taking that shit. It's bad news. I hate coke. I never touch the stuff, and neither should you.'

'I hear you …' Brian's voice was weakening. A delightful drowsiness was entering his spirit. He closed his eyes. 'Riddle me this, Batman: how come Adam and Eve have a belly button on every painting we see of them?'

'Huh …?'

'Exactly … a conspiracy … of biblical proportions.'

'That's fucking strange shit to be talking.'

'*I'm* feeling … strange, Doctor …'

'Doctor Strange … yes … Ditko's.' Kieran sucked heavily on the joint. Blew ghostly contrails down his nose. Smiled.

'Yes, I agree. Ditko was ... brilliant, but ... I always preferred Gene "The Dean" Colan's Doctor.'

'I ... have to differ on ... that ... dude. Ditko was ... a god before his time. A god before ... the New Gods ...'

'Differ ... differ all ... you ... want. Colan was ... was ...' Brian opened his eyes. Fog seemed to be coming in from underneath the door, like an old Hammer movie. 'Foggy fog ...'

'Froggy frog? I think ... I think I see it, too. Green and purple. Smiling with golden teeth. A hot ... little frog with silver hot pants on. Lovely legs. Cute. Sexy. It's ... winking at me.' Kieran inhaled deeply once again. 'Man, I am so fucking wasted ...'

Brian stood, his naked torso glistening with sweat. Placed the Superman cape over his shoulders, and stretched out his arms. They slowly began morphing into Mercury's wings. Seconds later, he was flying up the stairway to heaven.

* * *

Kieran awoke to a sound bouncing about in his swampy head. Croaking? Frogs? He looked about, expecting to be in a rain forest. Instead, his face was hugging the floor of the storage room, silvery strings of saliva dripping from his mouth.

'Brian ...? Brian? Where the hell are you, dude?'

The discordant sound seemed to be getting louder. It was coming from outside, in the street.

Standing, he walked unsteadily to the front door. Unlocked it. Just as it opened, he heard someone screaming to get an ambulance.

'What's going on out here? Brian …? *Brian!*'

Kieran dropped to his knees. Brian was sprawled out on the pavement, legs and arms knotted horribly. Blood was mingling with the Superman cape covering him.

'Brian! Brian!'

'Don't touch him!' someone kept shouting from the gathering crowd. 'The ambulance is on its way.'

'Brian! Talk to me. Please, dude, don't do this to me. C'mon, Brian!' Kieran squeezed his hand.

'Stop touching him! You'll make his injuries worse.'

'Brian, don't you die on me. Do you hear me, dude? I'll kill you if you die on me.'

'He must've thought he could fly,' a voice said. 'I saw him jumping out of the top room window shouting that he was Superman. Poor bastard.'

'Brian? You're gonna be okay. Do you hear me, dude? Why the hell did you have to open the cape in the shop? I told you it was bad luck.'

Chapter Ten

Somewhere in the ocean, a shark was missing its cold eyes because this man had them.
Steve Hamilton, *The Lock Artist*

Early next morning, Harry rapped on the door of Superintendent Winston McCafferty's office, waited a moment, then entered.

In his late fifties, McCafferty was thin in body structure, as well as hair-line and personality. A career cop, he had never spent a day on the streets fighting crime.

He was seated, a sheet of paper in one hand and a cup of tea in the other. He looked up at Harry in mock surprise, as if he hadn't summoned him to his office ten minutes earlier.

'Harry?'

Harry walked up to the large mahogany desk, the top of which was decorated with the many community awards McCafferty had gathered over the years. He loved nothing better than attending events and functions, tape-cuttings at new buildings, anything to keep him in the public eye. Harry liked to say McCafferty would show up at the opening of an envelope.

'You wanted to see me, sir?'

'Sit down and join me for tea.'

Are you for real? Harry thought, continuing to stand. 'I've a squad meeting going on down below. The Bank of New Republic robbery.'

'The bank – of course! That's what I wanted to talk to you about. How are things progressing? It's been what, three days?'

'Two, but we're moving along as well as can be expected. Slowly but surely.'

'Good. Glad to hear that. We need to get this cleared as a priority. Results, Harry. Results. Every second, every penny has to be accounted for. Ombudsman. Know what I mean?' McCafferty winked slyly. 'Not like the old days, eh?'

'I'm fully aware of that, sir. My men are working full throttle. In fact, we may have a breakthrough as we speak.'

'That's good news, Harry.' McCafferty smiled. It looked painful. 'Very good news, indeed. Well done.'

'That's why I'm in a bit of a hurry to get back downstairs to the briefing room.'

'Of course, of course! You will keep me updated on any new developments, won't you?'

'You'll be the first to know.' Harry kept the sarcasm low-level. 'Can I go now?'

'Yes. Thank you, Harry.'

The moment Harry left, a side door opened. A man stepped into the room. Tall with a wiry build, his face was as friendly as a drive-by shooting. His eyes were as menacing as a double-barrel shotgun. They seemed to have no eyelids, and had a predatory coldness, like those of a great white shark.

'We're not going to have trouble with Thompson, are we, Winston?'

'No … of course not.' Nervousness suddenly entered McCafferty's demeanour. 'I've got him firmly under control.'

'You better have, if you want to keep your arse in that nice, soft seat.'

* * *

Harry returned to the briefing room, where his crew were congregating in front of a large screen. He waited until the buzz of anticipation settled down before commencing.

'Okay. All eyes on the screen.' Harry hated using these modern contraptions, but had little choice. *You need to move with the times, Harry*, instructed the brass, more of a threat than a suggestion. 'Boyd, what was the outcome of the DNA tests?'

Boyd opened his notepad. 'The saliva belongs to a Jim McCabe, a jailbird who did time for a spate of armed robberies. Been in and out of prison since the age of sixteen. It's a second home to him. Out of prison for about a year, this time. According to his parole officer, our Jim was a model prisoner inside, and is keeping his nose clean while on the outside.'

Derisive laughter from around the room.

Harry pressed a button and a mug shot of Jim appeared on the screen. He looked grim and dangerous, as all good mug shots should.

'This photo was taken in Magilligan prison a week before McCabe's release. It's been circulated to all departments. Just make sure we're the department that secures his scalp.'

Harry turned his attention back to the screen. 'All of you, here's a list of associates McCabe knocked about with in prison. All have been released in the last year or so. Could be one or two of them were involved in the robbery. Perhaps none. See what we can glean from the list. It's a process of elimination, and I know it's time-consuming, but we work with what we've got.'

A series of names and photos appeared on the screen: Bernard 'The Bible' Blake, Henry Carlisle, Joe Gillespie, Peter 'Hardman' Hardy, Mickey O'Reilly, John 'The God' Paterson.

'Share the names between you, and hunt each of these miscreants down. Find out what they've been up to since the last time they took a shit. Weigh it, if you suspect they're lying about it. I want results. Big time results. Bill? What else do we have on McCabe?'

McCauseland flipped a page. 'He's separated, and has little or no contact with either his ex, Marianne, or ten-year-old son, Patrick. At present, his fixed abode is Steeple House, Victoria Street. That's a homeless hostel for men, run by the Charity of Christian Good. They enforce a strict policy of ten pm curfew, unless special circumstances arise.'

'Like, I need to go rob a bank, Brother McCauseland,' Boyd cut in. 'Hallelujah, Lord, and pass the guns and bags of stolen money!'

McCauseland grinned, before continuing. 'This jailbird seems to have flown the nest, for now. Arresting officers went to Steeple House in the early hours of this morning, but he wasn't to be found.'

'Was he there on the evening of the robbery?' Kerr said.

'No. Staff said he'd left the day before, and has yet to return. Management have been told to alert us immediately if he returns, but without the suspect knowing about it.'

'You think he'll risk going back to the hostel, sir?' Kerr said, looking directly at Harry. 'He already has a load of money at his disposal.'

'Bank robbers are risk-takers by nature. They don't abide by boundaries. The likes of McCabe would try anything, no matter how reckless and stupid it would seem to a normal person.'

Kerr scribbled in his notepad.

'Now, pay attention all of you.' Harry's his voice was no longer informal. 'What I'm about to show you, *does not* leave this room. If I find out what I'm about to say has been leaked to the press, I'll make sure the culprit's kicked out of the force with no pension or prospects, with the exception of a prison cell. Am I perfectly clear on this?'

Everyone nodded.

'We now have the bank's CCTV footage. Pay attention to it. Bill? Turn the lights off.'

The room went dark, and another screen started showing the bank's footage. Three wolves – one in a wheelchair – arriving at the bank's door, before splitting up and doing their thing. A gun-brandishing wolf running into Dana Robinson's office. A customer standing, confronting the wolf.

'That's Nolan, all right. Ballsy as always,' McCauseland said, a begrudging respect in his voice.

The scene continued, showing the verbal confrontation, then Nolan being smacked across the head.

'Ouch!' the group said in unison.

'Whichever robber hit that psycho, I take my hat off to him,' Boyd said. 'Must have a death wish, though. Nolan's not exactly the kiss-and-make-up type, is he?'

'More observation, gentlemen, and less talking!' Harry said.

Wolves One and Two run in panic as they discover the empty vault. Wolf One re-enters the office, saying something to Dana Robinson beneath the table. Wolf Two enters, waving signals to Wolf One. Wolf Two leaves. Wolf Three enters the office, waves a gun in the air, says something to Wolf One. Then, with sleight-of-hand, Wolf One takes Nolan's briefcase.

'Did you see that wee move with the briefcase?' McCauseland said with admiration.

'Lights please.' Harry clicked off the machine. 'As you can all see, Dana Robinson wasn't fully truthful with us when first questioned. She has now admitted that one of the robbers assaulted a customer, hitting him over the head with a gun. That customer, as we know, was Nolan.'

'What was Nolan doing at the bank, sir?' Kerr said.

'I'll get to that in a moment. As you all know, Nolan is the leader of the Brotherhood's execution squad in Belfast and beyond. A nice chap, he is not. Under the threat of being arrested and jailed for withholding vital information, Dana Robinson has been more forthcoming on why Nolan was there in the first place. He was making a deposit, when the robbers entered.'

'Did she say how much of a deposit, Harry?' McCauseland asked.

'A tidy sum in that briefcase of his, before it was removed by Wolf One. Half a million quid, in total.'

Everyone in the room looked gobsmacked. Harry savoured the look. They were back in the big league once again. If they could solve this, they would be back on the front page, instead of some overrated actor.

'I've agreed to overlook Dana Robinson's ... forgetfulness, provided she doesn't alert Nolan that we now know about him being at the bank, and his money being taken. To this, she has eagerly agreed.'

'Shouldn't we arrest Nolan, sir?' Kerr asked.

'For putting money in a bank, or for being robbed? At the minute, we don't have any proof, other than Dana Robinson's word, that Nolan even had this vast amount of money with him. No, we're going to let the hare sit for a while. Keep in mind, when we solve this – and nobody better be harbouring any doubts that we will – it'll be beneficial to us all. I want these robbers, and I want them before they get the chance to enjoy any of their ill-gotten gains. Am I perfectly clear on this?'

As one, the room said, 'Yes, sir!'

'Has anyone anything solid to add, before I dismiss you? No? Okay, get cracking. I want good news, and I want it soon.'

'Anyone need anything out of Tesco?' Boyd asked the room, exiting without waiting for a reply.

* * *

Outside the station, Boyd dodged manic traffic on the Antrim Road, before entering the supermarket directly opposite. Inside, he looked nervously about. Picked up the payphone near the exit. Inserted a few coins. Pushed some numbers. Waited. A few seconds later, whispered: 'Jim McCabe. Here's his details ...'

Chapter Eleven

*'I do not go without him. Efficient, lightweight, easy to unsheathe
… it fits easily into a holster!'*

Al Capone

Night security officer Peter Burns had just entered the
security office at Steeple House when the outside buzzer
sounded. The office had a total of twelve CCTV screens, monitoring all activity in and around the building. Burns looked at
the figure on screen number three, standing outside the entrance.
He didn't recognise the man. More than likely, someone looking
for a free bed for the night.

Bearded and wearing glasses, the man was well-dressed, but
that meant little. People always assumed that only homeless
people applied to get into the shelter. Ha! What a joke. The
amount of chancers chancing their arm at night never failed to
amaze and disgust Burns.

Tight-fisted businessmen were the capital offenders. They would
spin a yarn about having just been mugged, when in fact they had
probably been kicked out of the dodgy motel where they had been
staying with a lady of the night. Later, they would be spinning
another yarn to their loving wife about some business conference.

Burns lifted up the security phone from its cradle, deliberately slow.

'Hello? How can I help you, *sir*?' he said in a tired monotone, as if hating to use the obligatory 'sir'.

'Detective Peter Grogan, Musgrave Street. I'm here to ask a few questions about one of your clients.'

'Okay.' Burns hit the button beneath the desk and the door opened slightly with the jarring sound of grinding metal. 'Push and enter.'

Once inside, Rasharkin flashed his false police ID. Burns didn't bother his arse to look at it. Cops came and went in this place, almost as much as the nomadic residents. They were always investigating something or other, and trying to put the blame on Steeple House. Someone just got mugged? Blame it on Steeple House. Something was nicked from Castle Court? Must be a Steeple House resident. The economy going down the shitter? Must have something to do with Steeple House.

'How's it going?' Rasharkin asked, all-friendly.

'Ask me that in twelve hours, when my shift finishes,' Burns said dryly.

'I hear what you're saying. I do the graveyard shift, as well. You get no thanks, just all the shit.'

Burns half-smiled – unusual for him, except on paydays and the rare occasion when Liverpool FC won away from home.

From his inside pocket, Rasharkin produced a mug shot. Handed it to Burns. 'Know this chap?'

Burns looked at the photo. Nodded. Handed the photo back.

'Jim McCabe. There's still no sign of him. We've already been told to alert you if we spot him. What's he been up to, anyway?'

'Sorry, but I can't really disclose anything. You know the score.' Rasharkin pocketed the photo, which he had received less than two hours ago, along with all the info available on McCabe.

Burns nodded. 'Confidentiality? Same as here. You could have a bunch of sex offenders living in this place, but you can't disclose anything about them to the newspapers, or to the public. All hell would break loose if you tried to do the right thing by informing nearby schools and parents. The pervs have more rights than us.'

'I hear you. We both sing from the same hymn sheet.' Rasharkin winked. 'Now, about McCabe? Is there any chance I could have a look in his room? I know it's late and all, but I was hoping if I could get some clue as to his whereabouts, it might help get him off the streets. He's very dangerous.'

'Well … we're not really permitted to allow unofficial visits late at night, for security reasons. It's against procedure … Ah, fuck it! Why not? Another criminal put away, can't be a bad thing, can it?'

'Can't be a bad thing at all.'

'Okay. Let me grab a spare key.'

Burns accompanied Rasharkin up in the ancient lift, to the third floor.

'Take a left, then another left. Room twenty-two.' Burns handed Rasharkin the key, just as the lift door opened on the designated floor. 'Try not to be too long. And watch your back.

McCabe's got a few thuggish mates in here. They might try something if they see you going into his room.'

'Thanks for the warning. I'll be as quick as I can.'

Rasharkin walked down the narrow, claustrophobic corridor. The filthy carpet beneath his feet felt moist. Spongy with urine and dragged-in rain. The stench of unwashed flesh permeated the walls. For a second, the smell brought back bad memories of institutionalised hopelessness and horror.

Another smell lurked in the shadows, this one more malevolent. It stank like a combination of leprosy and liquorice, of skin gone to rot in an unhealed wound. The stench made him think of a man he once killed, throat slit in a ghastly goodbye. He was forced to sleep with the putrifying corpse for two days in scorching forest heat, while the man's heavily armed friends searched frantically, circling all around, calling his name: *Anthony ... Anthony ... Anthony ...*

It was one of the few names he remembered from his long list of the dead.

Once inside Jim's room, Rasharkin reached for the light switch. It dangled on one screw, next to the door. He jiggled the switch until the light came on, exposing the room's contents. It could have been a prison cell minus the bars.

He glanced about, quickly taking in his surroundings. Cramped. Stale body and cigar odour. Scant fresh air. Soft porn magazines scattered everywhere. Havoc in a hellish hovel.

Standing in the centre of the room, he studied what little furniture was offered. Where to begin? Was it worthwhile?

Would he find anything of value, not just fool's gold? His gut feeling said yes. It had never let him down before. From his pocket, he removed a pair of nitrile gloves and began searching.

Twenty minutes later, he found something of interest, crumpled up in a rusted wastepaper basket. The item was covered in used tea-bags, spittle and God alone knew what else. He sat down on the edge of the bed, gingerly flowering the paper open and reading.

A loud banging on the door disturbed his thoughts. He pocketed the paper, stood and walked to the door, easing it open.

Two men, a smorgasbord of scars on their faces, filled the doorframe. Menacingly. Like hired thugs from a bad movie set. They wore grubby T-shirts, their meat-cleaver arms sleeved with tattoos riding all the way up to their massive shoulders and beyond.

One was a skinhead, a mashed-in nose covering the centre of his pock-marked face, neck circled with painted rattlesnakes. The taller of the two looked even more intimidating. Gym-thick, with metal studs in ears, lips and nose, and double the amount of scars his mate had. His face looked like badly fried sirloin steak. Both gave off the stench of dangerous living and violent aspirations.

'Yes?' Rasharkin said in a calm, innocent voice. 'What seems to be the problem?'

'*You're* the fucking problem,' Rattlesnake snarled, revealing a cargo of rotted teeth. 'This is our mate's room. Haven't you fucking cops done enough harassment?'

'I was just finishing and –'

Rattlesnake pushed Rasharkin violently back into the room, while Stud Face slammed the door behind them.

'You're done finishing – *now*,' Stud Face said, placing a meaty hand on Rasharkin's shoulder, giving it a death-lock squeeze.

Rasharkin looked at the hand, then its owner. 'If that's meant to impress me, you'll have to squeeze a little harder.'

'How's this?' Stud Face squeezed harder, smiling a bottle-in-your-face smile. 'Looks like you need to learn your lesson the hard way.'

'Sorry, I should have told you I have learning difficulties.'

In a blink, the hand disappeared up Stud Face's back.

'*Fuckkkkkkkkkkkkkkkkkkkkkkkkkkkkkkkkk*!' Stud Face screamed, before an elbow connected with his forehead, followed by a fist square on the jaw. He collapsed like a busted accordion.

A look of amazement appeared on Rattlesnake's face. Before he could react, he was kicked between the legs, then cannon-balled off the wall. On the return journey, Rasharkin greeted him with a breath-removing punch to the throat.

Rattlesnake wobbled, then fell to his knees. He tried standing, but failed.

Rasharkin walked calmly to the door. Opened it.

'Fucking run!' Rattlesnake wheezed, suddenly producing a cutthroat razor and waving it in the air. 'I *ever* see you on the fucking streets, I'll cut your fucking throat.'

Rasharkin gently closed the door. Slid the bolt into its niche. Turned and faced Rattlesnake, before doing a little movement with the inside of his jacket. A small revolver appeared in his hand, filling the room with tangible fear. He walked over to Rattlesnake and placed the muzzle against the thug's nose.

'Did I hear correctly? You'll cut my throat?'

'I … I …'

'Open your mouth.'

A look of horror spread across Rattlesnake's face. 'Ppp … please … I … I … was just –'

'I'll shoot you, first in one eye, then the other.'

Rattlesnake's mouth opened slowly.

Rasharkin removed the razor from Rattlesnake's trembling hand. 'You like flapping that fat tongue of yours? Stick it out. Let me see what you're so proud of.'

Hesitantly, the yellow-tinged tongue emerged. Rasharkin rested the razor's edge gently upon it. For the longest time, he stared trance-like into Rattlesnake's petrified eyes, debating with himself on what tomorrow's newspapers would have in print, to be determined by his actions in this moment.

'You scream, I'll kill you. Understand?'

Rattlesnake blinked rapidly in acknowledgment.

Rasharkin pushed down on the razor. The plump meaty tongue offered little resistance. It sliced perfectly in two. Blood poured from the wound, like too much wine being consumed by a drunkard.

Rattlesnake collapsed to the floor, clasping his mouth, muffling all screams.

'Now you resemble a *real* rattlesnake.' Rasharkin unbolted the door before closing it soundlessly behind him.

Chapter Twelve

Dirty deeds and they're done dirt cheap.
AC/DC, 'Dirty Deeds'

In the bedroom of his *pied-à-terre* on the Antrim Road, a naked Barney Dennison was pouring himself a Gordon's gin, and a Tia Maria for his guest. 'West End Girls' by Pet Shop Boys was playing in the background.

Dennison was feeling damn good, and not just because of the gin's electric kick railing along his spine and buzzing the eye of his cock.

Sneaking a peek in the wall-mirror, he watched his guest on the bed, bending and stretching long, lovely tanned legs, graceful as a cat.

A sexy kitten deliciously created.

'I hope you're not trying to get me drunk, *Bern-ard*?' the guest said, smiling bleach-white teeth, skin perfectly golden.

Bern-ard. Just the way it was pronounced, with a hint of a French accent, made Barney's knees tremble, ballbag tighten, cock quiver like a dowsing rod indicating water.

'C'mon over here, *Bern-ard*. I want you inside me, all the way up until your hairy balls are crushing against my tender buttocks.'

Barney was feeling like a man once cursed with erectile dysfunction, now possessing a boner that could flagpole the Tricolour. Another hardener rising!

Years of tortuous impotence, not even helped by bottle-loads of Viagra. Now I'm Elton John, the rocket man, ready for take-off!

* * *

Just over a week ago, Barney was sitting drinking in the shadows of the Velvet Underground Rooms inside Ramsey's Kingdom – an exclusive, members-only club on the Lisburn Road, south of the city. For a long twenty minutes, he'd been surreptitiously eyeing a beautiful young creature by the sobriquet of Butterfly, doing his sexy thing on the tiny dance floor of weathered mahogany.

Butterfly had a face most women would kill to have – and the body. He wore designer jeans so tight they were practically criminal, leaving nothing to the imagination, back or front.

The young beauty was dancing with another young man, a narcissistic angel created by cock-teasing gods to torment people like Barney. Wild and torrid, there was something seductively hypnotising about the duo's dancing as they mounted each other in mind-bending manoeuvres a contortionist would be proud of.

Barney pictured himself forty years ago, up on the floor, dancing with the likes of Butterfly, hands and fingers running seductively over tight buttocks and bulging fronts.

He sighed. Stop it. Stop tormenting yourself. You'll only end up depressingly drunk, like every other lonely night.

Suddenly, the front door of the club opened. Barney held his breath. He instinctively ducked down behind the table, pretending to tie his shoelace while glancing nervously at the doorway. To his relief, it was just a couple of handholding old farts.

He knew he shouldn't be here, hidden in the darkest corner of the room, but it was more discreet and lesser known than the Kremlin, with its notorious poseurs, boasters of conquests real and imagined. Secretly, he had to admit there was a certain tingling thrill of darkness in living on the edge.

Provided, of course, he tread carefully and didn't fall off that dangerous edge, into the abyss of public mockery and shame. He shuddered at the thought, but knew that he wouldn't stop, regardless of the cost.

Ten minutes later, he stood, packing up for another lonely night at home with a farcical marriage montage for public consumption, a wife no longer there. Just as he slid his coat on, all hell broke loose on the dance floor. The two young lovers were pushing and shoving, screaming skin-tearing obscenities at each other.

Seated patrons either ignored the scene – bored of handbags-at-dawn squabbles – or giggled with amusement. Barney, however, took the unusual and dangerous decision to intervene in the squabble, an unwritten no-no that usually ended in bloody consequences for the intervener.

'I would have killed that bitch, if you hadn't got in the way,' Butterfly said a few minutes later, allowing Barney to lead him out into the cold Belfast night air.

'You could've been … hurt. Your face …'

'My face? What's wrong with my face?' Butterfly said defensively.

'Nothing. Nothing at all. It's … it's beautiful. I … I just … I didn't want to see it bruised, or worse, scarred. It's … so beautiful. The most beautiful face I have ever seen.'

Butterfly smiled. Tenderly kissed Barney's cheek. 'What a lovely man you are. Maybe we can go for a drink some time?'

* * *

'Here you go,' Barney said, holding the drinks, while awkwardly easing back down onto the welcoming bed.

'Too much alcohol, *Bern-ard*, means less sex.' Butterfly smiled mischievously, reaching over and fondling Barney's aging balls. 'We don't want that, do we?'

Barney's hands began shaking so badly, he spilt some of the drink onto his hardened cock.

Without missing a beat, Butterfly bent, and licked the liquor clean away.

'Waste not, want not,' Butterfly said, kissing Barney full on the mouth, his tongue darting in and out like a little sparrow feeding. 'I need to pee-pee. Back in a tick-tick. Keep dickie-dee nice and hard for me.'

'Hurry back … please …'

Butterfly slid off the bed, walking briskly out of the room, perfectly-shaped buttocks seesawing seductively.

'*Ooohhhhhhhhhhhh my* …' Barney voice shuddered weakly.

Less than a minute later, the sound of a toilet flushing brought Butterfly back with smile on face, condom in hand. A shake of the head threw his shoulder-length, jet-black hair into a sexy dance of dizziness.

'*Now*, I'm ready for action, my sweet *Bern-ard*,' he said, settling back on the bed. Tearing the condom's package open, he tongued the sheath perfectly into his mouth, smiling bizarrely at Barney like a blow-up doll on too much helium.

From a horizontal position, Barney's cock rocketed skyward, reaching an almost ninety-degree angle. He bit hard on his bottom lip, trying not to ejaculate as Butterfly's beautiful mouth began working wondrous wonders.

'You liked that, didn't you, naughty boy?' Butterfly said, emerging from down-under a few minutes later, while reaching over to the nightstand, grabbing a tub of Barney's *Slap Happy Masturbation Cream*.

'Can I … can I do it this time, Butterfly? *Please*,' Barney said, throat sandpapery dry with sexual anticipation.

'Okay, but be gentle with my beautiful *be*-hind,' Butterfly teased, turning over, offering his perfectly shaped, magnificent bottom to Barney's less-than-magnificent, imperfectly shaped face.

Please don't cum, Barney pleaded with his over-enthusiastic cock, while massaging the cream in and around Butterfly's dark heavenly aperture. *Not yet. Please not yet …*

'*Hmmmmmmmmmmmm.* I love the sexy smell of the cream.' Butterfly was purring, his back cat-arching, head on pillow, eyes slowly closing. 'That's *soooooooooooo* nice. You've an artist's hands, *Bern-ard. Ohhhhhhhhhh. Slooooooooooowly.* Nice and *slowwwwwww. Hmmmmmmmmmmmm.* That's the way … oh oh oh … baby …'

'I … I … can't hold back. I can't …' Barney said, frantically mounting Butterfly. 'Oh fuck. Oh fuck. Oh fuckkkkkkkkkkkkk-kkkkkkkkkkkkkkkk.'

Butterfly's hand reached round to his own buttocks, pulling on them, allowing them to flower open for Barney's cock to penetrate even deeper.

'*Hmmmmmmmmmmmmmm. Fuck me harder, you nasty old cowboy …* ' Butterfly whispered, voice filled with seductive need. '*Slap that little pony's ass.*'

Barney began slapping Butterfly's arse as if his very life depended on it.

'*Harderrrrrrrrrrrrrrrrrrrrrrrrrrrrrrr!*' Butterfly screamed.

Barney continued slapping and pumping, sweating like left-over cheese. His eyes felt ready to pop from their enclosures. Heart beating violently. A heart attack? He didn't care. This was heaven, this dark and forbidden bliss. If he died here tonight, it would be well worth it. To hell with the public shame. He'd be dead anyway.

While Barney slapped Butterfly's arse, someone suddenly began slapping Barney's – *very hard*.

'*Go on. Giddy-up. Ride that little pony's ass. Yee-haw, cowboy!*' whispered a voice close to Barney's left ear.

The voice was disconcerting. No matter how he tried, Barney couldn't stay focused. It was killing his rhythm. His boner quickly dried and died.

'What the …?' Barney froze at the face of Seamus Nolan glaring menacingly at him.

'Don't let *me* stop you, *Bern-ard*, you old cowgirl. You just continue digging yourself into that hole – and trouble.' Nolan winked, holding a snub-nose revolver in the crack of Barney's arse.

Barney and Butterfly became motionless.

'What … what do you want?' Barney's voice was teetering on tears.

'Not what you're having, that's for fucking sure. Listen carefully, I'm going to remove the barrel of this gun from your arse. You fart, I'll shoot you another hole.' Nolan slowly removed the gun. 'Dismount, and don't try anything stupid, *Bern-ard*.'

Barney dismounted in slow motion, horrified and trembling. His cock shrivelled to zero length, the filled condom dangling shamefully from it like an ancient mummification. He knew he looked disgusting and obscene. Wished for death.

'What … what the hell are you … doing here?' Barney was desperately trying to cover himself with a bedsheet.

'Just wanted to pay you a friendly visit, that's all.' Nolan held the sheet tightly, preventing Barney from procuring a modicum of dignity.

Butterfly quickly scrambled out of the bed, face angry. 'You took your time! I let you in over five minutes ago. You promised you would stop him in time, before he penetrated me.'

Nolan slapped Butterfly hard on the face. Grabbed his hair violently before ramming the gun against his left eye. 'Don't *ever* raise your voice to me, you little queen bee. Is that fucking clear, queer?'

Butterfly rubbed the side of his face. Nodded. Tears began forming in his eyes.

Bravely but foolishly, Barney made a move for Nolan.

Nolan let go of Butterfly's hair, quickly backhanding Barney across the mouth with the gun, splitting his upper lip. The violence of the blow stunned Barney into submission.

'Going to defend your girlfriend's honour, *Bern-ard*, after she set you up for a few quid? Think that was an accidental meeting you had in the Velvet Underground Room?'

Barney looked over at Butterfly. The young man was staring down at the carpet, refusing to meet Barney's shattered gaze.

Nolan hit Butterfly up the face with a crumpled-up twenty-pound note. 'Get your dirty arse out of here, before I put a different kind of hole in you. The next time I catch you selling yourself in a nationalist area, you won't be so lucky. You'll be going for a little swim. Got that?'

'Y … y … yes …' Butterfly stuttered, grabbing the money while reaching for his clothes.

'Not here. Get dressed in the street!' Nolan barked, kicking Butterfly up the backside, then shoving him violently towards the door.

Butterfly staggered out, leaving Barney alone with Nolan.

'Put your knickers back on,' Nolan snarled. 'You're disgusting to look at.'

Barney fumbled for his underwear, and quickly slid into them before wiping blood away from his mouth.

'What … do you want?'

'Some information.'

'What … what kind of information?'

'The good kind – the kind no one's supposed to know about, except for a select few.' Nolan tapped the side of his nose with his finger.

'What … what makes you think I'm privy to that?'

'A little bird told me you know about Doc Holliday, and all of Pope Conor's little secrets.' Nolan smiled. 'Good. I can see from the look on your gob that the little bird was correct.'

'Conor'll have you shot.'

'And what do you think he'll do to you, his favourite altar boy, spreading a butterfly's wings while dipping his wrinkled old candle into shitty hell?'

'I'm … I'm not afraid of you … or your blackmailing threats.'

'Of course you're not, *Bern-ard*.' Nolan grinned.

'Conor'll never believe you. He despises you.'

'Pope Conor isn't going to be in charge forever. Let me tell you something for free. They're tiring of O'Neill down south. New blood is coming *very* soon, in the form of yours truly. I'll remember those who stood by my side, when the time comes, and I'll especially remember those who *didn't*.'

'I'll never betray Conor for the likes of you.'

'How brave. How loyal. How pathetic and ridiculous. Well, then, let's see what arguments I can come up with to encourage you to change your mind.' Nolan pointed the gun at Barney's petrified face. 'I could shoot you.'

'No, please don't do –'

'I *could* shoot you, except I already have.' Nolan's free hand reached into his inside coat pocket. Removed an iPhone. Hit a button. 'Great little things, these. Have a good look at yourself, *Bern-ard*, in full-moon hi-def colour. No acting there. All natural. Even your grunting and loving words captured.'

Nolan held the device close to Barney's face. Put the sound up full blast. Barney quickly shied away from it.

'With the click of a button, this'll be all over the internet – and with an underage boy, into the bargain. Oh, you didn't know Butterfly is only sixteen?'

Barney paled. He slowly shook his head. 'No … I …'

'Try telling that to the cops when they come to arrest you. Makes you a child-rapist and paedophile in the eyes of the law *and* all your friends and family. Think what your hero

Conor'll do to you. Think of the irony of it. Me taking you out to some lonely forest and shooting you in the head, as ordered by your beloved pope.'

'Bastard …'

'Probably. Now, down to business. Tell me *everything* you know about Doc Holliday. Lie to me, and I'll make your life hell before I send you there.'

Chapter Thirteen

'I'll have his carcass dripping blood by midnight.'
Harold Shand, *The Long Good Friday*

Late on Thursday afternoon, Jim McCabe stood watching seagulls skimming and diving over the River Lagan, beside the impressive Waterfront at Belfast's Titanic Quarter. He had an appointment in an hour with the dreaded dentist, and hoped he had the courage to go through with it.

The accursed morning rain had finally drained itself for now, and the petrichor filled his nostrils. A large battalion of camera crews were gathering not too far away, preparing to drive out to Tollymore Forest – Ireland's oldest pine forest – to shoot a segment for *Game of Thrones*.

For the last couple of days, he'd been staying with different friends, sofa-surfing until things calmed down. The robbery – or *attempted* robbery, as the media kept referring to it – was no longer being mentioned, but Jim knew that retrieving the money would be a high priority for its original owner.

He had kept his ears firmly to the ground, but heard nothing relevant. That was until one of his mates from Steeple House contacted him, saying cops had called to the homeless shelter, looking for him. Then, the very same evening, another cop had come by, going to the trouble of searching his room.

'Don't worry, mate. We taught the bastard a thing or two,' Stud Face assured Jim. 'He'll not be showing his face in Steeple House, again – guaranteed.'

'Let me speak to Paul while I'm at it.'

'Er … Paul has an abscess on his tongue. He's … he's finding talking sore.'

'I can sympathise with that, mate. Okay, got to go. Anything else happens, let me know ASAP.'

Jim wondered how the hell the cops had got wind of him so soon? Perhaps they were just fishing, netting up the usual fishy suspects, which wasn't entirely unusual in a sea of crime.

He earnestly hoped that a fishing expedition was all it was, but had alerted Charlie for good measure, telling him not to be staying at home, just in case. Charlie had more or less laughed it off, saying if the cops were looking for him, they'd have been knocking on his door by now. However, he did agree to stay away from home for a few days, with the intention of eventually getting out of Belfast for good.

More worrying than Charlie's blasé attitude was the fact that Brian couldn't be located. Jim had quick-checked his flat, but he wasn't there. Called his mobile. No answer. He hoped Brian had gone to Dublin, attending one of those comic book conventions he loved so much.

He popped another couple of painkillers in his mouth. Just as he did, the rain returned. It was the soft, drizzly variety that would soak you right through to the bone. He quickly ran to the jalopy he had borrowed from Charlie. Once inside, he checked the gripbag, his cut of the money resting alongside all the weapons.

Jim didn't trust leaving the bag or the weapons with anyone. Too tempting. The bag had become his second skin, and would remain so until he got out of Belfast tomorrow. He would start a new life in London, or as far away from this shitty place as possible. Once away and secure, he would get money back to Marianne and Patrick. She would hate having to take it, but take it she would.

He tried starting the car. It jerked and coughed like an old man on the verge of death throes. After a few trying moments, it spluttered into life, farting out black smoke from the exhaust. He turned the heater up full blast, but no heat came.

'Piece of rusted junk!'

He hit the radio button. The crackly station was playing retro sounds from the seventies. The O'Jays, 'Back Stabbers'. He eased the car out, and headed towards the centre of town.

* * *

Ten minutes later, he pulled into the large car park at Castle Court. The facility was practically filled. Thursday being late-night shopping, hordes of people were coming into town early, all hoping to obtain a parking spot.

He exited the car, gripbag in hand, and began making his way through the crowds heading into the shopping centre. Three times he was actually elbowed out of the way for not moving fast enough. Twice he was bumped.

Finally, having reached the safety of the dentist's office, he started getting cold feet. He debated with himself. Closed his eyes. Sighed. Opened his eyes. Looked at the door. Entered.

* * *

Jim finally emerged over an hour later, face numb and rubbery, veins scaled with the lovely after-glow of Twilight Sleep sedation. He had to admit it wasn't the horror he had remembered as a teenager. In fact, it had all been quite pleasant.

Wouldn't mind having some of that twilight stuff in a bottle …

'Make sure you don't drive, or operate heavy machinery, for at least four to six hours,' the dentist advised.

'No … driving …' Jim said, words slurred.

No sooner had he left the dentist than a young female assistant shouted after him.

'Mister McCabe!'

'Wha … what?' Jim turned in slow motion.

'You forgot this.' She was struggling, holding the gripbag.

'What? Oh, thank you …' *Shit!*

He took the gripbag. Felt his heart race at the thought of losing it. In a careless second, his new life almost destroyed, gone forever.

The rain was becoming heavier. It bounced off the top of the car, with an annoying sound like kids with pellet guns. His hand fumbled, trying to get the key into the car door, but the sedative was making hard work of it. His fingers felt too big and heavy for his hand.

'C'mon the hell!'

Then, just as he was about to give up, the key slid in. He opened the door. Placed the gripbag in the back. Awkwardly plopped himself inside, his entire body feeling disassembled. Looked at his face in the mirror. Smiled. Pain gone. *Lovely twilight*. He wanted to sleep in the car, forever and ever.

Snap out of it. Go grab a coffee until this wears off.

But he didn't. He began easing the car slowly out of the car park, heading in the direction of North Queen Street, and evening's growing darkness.

He got as far as the Limestone Road, ten minutes into his journey, when one of the car's wheels started wobbling. Not thinking clearly, he slammed down on the brakes, sending the car skidding across the road, narrowly missing a telegraph pole, a telephone box and a barking dog.

'*Shit!*' Shock alerted, he managed to wrestle the car to a halt outside the rusted gates of an abandoned church. He sat there, tightly gripping the steering wheel, nerves frayed, staring out at the battered statue of a pensive-looking angel staring back at him.

That was too close …

He exited the car to have a look at the damage.

'A flat tyre … shit …' He kicked the dead rubber, then looked about at his surroundings. Deserted buildings and soulless streets. The church was covered in graffiti, most of it sectarian and political. All of its windows appeared to be smashed. A couple of leafless tress rubbed against it, as if offering comfort.

What if someone has seen me skidding along the road, and they're calling the cops right now?

Purgatorial rain was coming down, heavy as sin. He moved to the car boot for the spare. The thought of changing a wheel, with all this rain pissing down, put him in a foul mood. He opened the boot.

'What the …? I don't believe this! No spare wheel. You fucking moron, Charlie! If I had you right at this moment, I'd strangle you.'

He put his hand in his coat pocket for his mobile. He'd have to call Charlie or someone to come out and help fix the wheel, pronto. This area was unnerving. That's all he'd need, the cops driving by, finding the money and weapons on him. He didn't want to have a shoot-out with the cops, but if push came to shove, well then, so be it. He wasn't going back to prison, never again.

'Where the hell did I put my mobile …?' He began probing the rest of the coat pockets. Nothing. He ran back to the car, frantically searching to see if it had fallen behind the seats. Zero luck.

'I don't believe this!' He wanted to scream. He wanted to kill Charlie more than ever. He grabbed the gripbag, walking quickly to the telephone box he had narrowly missed.

Inside, he lifted the receiver.

'Fuck!'

He didn't know if he should laugh or cry, holding the decapitated receiver in his hand.

In the distance, a car appeared, its headlights dull and washed out by the rain. His hand went instinctively to the inside of the gripbag, the Magnum resting there.

'Cops ...?' He thought about hiding somewhere, possibly behind the old church.

The headlights became brighter, but it was still difficult to see what kind of car it was. As it neared the church, the car began to slow down. The driver looked apprehensive. He seemed to study the scene of chaos, then Jim glaring out at him from the vandalised telephone box.

The car began speeding away. Jim rushed out of the box, waving his hand frantically. 'Stop!'

The car kept going, picking up speed.

'Shit ...'

Then, just as he deflated with defeat, the car came to a stop a small distance away.

Soaked to the skin, with rain rushing into his mouth, and finding it difficult to breathe, Jim stood motionless, in case he scared the driver away again.

For the longest time, the car didn't move. Neither did Jim. Perhaps the driver was debating with himself on the rights and wrongs of helping a stranger in such a rundown part of town, on a terrible night like this?

'Please …' Jim whispered. 'Please …'

The car's backlights suddenly came on, and then the vehicle went into slow reverse.

'Thank you …'

The car came to a halt. The nervous-looking driver stared out at Jim, but did not crank the window down.

'Hello, mate,' Jim said, face near to the window. 'In a bit of a mess here. Got a puncture, and I've no spare wheel, no mobile.'

The driver glanced at Jim, at the gripbag, and then at the grounded tyre. By the look on his face, he didn't seem fully committed to opening the door.

For the longest time, the two men stared at each other, Jim's waterlogged face barely recognisable as human. Then, just when he thought the driver would drive off again, the door opened.

'Hop in.'

'Thank you, mate,' Jim said, barely catching his breath once inside the car. 'A flat tyre, and on a bloody night like this, into the bargain.'

'Isn't that always the way?' the driver said, still looking uncertain of his actions. 'Terrible night for any poor soul to be caught in.'

'I lost my mobile into the bargain. When your luck's dead, it's really dead.'

The driver finally relaxed with a smile. 'Had a few of those days myself recently.'

'Look, I hate to ask you this after you being so kind, but would it be possible to borrow your mobile? I need to call a mate to come and pick me up.'

'I'm sorry, I don't have my mobile with me, but if you like I can drop you off up the road? There's a petrol station there. They might have someone to fix your tyre. They should have a payphone, as well.'

'That'd be great. I really appreciate this.'

The driver was just about to drive off, when a mobile sounded. The driver reached into his inside pocket. Produced a mobile. Glanced at the screen.

Jim looked puzzled. 'I thought you said you didn't have your mobile with you?'

'I don't.' He handed it to Jim. 'This is yours.'

'Mine …?' Jim reached to take the mobile. A bad feeling immediately began washing over him.

The driver smiled, then administered a swift karate chop to Jim's throat.

For Jim, the darkness of the night suddenly became darker.

Chapter Fourteen

*'If you hold back anything, I'll kill ya. If you bend the truth or I
think you're bending the truth, I'll kill ya. If you forget anything,
I'll kill ya. In fact, you're gonna have to work very hard to stay
alive, Nick. Now do you understand everything I've said? Because
if you don't, I'll kill ya.'*

Rory Breaker, *Lock, Stock and Two Smoking Barrels*

Jim tried opening his eyelids. Felt as if they'd been glued.
Couldn't move or feel his body, but nevertheless felt acutely
alert. He had gone through these nerve attacks during adolescence. The doctor had called them sleep paralysis.

Just as he thought of the attacks, panic began eating into him.
Breathing was becoming difficult. Tried channelling the mounting pressure through his clenched jaw.

*Help me. Help me … I'm suffocating … one two three … try and
breathe … one two three … remain calm … one two three …*

'It's okay, Jim,' a composed voice said. 'Don't be alarmed.
Breathe slowly. That's good … nice and easy.'

His eyelids began opening. He blinked a few times before gathering in his thoughts and surroundings. The place had the triple
looks and smells of an old abandoned garage: Oil. Grease. Rust.

On the far wall, his distorted reflection spooned in the looking glass of some battered sign advertising car batteries. His eyes looked dazed. The look of a man that did not understand how he got here. Or where he was going.

He was seated upright, naked, strapped in to some sort of medieval chair covered in metal spikes, arms and legs clamped individually. A metal lever protruded from the side. Below the lever, bolts, spinners and tiny wheels rested in their designated places, like the exposed insides of a large antique clock. His entire being rested perilously on the spikes, but strangely he could feel no pain; feel no self.

A man's face came into focus. Jim recognised it as the driver's. Beside the man's feet, the gripbag lay opened, exposing money and weapons.

'What … what've you done to me?' Jim said. There was a terrible taste of burnt rubber in his mouth and gut. He needed to throw up. 'What … what's this all about?'

'Don't be coy, Jim. Francis Bacon didn't do handsome; I don't do bullshit.' Rasharkin said. 'In my business, time is money, and I don't let either get wasted without some sort of interest accruing.'

'You've got everything I possess in that gripbag. What else do you want?'

'Your two brave but foolhardy friends. That's the limit of what I request from you.' Rasharkin held Jim's phone up. 'Already I'm gleaning info from it. Your mates' phone numbers, for starters.'

'I've hundreds of names on that. Good luck finding them.'

'Save me time by telling me their names and I promise things will go a lot easier for you.'

'Misters Fuck and Off. How's that?'

'Okay, play it like that.' Rasharkin smiled. 'You're sitting on an eighteenth-century witch chair. Know what they were used for?'

'Sitting on?'

'Funny. I like a man who is able to keep his sense of humour under adversity. Specifically, these chairs were used to extract confessions from so-called witches. Quite barbaric, granted, but ultimately quite persuasive. At the moment, you can't even feel the metal spikes you're resting on. Not curious as to how that's possible?'

Jim forced a crooked grin. 'Witchcraft?'

'Ketamine.'

'Ketamine?'

'Horse tranquilliser – no, don't look so horrified, it's not as bad as it sounds. It's quite human-friendly, if correctly administered. I've balanced it with small amounts of common aspirin crushed up with baking soda to offset any complications. It'll keep you pain-free – at least for a while. The *for-a-while* part is very important for what we need to do.'

Rasharkin produced Jim's police mug shot. 'The photo really doesn't do you justice. The rosary tattoo looks well, though. Never understood ex-cons having tattoos. They stand out like red flags. Don't you know cops love nothing better than ex-cons with tattoos? They're treasure maps of betrayal.'

'You … you're a cop? You can't do this to me. I know my rights.'

'Wrong on all accounts. I'm *not* a cop; I *can* do this – and you have *no* rights. Whatsoever. You lost all rights once you stole money from those you shouldn't have.'

'Fucking drug dealers. Fuck them!'

'Drug dealers?'

'The owners of the money.'

'Is that what you think?'

'Yes.'

'No.'

'No?'

'No.'

'Who?'

'Brotherhood for Irish Freedom.'

'*Oh fuck …*'

'Oh fuck, indeed, Jim. Truly.'

'We … we didn't know. We wouldn't have touched it, if we'd known.'

'Ignorance creates no justification whatsoever when stock-taking. Accountability is the measure of all actions, eventually.'

'How … how'd you find me? I thought I'd covered my tracks pretty well.'

'Unfortunately for you, pretty turned ugly fairly quickly. I found the appointment letter for the dentist you had in your room, in the rubbish bin – that, along with all those bottles of black-market painkillers.'

'Fucking toothache …'

'Doesn't matter how tough you think you are when it comes to toothaches. They'd make an atheist believe in God. I figured you'd show up at the dentist on appointment day, no matter the risk – at least I *hoped* so. It was a gamble, and it paid in spades. You probably don't even remember me bumping against you, outside Castle Court?'

'I remember a couple of people bumping into me, but I took no notice.'

'That's when I pickpocketed your phone.'

'The tyre, and the missing spare? That was your doing?'

'I made a tiny incision into the tyre, and plugged it with Gorilla superglue. I knew it wouldn't be long before the plug would blow, under all that pressure of driving. The spare wheel is sitting back in the car park at Castle Court.'

Jim forced a smile. It looked wounded and sad. 'You know my reputation? You know you'll get nothing out of me, no matter what you do?'

'Oh, I know all about how tough you are; I know about you getting the shit kicked out of you for five days by the cops, when you did your first robbery at sixteen, and how you refused to give up the other robbers, despite having broken ribs and an arm snapped in three places. That's commendable, and I applaud you for your tenacity and courage. Unfortunately for you, I've a job to do. Very shortly, the Ketamine will be losing its comforting power.'

'Fuck you and your Ketamine.'

Rasharkin produced a knife. Brought it to Jim's face.

'This is a Fällkniven NL1 Thor hunting knife. Beautiful. Lethal. Efficient. I could remove a leg in less than a minute with this, cutting right through the bone, if I were that way inclined. It's the best lie detector created, sorting bullshit from the truth.'

'Fuck … you …' Uncertainty had now entered Jim's voice.

'Think you're *that* tough? This knife turns men into wee boys; wee boys who cry for their mothers, while pissing and shitting themselves. Trust me, I've had my fair share of so-called hard men laughing in my face, only to regret it later.'

'Fuck … you …'

'I'm not going to lie. There's no way out of this for you, even if you'd a godly wishbone rather than a courageous backbone. Regrettably, luck and God have both forsaken you.' Rasharkin slid the knife's blade under Jim's balls, making him flinch. 'You know, of course, that if you don't tell me, I'll have to bring these to Marianne and Patrick, see what *they* can tell me.'

Jim tried breaking free. Veins and muscles bulged in his neck and arms.

Rasharkin produced Jim's phone. Held the screen to his face. A photo of Patrick.

'He's a good-looking kid, Jim. Looks just like his mother, from the other photos I looked at. I can bring mother and son here. Make them take your place on the chair, have you watch while I –'

'You ... you put a finger on my son, and I swear I'll –'

'Yes, I know. You're going to kill me. Catch yourself on. This is cold-shit reality, not Hollywood fantasy. Liam Neeson isn't going to come crashing through that door to your rescue. No one knows where you are. They won't know until tomorrow, when I leave your body at a designated place. Now, where are your two friends?'

'You'll get nothing from me!'

'The chair's spikes will eventually porcupine themselves into your spine, your very soul. Pain you never knew existed in this evil world will come crushing down upon you. Do you really want that, knowing at the end of all this, you'll tell me what I need to know anyway?'

No response from Jim.

Rasharkin sighed, touched a lever on the chair, granting life to the dead metal. Wheels and cogs began turning. The spikes moved slightly, easing into Jim's skin.

Jim's face began transforming from forced steel calmness to a nervous twitching in the cheek bones. He gritted his teeth, trying to ward off the prickly pain now doing a slow-burn on his skin, as the Ketamine began fading from his bloodstream.

'The pain will start gradually, as your brain sends out defence signals. But that won't last long, as stocks run dry, and you're left bluffing on adrenaline and testosterone. You can still avoid all this pain. Just tell me where your two friends are, and it'll all be over quickly. You have my word on that.'

Jim's face knotted. Eyes squeezed tight.

'They … they're in … a … place called …'

'Called?'

'Called … Fuck … You …'

'Did I mention this old garage of mine is soundproof? You can scream away to your heart's content.' Rasharkin touched another lever. The spikes moved. Rivulets of blood-leakage began snaking down the chair and pooling at Jim's feet.

'Fuckkkkkkkkkkkkkkkkkkkkkkkkkkkkkkkkkkkkkkkkkkkkkkkkkkkkk-kkkkk!' Jim drilled his chin into his chest. Knotted fingers into fists.

After a few seconds, Rasharkin halted all movement in the chair with a tiny metal bar, pushing it through a bridge-hole.

'You don't have to go through with this, Jim. You don't have to prove your bravery. It's beyond doubt. You can stop the madness with a nod of your head. I promise you won't feel a thing afterwards. Pain gone forever.'

Jim shook his head.

Rasharkin released the bar. The cogs began moving again, in and out of the wheels, animating the spikes deeper into Jim's skin. Blood flowed more freely.

Jim sucked his lips into his mouth.

'Hhhum mmmmmmmmmmmmmmmmmmmmmmmmmmmmmm mmmmmm!'

'Think of Marianne and Patrick. Surely they mean more to you than your two friends?'

'Go to Hell!'

Rasharkin sat there in the claustrophobic silence, deep in thought, closely studying Jim. Only his eyes gave any indication of his thoughts, alternating from admiration to sadness.

'You're leaving me no option, Jim. Now I'm going to have to show you the truly dark side of pain, and what it really means to go to Hell.'

Chapter Fifteen

'Son, the greatest trick the Devil pulled was convincing the world there was only one of him.'
David Wong, *John Dies at the End*

Across town, at roughly the same moment, two other men were also about to get acquainted, this time at the Odyssey Arena, in the heart of the city.

Forget Disney on ice. This was pure gladiatorial violence on ice, between ice hockey teams the Belfast Giants and the Sheffield Steelers. The Giants had just had a player placed in the sin bin for what looked like a trivial interaction of bodies. Jeers from the home supporters drowned out the cheers from the Steelers' army of followers.

No one was jeering louder than Robert Boyd, standing and leaning over the packed seats in front. His voice could be heard over the tidal wave of moans, as if his very life depended on it.

'Get the ref a pair of glasses!'

Then, just as quickly as the commotion erupted, it faded, as one of the Steelers attempted a breakaway.

'Put him down!' Boyd screamed, watching in dismay as the player got clear of the defense, and headed straight for the goalie.

'Hook him! Don't just stand there, for fuck sake! Hook him!'

Total silence as the puck was propelled into the air like a rubber bullet during a Belfast riot. The goalie did a defensive 'X' shape, but all was lost as the puck flew between his outstretched arms and into the net.

Boyd slumped down on the seat in the dimly lit arena as if he'd just been hit in the forehead by the puck.

'Had a few quid on them myself, mate,' a voice beside him said.

Boyd turned his attention to his fellow loser. For the longest time, he stared directly into the face of Seamus Nolan, before glancing nervously to his left and right.

'It's okay, Robert, I'm on my own, with no malevolent intent. I'm here to make you an interesting and potentially lucrative proposition.'

'Don't ever let me catch you anywhere near me again, scumbag,' Boyd said, placing a hand inside his jacket, exposing the heel of his gun, as he stood to leave. 'Otherwise, you'll get a taste of your own medicine.'

Nolan smiled, held up his hands as if being arrested. 'Whatever you say, Robert. Just trying to help get you out of the jaws of all those loan sharks circling you, before they tear you to shreds. From what I've been told, they're going to be visiting you very soon. Like, twenty-four-hours soon. And you know those boys don't fuck about when it comes to money.'

'What the hell're you talking about?'

'Nothing. Just go your merry way. My mistake. I thought I was talking to a man with thousands in debt due to bad gambling, with the clock ticking towards final payment day; a man who could use a nice solid payment to get himself out of the shit he's in.'

Boyd slowly slumped back down in the seat.

'What the fuck do you want?'

'Just trying to be friendly, Robert. I know you're in debt to a certain organisation, and you're paying that debt off with inside information. If your boss, Harry Thompson, found out, he'd skin you alive. Public humiliation. Despised by your colleagues and friends. Then of course, a cop's worse nightmare: long years in prison with all the people you helped put there. Need I go on?'

Boyd seemed to sink deeper into the seat. For a long time, he didn't speak. When he eventually did, it was with a defeated voice.

'What is it you're after?'

'I think it's a bit too noisy and nosy in here, Robert. You don't want to be seen talking with me, and I definitely don't want to be seen talking with you. Why don't we go out to my car for some privacy, and speak inside?'

'Some fucking hope. You probably have a few of your mates waiting for me.'

'Don't be silly. I need you as much as you need me. Why would I want to kill my golden goose?'

'*Don't* ever call me that, scumbag.'

'Okay. No problem. Perhaps I should call you Doc Holliday, instead?'

'Bastard.'

'People have been calling me that a lot lately. Good job I'm not the sensitive type.'

'We'll use my car to talk in.' Boyd stood unsteadily. 'I'll leave now, and you can follow me out in five minutes. Make sure you use the front entrance, where it's all lit up, and I can see you clearly coming out the doors.'

'Aren't you going to tell me where your car's parked, Robert, so I can find it?'

'Think you're so slick?' Boyd eyeballed Nolan with a look of disdain. 'You knew where my car was the second I parked it.'

Nolan grinned. 'I see we're going to get on just fine, Robert. I know you, and now you know me.'

Chapter Sixteen

'How compliant are the dead. You can arrange,
like cut flowers.'
William Guy, *Twilight*

Breakfast time at the Thompson household in south Belfast found Harry bouncing down the stairs, fully dressed, and ready to face another day; another day to strike off his retirement calendar.

The aroma of an Ulster fry came ghosting over him as he entered the impressive open-plan kitchen.

Draping his overcoat over a chair, he walked to where his wife Elaine stood, and kissed her on the cheek. 'Morning, my dearest. Thought you had a committee meeting at the hospital this morning?'

'I postponed it until later. I wanted to be with you this morning.' Using one hand, Elaine cracked an egg on the side of the frying pan. 'You still had another twenty minutes in bed. I was going to bring breakfast up to you.'

'What're you up to, being so bloody nice?'

'There's that suspicious policeman's mind of yours working overtime again. I know you'll be in court most of the day, so I don't want to see you going hungry. Anyway, can't a loving wife keep her husband happy, do little things for him?'

'Your *little* things usually end up costing me *big* things.'

He sat down at the table. Reached across for the early edition of the *Belfast Telegraph*. Local journalists always seemed to know more about what was going on in the Force than he did. They got exclusives; he got excuses.

'One egg or two, love?'

He didn't really feel like eating this morning, but knew that World War Three would break out with Elaine if he didn't have some grub in his stomach before hitting the road. He'd rather face a squad of Brotherhood volunteers coming at him with Armalite rifles than a scowling Elaine coming at him with a frying pan.

'One, love, and go easy on the bacon.'

'Is that heartburn of yours bothering you again? Want me to bring back something from work?'

'I'm sound. Just trying to watch my figure, and trying to figure out what you're up to.'

Elaine placed the fry on the table. Ruffled his hair. Kissed the top of his head. 'Nothing wrong with your manly figure.'

'Nothing that two tape measures can't handle, you mean.'

'I like my man to be beefy.'

'Beefy, is that what it's called?'

Harry looked at the breakfast with dismay. Its size would choke a horse.

'Hope you're not chasing after one of those pretty little police-women in there.'

'If you think Hyacinth Bouquet is pretty, well, that's the dire selection I have to choose from.'

'C'mon now, I'm sure there're plenty of nice wee things in the station.'

'Yes. They're called guns.' Harry turned a page of the paper, scanning for news about the robbery.

'Did you hear any more about the Tom Jones tickets?'

Harry feigned deafness.

'Well?' Elaine said, snapping the newspaper from his fingers. 'Did you?'

'What?'

'The tickets for Tom Jones at the Waterfront? Any word?'

'So, that's it. That's why you're being so nice.'

'Well? *Did* you?'

'Sorry, love, but Murray said you and Brenda caused so much trouble the last time, he couldn't get any from his usual contacts.'

Folding her arms, Elaine frowned. 'What on earth is Murray talking about? We didn't cause any trouble.'

'That's not how he remembers it. He says that when you and Brenda threw your big-as-a-tent knickers at Mr Jones, they were so massive they almost suffocated the poor man.'

'*What?*'

Harry laughed.

Elaine punched his arm playfully.

Reaching into his jacket pocket, Harry pulled out an envelope. 'Two of the best seats in the place for Brenda and you. Right up front. You'll be so close, you'll need an umbrella to stop Tom's sweat from drenching you.'

Elaine grabbed the tickets. Kissed them, then Harry.

'I love you!'

'I noticed you kissed Tom before you kissed me.'

'Yes, but does Tom get this?' Elaine began kissing Harry's neck, while her hand reached down to the zipper guarding the front of his trousers.

'He better not, or his old home town will look a lot different by the time I'm finished with him.'

Elaine pulled the zipper down. Reached in. Began exploring.

'Do you have a search warrant, Madame? Legally, you could be charged with breaking and entering, or smash and grab.'

'If that's the case, shouldn't you be handcuffing me?' Elaine had managed to release Harry's excited cock from his underwear. 'Well? Shouldn't you?'

'Don't tempt me to –' Harry's mobile began ringing. 'Of all the bloody times …'

'Ignore it,' Elaine said, her fingers tightening on his fleshy manhood.

'You know I can't, love. Could be important.' Harry reluctantly answered the call. 'Kerr? Yes, what the hell is it?' Harry's cock instantly deflated at the sound of Kerr's voice, as if he was in the room watching.

'Sorry for disturbing you, sir, so early in the –'

'Just get the hell on with it.'

Elaine grinned, whispering into Harry's ear, 'I'm trying my best to do just that. If you'd stop fidgeting …'

Harry placed a finger on his lips, indicating for Elaine to hush.

'An abandoned car, sir, discovered near the Limestone Road. There was a naked body not too far from it. You'll never believe whose.'

'Are you going to tell me, or do I have to bloody guess?'

'McCabe, sir.'

'McCabe?'

'Jim McCabe. The suspect from the –'

'Yes, yes, I know who the hell he is – was.'

'Looks like he was badly tortured before being killed, sir.'

Harry pulled Elaine's hand out from his pants and quickly stood – with difficulty. 'I'm on my way. Do not do anything until I get there. Keep the press away from the scene.'

'I'm afraid they're already here, sir.'

'Who the hell alerted them?'

'I haven't a clue, sir.'

'You probably never said a truer thing in your bloody life, Kerr!' Harry angrily clicked the mobile off before turning to Elaine. 'Sorry, love. Have to run.'

'Just watch yourself.'

'I will.' He gave his wife a quick kiss, then grabbed his overcoat and rushed towards the door.

'Don't you think you'd better zip yourself up?' Elaine was trying to suppress a chuckle. 'You might get arrested for indecent exposure with your truncheon hanging out.'

* * *

Harry and his crew stood looking down at the naked body of Jim McCabe. It had been forced upright in a grotesque Cúchulainn-and-raven pose, beside a statue of a sorrowing angel in the derelict church. Horrific holes mapped his entire torso.

'He looks like a bloody pin cushion, poor bastard,' McCauseland said. 'Wonder what the hell caused all those holes? I'd bet my balls that fuckdog Nolan had a hand in this. Cert.'

'Or the other robbers,' Harry said, thanking the gods he had had the presence of mind to bring his overcoat to fend off the icy wind. 'No honour among thieves. A little bit of in-fighting goes a long way to increase the bank account.'

'Could be a smoke-screen created by someone with ulterior motives.'

'Whoever did this needed time. He was murdered elsewhere, his body dumped here. Why it was dumped here, I don't know, yet. Had to be more than one person involved, unless McCabe knew them. He wasn't the type of man to go like a lamb to the slaughter. Perhaps he got out to fix the puncture, and was nabbed?'

'I checked the boot, sir,' Kerr cut in. 'No spare. The boot had been opened, but could have been locals looking for stuff to steal.

An elderly lady across the street said the car was parked directly across from her house since early last night. Kids were jumping on it, as well as smashing the windows, so she called the police this morning. When uniforms came out, they discovered the body in the church yard.'

'You're being uncharacteristically quiet,' Harry said, turning his attention to Boyd. 'You here today, or what?'

'What? Oh! Yes … I'm here, sir. Sorry, didn't mean to drift.'

'Keep your drifting for when you're all-at-sea. What's your take on this?'

'Well … it does look like they've been fighting over the money. I'd say it was his mates who did this.'

'Thank you for that. It was very informative,' Harry said sarcastically, eyeing Boyd suspiciously.

'Sorry … sorry, sir. Have a few things on my mind …'

'Door-to-door questioning done, Kerr?'

'Being carried out right now, sir, by four uniforms.'

'Is this McCabe's car, Bill? Do we have a record of him owning one?'

'We're running the plates. Also, Forensic will be going over it – though it'll be a mess with what the young louts did to it, pissing and shitting on the seats, taking a dump in the dump.'

'Dirty wee thugs. CCTV?'

'In this area? Ha! They'd steal them. I checked a couple of local shops, but they only have dummy ones. Say no more.'

Harry shook his head with disgust, walking back towards his car.

'Bill? Bring Mister Nolan in for questioning.'

'A pleasure. Want me to rearrange his features, in the back room?'

'No. Rough stuff's out – for the moment. Kid gloves now; knuckledusters later, if needed. Bring him in discreetly. No press alerts.'

'Okay.'

'I'm heading off to the High Court as a witness for the prosecution. Probably be there most of the day. A waste of time. A dirty deal is always done near the end, wasting everyone's time. Also, make sure you track down the owner of the car, if it turns out this wasn't McCabe's or – Jesus, I don't believe it. Is that who I think it is?' Harry indicated with his chin at a man across the street carrying a doctor's medical bag.

McCauseland looked across the street, nodded. 'Frankie Flanagan, of all people.'

Flanagan was in his late fifties, immaculately dressed and sporting gold-rimmed spectacles. He resembled a doctor making house calls.

'Flanagan!' Harry voice trumpeted.

Flanagan appeared deaf to Harry's booming voice, but his walk sped up dramatically, until his feet were practically doing a jig along the street.

'Don't have me going after you! Get your arse over here – *now*!'

Flanagan slowed down to a reluctant crawl. Came to a complete stop. Turned, then made his way across the street to where Harry waited. He looked uncomfortable under Harry's interrogatory gaze.

'Oh, hello, Mr Thompson … didn't notice you … I … was deep in thought.'

'Deep in thought!' Harry harrumphed loudly. 'The only thing deep about you are your pockets – or the shit you get into, burgling the homes of the rich.'

'I haven't done that in three years, Mister Thompson.' Frankie sounded hurt.

'Because you've been in bloody prison down south for the last three years, *that's* bloody why! When did you get out? I thought you had at least another year to do?'

'Good behaviour.'

'Good behaviour, my arse. Good behaviour so you can return to bad behaviour.'

'Honestly, Mister Thompson, those days are behind me.'

'Why are you shaking so much? Nervous?'

'I'm ball-freezing. Can't afford a good heavy coat like yours, Mister Thompson. You know what they say: you know it's cold outside when you go outside and it's cold.'

'So, if I asked you to open up your bag of tricks, there would be no tricks in it?'

'I'll prove it to you.' Frankie started opening the bag.

'Forget it. I'll give you the benefit of the doubt – this time. not the next.'

'Thank you, Mister Thompson. I really appreciate that, it helps me believe that society is not out to persecute a person who has seen the errors of his past ways, and –'

'Save the bullshit for the next time I see you in a cell.'

'Can I go, now, Mister Thompson? I've an appointment with my parole officer, and I don't want to be late.'

'I suppose you know nothing of the body found at the church?'

'Body? What body?'

'What did you think was under the cover, right behind you?'

Frankie's body didn't move an inch, but his eyeballs did a peripheral three-sixty-degree movement.

'As God is my witness, Mister Thompson, that's the first time I've laid eyes on it.'

'Lucky for you, I believe you. But take heed: I'll be keeping *my* eyes firmly on your future behaviour. Now beat it.'

Harry waited until Frankie had moved on before getting into his car. He adjusted the rear-view mirror, pinning its reflection on Boyd standing off to the side, a worried look on his face.

You're up to something, Boyd, and I intend to find out what the hell it is.

Chapter Seventeen

Did you ever want to forget anything? Did you ever want to cut away a piece of your memory or blot it out? You can't, you know.
Al Roberts, *Detour*

Having spent most of the day forensically cleaning the converted garage, Rasharkin returned to his apartment, two streets away, just as night lights were coming on.

Once inside, he hit the button on the TV remote, closed all curtains, stripped, then entered the shower.

He turned the shower up full blast, allowing the propulsion of hot water to attack his skin. Pushed the hot water button a fraction. The water intensified its heat, forcing him to grit his teeth. Pushed the button again. Longer this time. The scorching water was turning his skin wound-raw. Unbearable to most human beings, he stood there in defiance.

Despite living in a world void of excuses, focusing only on what was clear and incontrovertible, guilt was seeping into him. It didn't matter how hard he fought to hold it at bay. He tried to empty his mind, to clear the emotional debate, knowing it invited weakness and vulnerability, but a newscaster's accusing voice was steadily filtering through the walls:

Police still have not released the name of the murder victim whose body was discovered this morning beside a derelict church in the north of the city. Unconfirmed reports suggest the man had been tortured, as well as –

'Damn you, McCabe!' He slapped the wall violently.

Something in McCabe's face and demeanour had unnerved him. Yes, he had eventually gathered all that he needed, info-wise, but at what cost? Torture? Was that his net worth now? Dust from a dead man's pocket? In the past, he had always managed to break a man – *any* man – with psychological terror alone. He had never had to resort to actual physical torture, using fear as a weapon to glean information. Ultimately, brain had always triumphed over brawn, but not this time. No, not this fucking time.

'Damn you …'

He had never met a man like McCabe before. Even when he threatened to remove his balls, he still resisted. Until resistance became futile, and the bluff of bringing McCabe's wife and son into the equation finally sealed the deal *and* McCabe's fate.

Turning the shower off, he stepped from its enclosure. Dried. Made his way to the bedroom. On the bed, he considered the two names, and the details he had on each of them: Brian Ross and Charlie Madden.

Quickly dressing, he headed out into the night.

Chapter Eighteen

'This town stinks like a whorehouse at low tide.'
Jim Malone, *The Untouchables*

It was late by the time Harry returned to the station from court. As predicted, it had all been a waste of time, with dirty deals being agreed to, all to save time and money. Justice, as usual, ran a poor second.

Boyd greeted him as he was about to enter his office.

'The *Tele* has McCabe's murder on the front page, sir. They're saying it was drug-related, and his accomplices are chief suspects in his murder.'

'Almost as imaginative as your response when I asked you this morning.'

Boyd's face flushed. 'I'm sorry about –'

'Any news on the car?'

'Nothing … nothing yet. On a plus side, we have Nolan downstairs. Arrested an hour ago at home. Came without a struggle. He's saying nothing, as usual.

'We'll see if he still feels like doing Harpo Marx impersonations after a few days down there, sleep deprivation and lights burning the eyes off him.'

'He wants his solicitor.'

'I know what he wants, and it's not a bloody solicitor. Anyway, if he's not talking, we can't hear him.'

'Scarface Logan and a couple of his associates have been arrested, also.'

'That low-watt lightbulb? Why? What's the charge?'

'They're being questioned about the murder.'

'What? Who the hell gave the orders for that bullshit?'

Boyd pointed upwards. 'McCafferty.'

'McCafferty's as useful as a concrete pop-up book. Logan's only interested in drugs, not blood. Bad for business. And he certainly does *not* do bank robberies. Wouldn't have the balls.'

'McCafferty's left word he wants to see you, as soon as you come in.'

Harry sighed. The last thing he wanted was another meeting with McCafferty, and his litany of official bullshit. He had gone through enough bullshit in court to last a month.

'I need to talk to you first. In my office.'

'Can it wait? I'm finishing the report on McCabe and –'

'*That* can wait. What I've to say can't.'

Boyd followed Harry into the office.

'Close the door.'

'Anything wrong?'

Harry folded his arms, looked directly into Boyd's face. 'You tell me.'

'I … I don't know what you mean.'

'No? Two years ago, I stuck my neck and reputation on the line for you, when they tried to kick you out of the Force for gambling. No other squad wanted anything to do with you. Remember?'

'Of course, and … and I'm eternally grateful for that.'

'Not grateful enough, it would seem.'

'What's that supposed to mean?'

'You're the detective. You tell me.'

'I don't know.'

'Want to really piss me off? Keep playing dumb.'

'I'm not trying to piss you off or –'

'You haven't been gambling? Part of the deal was that you'd never be involved in *any* sort of gambling again.'

Boyd's left cheek did a little nervous tick.

'I swear to God, I wouldn't –'

'Don't finish. I'd hate to think you'd look me in the eyes, and lie like a mongrel dog.'

'I … I … wouldn't. I owe you too much.'

'That's right, and never bloody forget that. Something's going on with you. Your work's getting sloppy again, just like when you were pissing your wages into every loan shark's bank account. I need intelligence, not indulgence. How long's it been since you were at GA?'

'How long?'

'Is there a bloody echo in here?'

'A … few weeks … a month, maybe.'

'Actually, it's been two months. I checked. That was part of the deal, also, you to attend Gamblers Anonymous. *Every* week. *Every* meeting. *No* excuses. What part of that agreement did you not understand?'

'You're right. What can I say? I've let you down by not attending. I'm sorry.'

'Never mind the drama and bullshit. I get enough of that from McCafferty. From here on in, you attend *every* Thursday night. I'll be checking, so don't try being a crafty bastard by getting someone else to sign in for you. One more slip-up, and you're gone. Out on your arse, and you can bet on *that*. Do I make myself clear?'

Boyd couldn't hold Harry's glare.

'Yes, sir … perfectly.'

'I'm putting you on evening duty for the next two weeks. Any problems with that? Because if you have, you can always ask to get transferred.'

'No … no problems, sir.'

'Good. Now get the hell out of my sight and start producing results.'

Harry waited a few moments after Boyd had left, then made his way upstairs.

Outside McCafferty's office door, a man, tall of build, stood stoically, like a silent sentinel of cement and steel. He ignored Harry's friendly nod.

Harry knocked once on McCafferty's door, then entered.

'You wanted to see me, sir?'

McCafferty looked tense. A copy of the *Belfast Telegraph* rested on his desk.

'Close the door, please, Harry. Have a seat.'

Harry closed the door. Remained standing.

'Got a bodyguard looking after you now?' Harry forced a smile.

'Pardon?'

'The Brother Grimm, outside the door.'

McCafferty ignored the quip. Held the newspaper up, showing a photo of Jim McCabe's covered body. 'Grisly stuff. What's your take on it?'

'Too early to draw conclusions. In-fighting, perhaps; maybe a smokescreen for someone else's bloody hand. I see you gave the order to arrest Scarface Logan? You don't seriously believe he's involved?'

'A bone for the press to gnaw on, keep them happy for a few days, before we release him on bail with some sort of drug offence.'

'I already have the main suspect: Seamus Nolan. He's waiting patiently for me, down in the dungeons. I suspect his involvement in this, somewhere. I was just about to interrogate him.'

'You need to release him.'

Harry looked as if he'd just been kicked in the balls. Twice. Hard.

'Release him?'

The side door opened, and the man with shark eyes walked into the room. Harry felt a tightness in his stomach; suspected the smirking face was a precursor of something ominous about to be announced.

'You don't look too pleased to see me, Thompson, I'm pleased to say.'

'What the hell's this got to do with you, Purvis, *or* MRF?'

'I don't have to explain anything to you, but I will, out of professional courtesy. First of all, Brother Grimm, as you referred to him, is Carson McComb, one of my team of investigators.'

'Investigators? Good to hear you got yourself a wee gang. You deserve it, after being sidelined so many times for recurring failures.'

'Still Mister Smart Mouth, eh, Thompson? One day your smart mouth is going to walk you into trouble; trouble you'll not be able to talk your way out of.'

Harry was about to snap a reply, but McCafferty moved to deflate the tension.

'Gordon and his team have been observing Nolan for quite some time, Harry, and the people he's associated with.'

'That was until you messed things up.' Purvis pointed his finger inches from Harry's face. 'Now you've turned the whole thing into an unmitigated disaster, jumping in and arresting Nolan.'

'He's a suspect in a brutal murder. Normally, that's what we do with suspects in murder cases. Arrest them. I know that might be difficult for *you* to understand, having screwed most things up throughout your career.'

'Okay, Harry, enough,' McCafferty said. 'Let Gordon finish what he has to say.'

'We suspect Nolan has sympathies with others opposed to the Good Friday Agreement,' Purvis said. 'And in fact, that he is channelling money and weapons to them.'

'Now, I thought all the weapons were destroyed? You boys were supposed to be overseeing that, right?'

'Realistically, it was never going to be possible to account for every weapon, or every ounce of explosive. Of the tons that *were* destined to be destroyed, some inevitably managed to slip through the net, and into the hands of people like Nolan. That's why we need him released ASAP, to continue our investigation and monitoring.'

'Monitoring? Is that what you call it? Like monitoring him depositing his pocket money at the Bank of New Republic, before it was liberated by Larry, Curly and Moe? Are you saying that it was all done right under your nose?'

Purvis bristled. 'You can hardly talk. By the looks of things, you've already lost one suspect who won't be getting interrogated. I'm here to see it doesn't happen again.'

'What's that supposed to mean?'

'I'm taking over the Bank of New Republic case. I need you to turn over all files and evidence you've gathered on the robbery.'

'Adding brass to your balls asking me to –'

'Actually, the asking's over; I'm *telling* you.'

'You get to tell me *nothing*. I'm still in charge of this case.'

'I'm stationed on the fifth floor, Thompson. In Jackson's old office. I expect everything filed about the robbery to be on my desk by tomorrow morning.' Purvis turned and left by the front door.

'What the hell's he on, talking shit like that?' Harry looked at McCafferty. 'What? What's the look for? I *am* still in charge, right?'

'This has come from the very top, Harry. MI5 are involved now. It's out of my hands. I don't have a say in it, whatsoever.'

'But Purvis, of all people. That bastard's always been a force-within-a-force, operating unrestrictedly.'

'Look, Harry, I know you two have history, but Purvis is good at what he does.'

'Murdering an old cop because of his religion?'

McCafferty's face tightened. 'Those allegations were never proven, and you shouldn't be repeating them – especially in my presence.'

'Oh, *I* know he did it. We all do. One day, I'll prove it. Justice will be served, one way or another.'

'I could repeat the same question you just asked me. What the hell are *you* on, talking shit like that, making veiled threats?'

'Will that be all, sir?' Harry walked to the door, and opened it.

'Look, at the end of the day, Harry, there's nothing you or I can do about the present situation. He's in charge, until new instructions come through. Let him have all the pressure. You've only a handful of weeks before retirement. Sit it out.'

'Thank you for your support, sir, and fighting so hard for me. Now, if you'll excuse me, I've got important matters to attend to, like parking tickets and drunken brawls in pubs.'

Chapter Nineteen

She was trouble looking for somebody to happen to.
Ross MacDonald, *The Wycherly Woman*

It was nearing midnight. For the last hour, Rasharkin had stood in a filthy entry, like a lone exclamation mark, studying the barren wasteland across the street.

The word street was an overstatement; more an apocalyptic scene from a war movie, with pyramids of muck and crushed bricks coiled in desolation alongside rusted machinery.

The Maddens' house was in total darkness. Outside in the street was a similar story, the handful of streetlights still standing decapitated by vandals. Fifty feet away, an almost identical house, lights flickering from the weak afterglow of TV, bookended the street, or what was left of it.

He wondered if Madden and Ross had somehow figured something out about McCabe, and fled? Did they have a secret warning signal in the event of one of them not showing up at a designated meeting place?

Ross' flat in the city centre was also deserted when he had visited a couple of hours earlier, so the possibility was strong. It was something he would have to seriously consider, regardless of how unpalatable it tasted. Yet, despite what he had witnessed, he was confident that Ross would be back. Ultimately. Of that he had little doubt. Madden? Perhaps never.

He walked back to the car, and once inside made a phone call.

'Yes?' Conor O'Neill said.

'One of the three suits you left for cleaning is ready.'

'How does it look?'

'A couple of threads missing, but nothing serious. A very stubborn stain gave resistance, but I was able to break it down, eventually.'

'How're the other two coming along?'

'Unfortunately, they're offering a bit more resistance.'

'I see … that's not the news I was hoping for.'

'One of them, I'm confident of eventually cleaning. Just need a bit more time. I'll give due attention to the other one first chance I get, but just letting you know to be prepared in case I can't mend it.'

'I know you'll do your best, as always. Two out of three I can live with. That would be acceptable.'

The conversation ended, Rasharkin drove off, heading over to the affluent Malone Road area in the south side of town.

He parked the car at the side of a large detached house-cum-bordello. The impressive Victorian abode was camouflaged by Ent-like ancient trees, alongside expertly trimmed shrubbery.

Exiting the car, he admonished himself for his previous uncharacteristic bout of weakness in the shower concerning

McCabe. McCabe was a distant memory. A man who lived and died by his mistakes, by his own choice of path. A name on a long list of names fading into the past, soon to be forgotten. That was why he was here, and McCabe there.

At the imposing wrought-iron gates, he pressed a brass button. The gates opened soundlessly. He walked up the pathway to be met by two large mahogany doors. One slowly opened. A woman appeared.

'Good evening, Mister Bailey.'

The voice belonged to Louise, the madam of the establishment. Attractive. Mid-forties. Elegantly dressed in sombre attire of black and red silks, providing ample but tasteful cleavage.

'Good evening, Louise.' He stepped inside.

'Your usual room?'

'Not yet, thanks. I'm going to have a drink first.'

'Just let me know when you're ready. I'll have everything prepared. Take a seat and I'll send a girl over to serve you.' Louise smiled and left.

He found a seat and table of his liking nestled in the far corner, and made himself comfortable. Soft music was everywhere, mixing seamlessly with the pleasant ambience and voyeuristically inclined vignettes of beautiful courtesans fussing over smartly dressed punters, most of whom originated from high-paying professions such as law, medicine and business. Ironically, probably not one John among all the johns.

No names. No identities. No existence.

However, despite the dimmed lights and strict rules guarding privacy, he recognised a few of the faces from earlier visits over the years.

'What would you like to drink, sir?' an attractive young woman asked, appearing at his table, face smiling an official enjoin.

'A Lagavulin single malt please.'

She returned two minutes later, drink perfectly balanced in the centre of a silver tray. He didn't mind the wait, having occupied himself watching – à la *Rear Window* – the comings and goings of the inhabitants, lips mouthing surreptitiously into ears, mysteries and secrets revealed and discussed.

He tipped the young woman generously. She smiled again, but this time it was authentic.

'*Anything* else, sir?' Her eyes were inviting in a shy, tentative way.

'What's your name?'

'Candice,' she said, with just the slightest hesitancy in her voice.

He doubted very much she was a Candice. Everyone here was a pseudonym living inside a matryoshka doll.

'Well, Candice, if I *should* need anything, you'll be the first to know.'

He watched her walking back across the floor. Confident. Elegant. Halfway there, she tilted her head slightly. He was certain she was watching him from her peripheral. He raised the glass in a friendly salute, then brought it to his lips, swallowing half the contents in one gulp, no grimace.

He was just about to order another from Candice, perhaps discuss spending the night with her, when he saw a figure over near the impressive winding mahogany staircase.

Without warning, his breath caught hard in his gullet. Cleared it with a cough while keeping his eyes on the woman at the staircase. Even from this distance, the resemblance was uncanny. Chillingly so.

A nervous smile skittered across his face. He glanced at his hands. Uncharacteristically, they were trembling slightly.

'Mister Bailey? Are you okay?' Louise broke his thoughts.

'That girl ... over by the stairs. What ... what's her name?'

Louise turned her head, and looked over towards the stairs.

'Alice? She's only been with us a couple of weeks, but she's proving to be *very* popular. Gorgeous, isn't she?'

'Beautiful ...'

'Would you like *her* to prepare your room?'

For the longest time, he couldn't take his eyes off Alice. Finally, he answered: 'I want to bring her home. Would there be a problem with that?'

'No problem whatsoever. I'll arrange it immediately.'

Chapter Twenty

And you've just had some kind of mushroom …
And your mind is moving low.
Jefferson Airplane, *'White Rabbit'*

'**W**ow!' Alice said, entering the apartment, taking in its opulence in one sweeping gaze. 'What a place you have, Mister Bailey.'

'Jack. No Mister.'

'Okay, Jack.' She smiled coyly, making her way over to the enormous show-window centred in the living room and gazing out on the panoramic night view. 'Who'd have thought dirty old Belfast could look this beautiful?'

Down below, the streets, fast-moving wisps of car lights brushed against the darkness, all forming a conglomerate of electric join-the-dots.

'Distance gives a cleansing appearance.' He reached towards the drinking cabinet. 'Would you like something to drink?'

'No thank you.' From her handbag, she removed a Betty Boop lighter and matching cigarette case. Clicked the case open, exposing a family of homemade reefers. 'I prefer these. Do you mind if I smoke?'

'Can you do it out on the balcony? I've numerous paintings that are sensitive to the slightest change in their environment. I have to be careful with them.'

'Not a problem. I like that in a man.'

'What?'

'Sensitivity and caring.'

They both stepped out into the balcony. The night air was cold, but in a refreshing sort of way. She held the Betty Boop case out to him. He declined. She selected a reefer. Lit it, then inhaled deeply, holding the smoke in her mouth for a few seconds, before sending contrails down her nostrils.

'You look like you needed that.'

'I did.' She sucked on the reefer again, closing her eyes, allowing the smoke to slowly filter from her mouth in a very sexy, seductive manner. 'Helps me …'

'Helps you … face the likes of me?'

She opened her eyes, now slightly glazed. 'What's that supposed to mean?'

'It can't be easy, what you do.'

She shrugged her shoulders. 'It's a business. I'm a professional. I make good money. Pays the bills. Anyway, if all my clients were like you, well then.'

'The money, you mean?'

'Not just that. Your whole persona, style, good looks.'

'Good-looking, I am not!'

'Oh, you don't know just *how* good-looking you are.

Men like you attract women, like moths to a flame. There is something dangerous about you, something that says "fuck with me and suffer the consequences".'

'Don't hold back.' He laughed. It sounded rusty, unused and foreign.

'Plus, you smell nice.'

'Is that an essential requirement?'

'It helps! Some of the men I'm introduced to haven't washed in days. They sit in the club, smelling of sour sex and stale alcohol. And some of them can be mean.' She leaned in and kissed him. 'But not you. You're kind.'

'You know me how long? Less than an hour?'

'Don't smirk. I can tell you're kind. I'm a good reader of people. There's a sorrow in your eyes. Even when you smile, it remains. Something … wounded. You've suffered in the past, but your kindness is there, in the darkness.'

He suddenly felt uncomfortable.

'Let's go inside.' He guided her down a landing, and into the master bedroom.

'It doesn't disappoint, Jack. For a single fella, you've got great taste.' Alice nodded approvingly, all the while teasingly discarding most of her clothing via a seductive, Salome-like dance, which transported her steadily across the floor toward the king-sized bed.

Rasharkin watched, spellbound. He thought of the young seductress, clutching the Baptist's decapitated meaty head, well worth Herod's bloody payment for her services.

Alice stood semi-naked at the side of the bed, before flipping playfully onto it, backwards, as if diving into a swimming pool. She patted the top of the sheets. Winked. Smiled so fucking innocently sweet, while whispering a double entendre: *'Coming, Jack?'*

'One second.' He pressed a button on a remote control. A few ceiling tiles above the bed parted, leaving a square of darkness peering down at Alice like a chunk of moonless sky.

Looking nervous, she pointed at the gap. 'What's that? I hope it's not some sort of camera? I don't want compromising pictures of me out there. It would kill my mum and dad if they knew what I do.'

'No, nothing of that nature, I assure you. This is private. You and I. You have my word on that. Just relax. It's an old projector, showing old movies.'

'Old blue movies? Well, I can't moralise. Last week I went to bed with twins just to see if their cocks were identical. And guess what?'

'I'd rather not.'

'They were!'

He knew he should have laughed, but puzzlingly, a dull coin of resentment entered the pocket of his feelings.

'You'll have to close your eyes for a few moments, until they acclimatise to the brightness. The beam of light from the projector can be quite sharp at the beginning.'

'You … you're not going to tie me up, are you?'

'No, I'm not going to tie you up.'

'I don't like to be tied up … I had a bad experience with a client … he was very cruel to me.'

'Don't worry. I won't do anything you don't want to do. I'll stop it the moment you become uncomfortable. You have my word on that.'

'Okay …'

From a drawer, he removed the gold box. Flipped it open with a two-thumb push. Retrieved an LSD/BBC stamp.

'What's that?' she asked.

'My ticket to worlds of wonders.'

'A ticket to *ride*?' Her eyes were twinkling mischievously. 'Can I accompany you on the trip? I promise not to take any clothing with me.'

He shook his head. 'This isn't weed. It's LSD Prime, mixed with coke. A major-league fuck-with-your-mind, if your mind isn't strong enough to be fucked with. It's dangerous, it takes no prisoners.'

'I'm a big girl. I like danger. It excites me. That's why I really like you. Besides, I can fuck with the best of them.'

He was hesitant.

'C'mon! Don't destroy the moment. Why should you get to have all the fun? *Pleaseeeeeeeeeee*! Pretty please?'

'Okay. Take it.'

Giggling excitedly, she removed the stamp from his fingers.

'What do I do with it?'

'Place it *under* your tongue. It'll dissolve in a few minutes. Then, just lay back, relax.'

She did as instructed. While waiting for the magic to happen, she hoisted her hips and wriggled out of her panties, becoming completely naked.

He listened to their silky sound as they slipped down her long, beautiful legs.

'I don't shave my pussy,' she said, running her fingers through her natural overgrowth.

'That's okay. I don't shave mine, either.'

She laughed.

He began removing his clothes.

'*God* … all those scars … what … what happened?'

'Nothing. Just old wounds from old wars. Don't be put off by them.'

'I … I'm not. Anything but.'

He removed two stamps from the box. Popped them in his mouth. Pressed the remote. The projector began beaming grainy images onto Alice's body. He selected a song from his music collection.

'A song for you, Alice.'

'Me?'

The room was filled with the hypnotically quivering voice of Grace Slick's surreal 'White Rabbit'.

One pill makes you larger, and one pill makes you small … And the ones that mother gives you, don't do anything at all … Go ask Alice, when she's ten feet tall …

'It might be the LSD, but that beam of light from the projector is tickling my pussy.' Alice was giggling, while pushing her bush towards his face. 'Can you lick her for me? Taste her. Tell her not to be nervous …'

He bent into her crotch, whispering, *'Don't be nervous, little bush.'*

Alice giggled again, louder this time. 'That's even more ticklish.'

He placed a hand at the small of her back where it flowed into her buttocks, then began kissing her inner pinkness until she was wet with excitement.

'Ohhhhhhhhhhhhhh …' She groaned, thrusting herself further into his face.

And if you go chasing rabbits, and you know you're going to fall … Tell 'em a hookah-smoking caterpillar has given you the call … And call Alice, when she was just small …

He came up for air, lips glistening a silvery sheen. The projector's images continued dancing on her skin. The Jane Russell lookalike appeared, smiling.

He positioned Alice's body until it was in perfect alignment with the woman on the screen, becoming one, like clones in light and flesh.

A man's voice in the background faded the moment. Rasharkin muted the sound.

'Now play with yourself …' His voice was low.

Alice and the woman let their fingers do all the work.

'Harder! Fuck yourself harder!'

Alice began thrusting harder and harder, her face intense. Teeth pressed tightly against lips.

'I … want you to … to fuck me in the mouth. Say it.'

'I … want you to … to fuck me in the mouth.' Alice and Jane's lips worked in perfect sync.

'Then … then in the ass. Hard in my ass … with … with that big cock of yours. Say it!'

'I … want you to … to fuck me in the mouth, then in the ass. Hard in my ass with that big cock of yours.' Alice's body was trembling. 'Hurry, Jack. Hurry … I can't hold off much longer … *fuuuuuuuuuuuuuuuuck me …'*

When the men on the chessboard get up and tell you where to go … And you've just had some kind of mushroom, and your mind is moving low … Go ask Alice, I think she'll know …

He eased in beside Alice. The woman on the screen was laughing. Harder, she mouthed. Harder … in the ass …

Remember what the dormouse said … Feed your head, feed your head …

* * *

While Rasharkin was having sex on Alice's epidermis canvas, Alice went traversing down the rabbit hole via her first Astral Projection. Exiting at the other end, she found herself naked, sprawled out on a lawn, with the sun beaming down upon her. Two figures stationed at a picnic table watched her, crafty bemusement on their bizarre faces. March Hare and Mad Hatter.

Hare was the first to sing a comment:

'A naked Alice with exposed titties releasing fragrance!

How titillating! What a heavenly entrance!'

Hatter quickly joined in:

'And such a hairy ranch, a lovely spread for all to see!

One could make a hat from it, or at least a fine toupee.'

Alice quickly tried covering up her nakedness, but what covered one part exposed another.

Hatter and Hare pushed away from the table. Stood towering over her. Hatter was naked, except for his hat hanging on his half-cocked cock. Hare was naked also, except for a dickie-bow on his rather long carrot-shaped dickie, with what looked suspiciously like Hatter's teeth-imprints nibbled into it.

'You won't hurt me, will you, Mister Hare? *Boop oop a doop.*' Alice sang, eyelashes fluttering seductively like Betty Boop.

Hare didn't respond, but a sinister smirk crawled over his face as he bent down, and slowly parted her legs. 'Your clit looks suspiciously like the Caterpillar – and equally fat and juicy.'

'*You* won't hurt me, Mister Hatter, will you?' she said, glancing behind Hare's shoulders at voyeuring Hatter. 'Please say you won't hurt me.'

'Do not fret, sweet Alice, I'm not into girls and their moist little split,

Boys are a tastier dish, their pickle-onions and wieners held in my fist.'

The last Alice remembered was a naked Rasharkin running towards the scene in slow motion, double-barrelled shotgun blazing buckshot at Hare and Hatter, turning their heads into rice pudding confetti, pouring all over her face.

* * *

'I don't know who you were fucking back there, but it wasn't me,' Alice said, an hour later, watching Rasharkin dressing. 'Not that I'm complaining, mind you. That was the best – *and weirdest* – fuck I've *ever* had. Want to tell me her name?'

'Whose name?'

'The beautiful woman in the old film.'

His back tensed. He said nothing.

'Okay, I understand. We all have our private fantasies we like to keep for our darkest thoughts. Shit, we all need our secrets, don't we?'

He stood. Finished buttoning his shirt. Turned and looked at her, a strange smile on his face.

'I couldn't agree more.'

Chapter Twenty-One

It is the bungled crime that brings remorse.
PG Wodehouse, *Love Among the Chickens*

Evening visiting time at the Mater hospital was buzzing with visitors. Charlie walked down the corridor, brown bag under his arm bulging with fruit, Lucozade and a newspaper.

Brian's partially bandaged face produced what looked like a slit for a grin, the moment he spotted his old pal approaching the bed.

'Charlie! You're a sight for sore eyes. And a busted arse.'

'Jumping out a bloody window? What the hell were you thinking?'

'I *wasn't* thinking. That's why you're standing there with a bunch of bananas in your hands. Good job I was stoned out of my mind. Didn't feel a thing.'

Charlie rested the bag on top of a side table, then leaned in towards Brian, whispering, *'You haven't heard the news?'*

Brian shook his head. 'They've had me doped to the eyeballs with painkillers. It's only been a few hours since I've started to think straight. *Is it the robbery?*

'Jim.'

'Jim? Fuck! Did they arrest him? Where? When?'

'He … he's … dead, Brian. Murdered.'

'What …? What're you talking about? Have you been boozing?'

'They tortured him, and then murdered him.'

Brian looked in a daze. 'Who … who murdered him? You're not making sense, Charlie.'

'Drug dealers. Threw his naked body on the street, like garbage. They arrested that piece of shit, Scarface Logan.'

Charlie removed the newspaper from beneath the bag. Showed Brian the headline.

LOCAL MAN'S TORTURED BODY FOUND AT DER-ELICT CHURCH: Drug deal gone wrong? Scarface Logan arrested.

Brian grabbed the paper. Started reading. Tears began welling up in his eyes. He angrily brushed them away.

'I tried calling him on his phone, to let him know I was in hospital, but I got no answer, only a dialling tone. I tried calling him again, a bit after that, but his phone had no tone whatsoever. Aw fuck, Charlie, they must have had him by then.'

Charlie nodded. 'Jim called me a couple of times, warning me to stay away from the house, in case the cops came. Little did any of us know, it wasn't the cops we had to worry about.'

'How did Logan and his gang catch up with him so soon?'

'I don't know, but what I do know is, if they got Jim, we'll be next on their list. They might have Logan in custody, but his gang are still out there. You've got to get out of here.'

'I can't – at least not right now. The doctor's coming in the morning to check my ribs.'

'To hell with the doctor. I think you should leave now. I really do. First chance I get, I'm heading out of Belfast, for good, me and Rosie, we're never coming back. We're going to buy a barge, and head down south to live in it. Hope to have it in a week's time. We're staying at a hotel for a couple of days, over at –'

'Don't! Don't tell me where you are. Best I don't know. Look, Charlie, they're not going to try anything in a hospital. This is probably the safest place for me at the moment.'

'There are other hospitals, far away from here. With the money, you can book yourself into a private one, down south.'

'Fuck that. I'm not leaving Belfast for anyone. I respect your decision to leave with Rosie, but it's not for me, mate. I love Belfast, warts and all.'

'Don't be stupid. It's not worth it. We don't know what Jim told Scarface and his gang.'

'What? What the fuck did you say? Fuck you, Charlie Madden, for saying that! Jim would never squeal on us.'

'They tortured him! Holes all over his body. Read the paper.'

'I don't need to read anything to know he would never give us up. You, on the other hand, would sell your granny for a slice of hairy bacon.'

'Why, you little fucker. I shouldn't have come here. I risked my neck coming here to –'

'You risked fuck all, you ball-less bastard. You only came here to clear your guilty conscience for not watching Jim's back. Now fuck away off to wherever the hell you're going, you and your rowing boat.'

Charlie's face knotted with anger. *'I ought to –'*

'You ought to get the fuck out of here while you have the chance! I'll give you five seconds to get your cowardly, bony arse in gear, before I crack this over your skull.' Brian secured a lethal blackthorn steel-knobbed walking cane from the side of the bed, and began waving it angrily at Charlie's face.

Charlie backed away, agitated and angry. 'Fuck you.'

'Fuck you double! And shove these cheap rotten bananas up your arse as far as you can get them. They're as yellow as you!' Brian shouted, throwing the fruit at a fleeing Charlie. Bemused patients and their visitors looked on, some laughing, grateful for the unexpected entertainment in that sombre and depressing place.

Chapter Twenty-Two

The legend has it, Ossian lies
beneath this landmark on the hill,
asleep till Fionn and Oscar rise
to summon his old bardic skill
in hosting their last enterprise.
John Hewitt, 'Oisin's Grave'

In the parlour of his modest, one-bedroomed flat, Conor O'Neill placed a cup of tea and a plate of McVitie's Digestive biscuits on a small table. The table was one of the few pieces of furniture he possessed, a purchase from a local charity shop.

A woman seated at the table reached and took the cup of tea, thanked him, but ignored the biscuits. She was in her late forties, and despite the devastating attacks of cancer and the counter-attacks of chemotherapy, Fiona Harrison's legendary beauty still dominated her features.

A winner of Miss Young Ireland while in her early teens, she was also a past member of the republican movement. Her disillusion-ment with the movement followed on the heels of teenage son Michael being labelled an informer two years previously. He and his family – especially Fiona – vehemently denied the accusation.

An order of execution was commuted to a lifetime banishment from Ireland, only after the influential intervention of Conor brought an eleventh-hour reprieve for the lad.

Also in the room was Barney Dennison, standing leaning against the far wall with arms folded, looking uncomfortable each time he moved.

'For God's sake, have a seat, Barney,' Conor said. 'You're shuffling about as if you've a bee in your arse.'

'I … I'm okay standing, for now.'

Conor's two rescue cats, Tiddles and Chairman Meow, watched the gathering with sleepy eyes of indifference.

'Okay, Fiona. Now, what makes you think Michael has returned to Belfast?' Conor asked, sitting down opposite.

'A mother's intuition maybe? Call it what you want, but I *know* he's returned. We tried not to let him hear about my cancer until it was absolutely necessary, but an aunt let it slip when she spoke to him on the phone a couple of days ago. He told her he was coming back home, first chance he got. He's no longer in his Liverpool flat.'

Dennison quickly cut in: 'You think he'd come back here, knowing the consequences?'

Fiona glared at Dennison. '*Regardless* of the consequences. A mother and son's love. Something the likes of *you* wouldn't have a clue about. Don't think I don't know you were the ones who accused my son of being an informer.'

Dennison looked as if the gun-in-the-bum torture was being

administered again. 'You … should be very … careful of those accusations, Fiona.'

'Why? Going to have me shot, like the big man you aren't?'

Conor quickly interceded with a quiet but commanding voice. 'Okay, enough. Let's calm the situation down. We'll get nowhere with acrimonious jousting.'

Dennison, unable to hold Fiona's stare, looked even more uncomfortable, glancing around the room.

'What exactly do you want us to do, Fiona?' Conor said.

'*You*, Conor. No one else. What I want *you* to do is get word out – Michael's not to be touched. He's here on a mission of mercy. You can do that, can't you?'

From his ageing waistcoat pocket, Conor secured the Caminetto pipe. Rubbed its textured bowl with forefinger and thumb. He seemed to be pondering the question before answering.

'Yes … I can do that – *if* he's in Belfast. But if he's outside the city, then it's a different story.'

'I want to talk to him, before he's forced to leave Belfast, *again*.'

'You're putting Conor in a terrible fix, a no-win situation.' Dennison mumbled. 'No one can guarantee you a sit-down with your son.'

Fiona, ignoring Dennison, kept her eyes resolutely on Conor. 'Well, Conor?'

'Barney's right, Fiona, nobody can guarantee it.'

'You're not nobody. You can, and you will. For me. The movement owes me that much, don't you think?'

After a few seconds, Conor nodded. 'Okay. If we can find him, I'll make sure you get to talk to him.'

'But, Conor,' Dennison began, 'you can't –'

'Get word out. He's to be held in a safe house until I arrive, if we locate him. No harm comes to him. That's a direct order from me.'

Dennison looked on the verge of saying something. Glanced over at Fiona, then at Conor, before leaving the room without saying a word.

'God, how I detest that vile creature,' Fiona said, the moment Dennison closed the door. 'An opportunist coward who didn't lift a finger to fight when the war was raging. Of course, now that it's over and he hasn't a hope of being harmed, he's walking about like the last Spartan.'

Conor false-shuddered. 'Shame on you, Fiona Harrison. You just placed an image of Barney in Spartan underwear before my eyes!'

For the first time since entering, she laughed. 'The thought!'

'Regrettably, the movement is now filled with Barney-clones, and there's very little that genuine republicans can do about it. Anyway, how are you doing? *Really?*'

'Really? Terrible. I know I'm supposed to come out with brave statements about fighting cancer, how I won't give in, but to be honest, Conor, I've already given in and made my peace with the Man – or Woman – Upstairs. I'm too tired for it all. I just want to see Michael before I die. Is that too much to ask? From me, to you?'

Conor looked at the pipe in his hands, as if suddenly seeing it for the very first time.

'What an insensitive idiot I am. I shouldn't have brought this out in your presence. I wasn't thinking. Sorry about that.' He quickly moved to return the pipe to his pocket.

She reached and stilled his hand, holding it gently but firmly. 'It's okay …'

'You sure? I can wait until you leave.'

'The smoke's hardly going to make any difference now, is it?' She offered the palm of her hand. 'Let me light it, the way I used to, when I first bought it for you.'

Hesitantly, he brought the pipe's bit to his mouth; fished out the box of Swan matches from his pocket; placed the pipe's bowl on her palm.

She removed a single match, flaming it to the pipe, while he sucked life into it, never taking his eyes off hers. Smoke began drifting over them, like an old crime noir movie.

Fiona inhaled the smoke up her nostrils, closing her eyes. When they opened again, she was smiling the smile he loved, from a distant time.

'I miss the aroma, Conor. Brings back happy memories.'

He removed the pipe. 'No point in raking over old ashes from years ago. They only burn the soul.'

'Sometimes I think smouldering memories are all I have now. Warm nights in Cushendall. Summer walks in Glenariff Forest. You reciting "Oisin's Grave" while us picnicking with Hartley's strawberry sandwiches and Lyons tea.'

A sadness entered his eyes. 'Yes, well …'

'To be honest, I thought you'd have dumped the pipe.'

He couldn't contain the bitterness in his voice. 'The way you dumped me?'

She looked stunned. 'That ... that was unfair.'

'I couldn't agree more.'

'You know what I meant. I left you because I loved you. You knew that.'

'Did I? Strange way of showing it.'

'The scandal would have destroyed you, made you weaker in the movement, especially so soon after Bridget's death. *That's* how much I loved you, even though it broke my heart, having to return to Paddy.'

He took a long suck of the pipe while looking across at her. Directed smoke towards the ceiling with the side of his mouth. Sat the pipe down on the table.

'Paddy's a good man. A better man than me. I know he still hates me, and who the hell can blame him?'

'He has no hate in him. Never had. He doesn't even think of that time any more.'

'Ha! Don't fool yourself. He thinks of it always, like an unhealing cut, gnawing at his skin. No man forgets a blow so personal, so close to the heart.'

'He ... he hasn't come near me in a year.' She was blushing, as if confessing some unpardonable sin to her confessor, seeking absolution. 'Sometimes he acts as if he's going to be contaminated just by touching me. Can't blame him, I suppose, the way I look.'

'You look as beautiful as the first time I met you, in that old hall on North Queen Street, doing our training for Saint John Ambulance. Remember?'

She smiled. 'I'll never forget it. each of us on a secret mission to learn first aid, to help volunteers who'd been injured in gun battles. You thought you were all that, because you were a natural at it. A bit of a show-off.'

'Was I?' He grinned.

'Always contradicting an instructor. I had to remind you that it was supposed to be secret, and that you were doing everything but keeping a low profile.'

'You're right, I was full of myself, but for thinking I had a chance with Miss Young Ireland!'

She started laughing, then her face suddenly tightened with pain. She began coughing. Conor sprang up to get water, but she grabbed his hand.

'No … it's … it's okay. It'll go … go away in a few seconds.'

He looked concerned. Remained standing, watching, and gripping her hand.

The coughing eventually stopped. She stood. 'I need to be getting ready to go. Paddy'll be here shortly to pick me up.'

'Shouldn't you sit a while, until the coughing subsides? At least let me get you some water?'

'I'm okay. Really.' She looked intently at him. 'You *will* find Michael, won't you? Keep him safe. Promise me, Conor.'

'I'll do my damnedest.' He squeezed her hand. 'You have my word.'

'That's good enough for me. I'm thankful I came to see you. You've made me feel so much better – in every way.'

'I'm glad you came. It's been too long. I've never stopped thinking about you.'

A car horn beeped three times.

'That'll be Paddy,' she said.

'I … wish things were –'

She placed a finger over his mouth, preventing the words from forming.

He gripped her tightly, and was immediately shocked by how emaciated she was under all the sweaters. Ribs. Nothing but ribs. Emotion rode up his chest. He swallowed hard, hoping not to cry in front of her, never wanting to let her go.

The horn beeped impatiently, another three blasts.

She quickly kissed him, then pulled away, leaving him in the ethereal presence of her perfume, clinging to his clothes.

Chapter Twenty-Three

We have never heard the devil's side of the story,
God wrote all the book.

Anatole France

Night time in Belfast. Scarface Logan squeezed out of a brutish four-wheel drive, and stood outside his large, ivy-covered Antrim Road house, observing it as if for the first time.

'Always good to be home after a hard day at the office …' he said to no one in particular, wry grin on lips. Logan looked every part the evil drug baron the press had painted him, his face a double cross of scars from a double-cross.

Rain was coming down in whiplash formation. The vehicle rolled away smoothly, leaving him in the neon streetlights with their hoary hues and secretive shadows.

Logan stood staring up at the sky, allowing the rain to pound his face, as if hoping to dilute the stench of a grim police cell filled with some stranger's vomit, piss and blood.

Once the four-wheel drive was out of sight, the only sounds the street surrendered were the wind and rain, unified and purposeful in the eerie calm. He listened to the downpour for a few moments more, before proceeding up the steps to the front door, tapping the touchpad in the Yale KeyFree digital door lock.

The door opened without a sound. He stepped into the hallway, only to be shoved roughly sideways, something hard pressed against the back of his head.

'Hands high, scumbag! Don't turn your head or I'll blow it clean off your shoulders,' a balaclava-clad Brian Ross hissed, slamming the door shut while keeping the blackthorn steel-knob pressed against Logan's neck.

Logan raised his hands.

'What's this all about?'

'Shut up.' Brian's free hand quickly searched Logan's clothing.

'I don't carry a gun, if that's what you're searching for, mate.'

'I'm not your mate, scumbag. Move slowly – *very slowly* – into the living room.'

'What's this all –?'

'Shut the fuck up! Walk!'

'Okay … easy … no problem …' Logan began walking towards the enormous living room. 'Look, see? I'm complying. Let's not do anything foolish, or –'

Brian cracked Logan over the head with the cane. It made a horrible dull thud as metal connected with bone. Logan hit the floor face down, out for the count.

From a gripbag, Brian removed a smoothing-iron and a roll of duct tape. Expertly securing Logan's ankles and wrists with the tape, he dragged him towards a large mahogany dining table.

Satisfied, he found himself a comfortable seat, removed the bala-clava, and began wiping the sweat from his face.

* * *

It wasn't long until Logan – now bound and stretched out like a corpse on the dining table – started regaining consciousness.

Quickly re-hooding, Brian stood, towering over the drug dealer.

Regardless of his reputation, Logan's face held the look of a man already at his sell-by date. Despite this, he gave an attempt at bravado. 'Ever have one of those days when everything goes according to plan and turns out great? Yeah, me neither. Can I ask why I'm being tied up like this?'

'You've heard of waterboarding? This is the Irish equivalent. Ironing-boarding. *I* ask the questions; *you* supply the answers. I want you to tell me *everything* about the murder of Jim McCabe.'

'Jim Mc … oh, you're going by all the bullshit in the *Sunday Truth*. Right? Top drug dealer arrested, blah blah blah, suspected in murder, blah blah blah.'

'You're just a poor scapegoat?'

'Scapegoat and usual suspect when the cops and that shitty rag want to make it look like they know something. Helps convince the gullible public that they're getting their money's worth, and they can sleep peacefully in their beds at night.'

'Cut to the chase.'

'There is *no* chase to cut *to*. The cops know I had nothing to do with any murder. I'd never even heard of Jim McCabe until they arrested me a few days ago and mentioned his name. It's not the first time they've tried to set me up for someone else's dirty deeds, despite all the backhanders they take from me. That's why they had to release me this morning on bail, on a lesser charge of possession of marijuana.'

'If that's your final answer, don't say you weren't given the chance to come clean.' Brian inserted the smoothing-iron plug into a socket on the wall, then slapped a patch of duct tape on Logan's mouth.

'Hmummmppppppppppppppppphhhhhhhhhhhhhhhhhhhhhhhhhhh-hhhhhhhhhhhhh!'

Brian turned the iron's dial up to full blast. A few seconds later, he spat onto its smooth metal face. The spittle sizzled and fragmented into marbleised spheres before skating off the hot metal edge.

'Perfect. Time to iron out all those wrinkles in your story and ballbag.' Resting the iron on its side, he reached over and unbuckled Logan's belt, pulling down his jeans.

'Hmummmppppppppppppppppphhhhhhhhhhhhhhhhhhhhhhhhhhh-hhhhhhhhhhhhh!'

'Very kinky. Commando *and* Brazilian, eh? Well, by the time I'm finished with you, you're going to have a ballbag smoother than a baby's arse to go along with your pampered cock.' Brian brought the heated iron perilously close to Logan's exposed balls.

Logan's eyes widened in horror. He wriggled frantically, trying to snake free, but the restraints tightened their grip.

'*Hmummmpppppppppppppppphhhhhhhhhhhhhhhhhhhhhhhhhhhhhhhhhh!*'

'Sorry, I don't understand a word you're muttering. Now, where was I?'

The tip of the iron touched Logan's ballbag. Logan jerked stiffly, as if hit by bolts of electricity.

'*Hmummmpppppppppppppppphhhhhhhhhhhhhhhhhhhhhhhhhhhhhhhhhhhhhhhhhhhhhhhhhhhhhhhhhhhhhhhhhhhhhhhhhhhhh!*'

Brian violently pulled the duct tape off.

'Ready to talk?'

'*Fuckkkkkkkkkkkkkkkkkkkkkkkkkkkkkkkkk!* My balls are on fire, you fucking maniac!'

'That's right. I *am* a fucking maniac. Now, if you didn't murder Jim, who the hell did?'

'How the fuck would I know? I'd nothing to do with it.'

'Have it your way.' The tip of the iron touched the ballbag again, this time for a longer period.

'*Arghhhhhhhhhhhhhhhhhhhhhhhhhhhhhhhhhhhhhhhhhhhhhhhhhhhhhhhhhhhh! Fuckkkkkkkkkkkkkkkkkkkkkkkkkkkkkkkkk!*'

'You get one last chance before I turn your cock and balls into an Ulster fry of sausage and black pudding. If this doesn't work, I have gunpowder and touch paper left over from Halloween. I'll fill the eye of your cock with the gunpowder and touch paper and light it up like a firework. Now, for the last time, who murdered Jim?'

Logan's face was raw. He was perspiring terribly. 'I ... I can't give you an answer to something I ... know nothing about! For fuck's sake, you ... you've got to believe me! Think ... think I want my balls fried or dick blown off? I've tons of money. Name ... name your price.'

'I wouldn't touch your filthy money with a barge pole. I hate drug dealers, what they do to kids.'

'I don't sell to kids. That's a fact.'

'A drug dealer with a conscience?'

'I ... only sell blow to university students, teachers, hippies ... people of that nature and inclination. Nothing heavy. No H or coke, none of that heavy-calibre crap. All that shit in the papers about me? That's all it is. Shit and lies.'

'Shit and lies? Yeah, I can see that from your humble abode and humble lifestyle.'

'Okay, I make a few quid on the exporting side, but that doesn't make me a bad guy. I've a good heart. I help the homeless; I give to charities. I can tell you're not a bad guy, either. You don't want to kill me. You're wearing a balaclava. You want to walk out of here without me recognising you. Right?'

'Shut the fuck up!'

'I don't believe in violence, either. I've never used it in my life.'

'Well *I* have, and I'm about to re-commence if you don't come up with an answer.'

'Look ... all I know ... one of my cop insiders told me there was speculation about a certain scumbag being robbed in that bank robbery, the Bank of New Republic. You must have heard about it?'

Brian felt his ribcage tighten. Skin began tingling.

'Go on … what about it?'

'Ever hear of Seamus Nolan?'

'Nolan …? Don't think so.'

'Just Google his name. If you've ever had a nightmare, he was probably in it. A real psycho and a leading member of the Brotherhood.'

'Brotherhood …?' Brian felt a chill on his neck.

'Three things in life always lead to the grave: God, undertakers – and Nolan. One of their top killers. Takes no prisoners. Does all the Brotherhood's nutting – hence the nickname, Nutty Nolan. Apparently – and I can only go by my cop contact – he was inside the Bank of New Republic when it was hit by the robbers.'

Brian's knees suddenly rubberised. The balaclava seemed to be tightening, suffocating him. He was finding breathing difficult.

'It gets better,' continued Logan. 'They robbed Nutty of a load of cash. Then had the audacity to slap him about. Fuck, how I cheered when I heard that. I had a couple of run-ins with him, in the past. A couple of years back, he shot me in the knee, and exiled me out of Belfast. Said if I ever came back, he'd personally shoot me in the face and watch me leak to death.'

'Leak to death …?'

'He's that kind of psycho. As sharp as a beach ball, and there's more brains in a Halloween mask, but he's relentless. Like the Terminator with a Duracell battery shoved up his arse. Just keeps coming for you. Shit, for all I know, he's looking for me now,

now the cops and media have blown my cover that I'm back living in Belfast. Which begs the question, how the hell did you know where I was living?'

'The local BBC released it when you were arrested. Then you got bail this morning. I waited all day in the pissing rain, to see if you'd show up. That's how badly I wanted you.'

'You're talking past tense. I like that. Shows positive thinking for the future.'

'Don't bet on it. You're far from off the hook. What … what else did the cops say about the robbery?'

'There were three robbers. I would say this poor bastard Jim was the first to be hunted down by Nutty. The guy was horribly tortured, they say. Another of Nutty's calling-cards.'

The room span into a queasy vertigo. Furniture was dancing in slow motion. Brian sat down on a large Victorian armchair, wishing this was all a bad dream. No bank job. Jim still alive. No psycho who likes to watch people leak to death, searching for him.

'If *I* were one of the lads who robbed that bank?' Logan said, staring into Brian's eyes. 'I'd make sure I was armed to the teeth. At least give myself a fighting chance when Nolan comes a-knocking. And a-knocking he will come, make no mistake about that.'

Brian was trying to kick-start his brain into gear, weighing up the pros and the cons.

'What if these lads didn't have guns?'

'Forgive the pun, but I could fix that in a shot.' Logan's eyes started dancing with hope. 'Any weapon, any shape, size or weight – I'm your man with a plan.'

'Thought you said you didn't believe in violence?'

'I … well … I don't, but I'm not a fool. In my business, I have to protect myself against those who *do* believe in violence. Everyone has the right to defend themselves, especially against a nutter like Nutty.'

'And I'm supposed to trust you?'

'At the moment, I may be dangling by my balls, but you're dangling by a thread. Necessity outweighs trust. So, what do you say about our newly formed alliance?'

'I'll have to give it some thought.'

'While you're thinking about it, any chance of pulling my pants up? It's getting awfully chilly in here, stretched out naked with my cock and balls exposed. Being watched by a man with a sock over his head is also pretty unnerving.'

Chapter Twenty-Four

'Morning, gentlemen. Nice day for a murder.'
Rocky Sullivan, *Angels with Dirty Faces*

Billy 'Goat' Butler sat waiting in the driver's seat of the car, lapping up the rare piece of Belfast sunshine that was beaming through the windshield.

In all honesty, the driver's seat was the last place Billy should have been sitting, having suffered from narcolepsy since he was a teenager. It was a dark secret he kept from everyone, despite the long list of near-disasters he had had as an active volunteer in the Brotherhood for Irish Freedom, many moons ago.

Three times he had fallen asleep while making bomb components, almost blowing himself and everyone within a mile radius into an early grave. He finally decided to seek medical help, but only after falling asleep on his most important mission: to blow up the British Ambassador on a lonely rural road, using a hidden command wire leading to a 200-pound bomb hidden inside a culvert.

Camouflaged in a leafy hillside in south Armagh, waiting in ambush in the early hours of a Sunday morning in July, he fell into a state of zombie-like unconsciousness. While in the land of nod, a stray mountain goat arrived on the scene and chewed through the command-wire hidden in the grass, saving the ambassador's arse and giving Billy the moniker of a lifetime.

Thankfully, the medication now available to him was working miracles, keeping him awake for hours on end. The only side-effect was that sometimes it left him jittery and excited, with the occasional outbursts of mad laughter when he was feeling nervous or under stress.

Normally, he loved his cushy job, chauffeuring pampered Stormont oligarchs and their families wherever their dear hearts desired, be it to their favourite restaurant, drinking den or bingo parlour. However, this particular member always made his stomach flutter like a cave full of nervous bats. Not that Billy had anything to hide, especially anything hinting towards insubordination or free thought. God the night, no! Perish the thought.

Suddenly, someone tapped sharply on the car's window, unsettling Billy's already unsettled soul and stomach. He made an attempt to get out of the car to open the passenger door, but it was too late. Seamus Nolan had already seated himself in the back.

'Afternoon, Seamus.' Billy forced a smile. 'Not a bad day for the first day of November, eh?'

Nolan, ignoring both the greeting *and* Billy, opened a copy of the *Andersonstown News*. Began reading.

Dear God, this is going to be one hell of a long journey, with Darth Vadar lurking in the back. Billy eased the car out of Nolan's driveway, and headed south for Dundalk, taking the back-roads less travelled for security reasons, to avoid running into roadblocks.

The journey *was* long, and silent and unpleasant. A few times, Billy thought he could feel Nolan's interrogatory eyes drilling into the back of his skull, as if searching for his most oily thoughts.

An excruciating hour later, they reached their destination – an abandoned one-time church nestled in a desolate wooded glen. The gothic structure rested silently, like a disease yet to be discovered, in the middle of a graveyard of abandoned husks of rusted cars.

Billy had been here a few times before. It never failed to give him the creeps. Like the house in Hitchcock's *Psycho*. Regardless of how he tried, he could never erase other church smells and their associations from his memory: the faded aromas of candle grease, rotted pews and dried-out varnish from confessionals.

And this place was another confessional, one where false confessions were forced from mouths, where hope was destroyed and prayers were rarely answered. A place with only two consequences: the dreaded 'six pack' – shot in both ankles, knees and elbows – or the more final and absolute OBE – one in the back of the ear.

Nolan exited the car; stood pensively, as if taking in the sun's warmth.

'Finished with your *Andytown News*, Seamus?' Billy asked, sticking his head out the window.

'Take it.' Nolan replied disdainfully. He walked off in the direction of the church, much to Billy's relief.

With Nolan out of sight, Billy stretched over the seat, grabbed the local newspaper and quickly exited the car. His stomach rumbled a warning. He farted, loud and watery. Prayed he hadn't shat himself in the shadow of the church.

Desperately bursting to take a shit, but somewhere out of the way, he ventured up an old pathway, covered in a jungle of weeds. That's all he'd need – Nolan literally catching him with his trousers down.

He headed around to the back of the church, to a nice wee spot he had used before, to fertilise the sacred ground, so to speak.

* * *

Inside the old church, Nolan walked to the middle of the bare floor, a cowl of darkness flowing over him, like the notorious Dominican, Alonso de Hojeda, the Brother of Death.

A table and a family of five chairs dominated the floor, and a crew of sombre-looking men occupied four of the chairs, their sharply curving shadows seeming super-real in the tangible tension.

Nolan sat down in the fifth chair, without offering or accepting a greeting.

Above in the apse, abandoned icons of wide-eyed angels and peeling-faced saints looked down on the gathering with a mixture of curiosity and anxiety. A cloying smell of something long dead mixed with the redolent stench of animal excrement and urine.

'Never thought you'd have the balls to return to Belfast, wee Mickey,' Nolan finally said, his eyes drilling into the face of a pale and shattered-looking Mickey Harrison.

'I had to get back home … no matter what.'

'Wasn't very smart of you, getting a black taxi from the airport, two nights ago, was it? We have plenty of people driving those. Surely you knew we'd hear about it?'

'I didn't care. I needed to get home, as quickly as possible.'

'Your touting put good men and women in jail. Wrecked families. The repercussions of your treacherous acts are still being felt to this day. Suicides, drugs, depression, to name a few.'

'I never touted. No point in saying I was set up, Sean, and totally innocent, is there? You wouldn't believe me, anyway. My mum … she's dying … cancer … That's the reason I came back.'

'Sorry to hear that. Fiona was a good republican. A good supporter, until you fucked things up. Then it became personal with her, hating us for something *you* did. How long's she got?'

'A few months at most. All I'm asking is to be at her side, when she dies. Then … then you can shoot me, if you want. I'll not run. I'll hand myself over to you.'

'I doubt that.'

'I swear to God I will! I will, Sean. I will! I'll do whatever you –'

'Calm down. You're not going to be shot. Okay? You've got my word on that. Besides, those days are over. You can thank your lucky stars and the Good Friday Agreement for that. Not forgetting Conor O'Neill, of course. He seems to be very concerned about getting you back to Belfast in one piece. He has a soft spot for you, apparently. Why's that?'

Mickey shrugged. 'Don't know.'

'If you had something on O'Neill, of course, I would be extremely interested to hear it. It would be beneficial for you, also.'

'I … I hardly know him. I've never met him.'

A silence descended on the space. There was only the raucous sound of crows gossiping somewhere outside, and the distant hum of traffic way off on a motorway's edge.

'Okay, here's the score,' Nolan finally said, pointing his finger into Mickey's face. 'You get to stay until Fiona's death and her funeral. Not a second more. Clear?'

Mickey nodded. Relief transformed his young face. 'Thank you for that, Seamus.'

'Keep your fucking thanks. I don't want *anything* from a scumbag like you. There are lads in Belfast who'll be pissed off if they ever find out we let you live after coming back.' Nolan stood, as did the rest of the group.

'What happens now?' Mickey asked.

'You're going to be blindfolded and let out the back way. Don't take the blindfold off until you've walked for at least five minutes. *Do not look back.* If we catch you trying to note this location, you *will* be shot.'

'I swear to –'

'Shut up! Just shut the fuck up and listen. You'll hear traffic leading to the main road. Hitch a lift to the train station a couple of miles away, or walk to it. I don't care how you get there, just get there. Make sure you *stay* low until your ma's funeral. After that, you're on your own. I can't guarantee your safety, if you're spotted by any of the lads.'

'Thank you, Seamus. Thank you.'

Nolan, ignoring the words, nodded to one of the others.

'Bag him.'

A cloth bag smelling of decayed spuds was pulled over Mickey's head, then tightened with a filthy cord. He was pushed roughly to the open back door, and eventually led out into a field. A hand grabbed his arm roughly, guiding him over uneven ground in a minefield of loose stones and knee-high weeds. In the distance, a train's faded whistle could just about be heard. It seemed to be saying something. Soulful. Forlorn.

A couple of times, Mickey stumbled clumsily, but was quickly steadied by the same guiding hand. After a couple of minutes of walking, he was suddenly stopped, cord loosened and bag pulled from head. He squinted as sharp sunlight hit his eyes, partially blinding him.

'Do … do I just keep … keep walking straight ahead?'

'No more walking needed, Mickey. You've come to the end of your journey.'

'Seamus?'

'You didn't really think we'd let you get away from us twice?' Nolan smiled, gloved hand pointing a gun at Mickey's face. 'Are you really that thick?'

The stench of human and animal excrement began filling the air. Poisonous gas fumes, faintly transparent and ghostly, misting over a swampy cesspool.

'I … I guess I am thick, believing I could trust you.'

'I always keep my word. I'm not going to shoot you, because I wouldn't waste a bullet. You're going for a little swim in my private pool. Enjoy.'

Nolan kicked Mickey full in the chest, sending him tumbling backwards into the large, open cesspool.

Mickey hit the swampy mush inverted, disappearing for what seemed like minutes. Suddenly, his face burst through the brown, putrid ceiling, gasping and spluttering for air as the foul substance seeped into his mouth. He was unrecognisable as anything human, more like some gothic swamp creature bawling for its god, trying desperately to swim free of the nightmare.

'See anyone you know in there, Mickey?' Nolan laughed, as two of his companions pulled the cesspool's heavy metal cover back over the opening, drowning out Mickey's dreadful screams. 'Don't worry, I'll send a wreath to Fiona's funeral with your name on it.'

'He didn't put up much of a fight,' one of the crew said, a few minutes later, wiping his hands on baggy jeans.

'That's the idea. Always keep them calm, until you no longer need their calmness.'

'Anything else, Sean?'

'No, that's it. Job well done, lads. One less tout to worry about.' Nolan handed the gun over. Removed the gloves. 'I shouldn't be telling you this, but big changes are coming. I've been told through the grapevine, I'm about to be promoted and O'Neill demoted.'

'Congratulations,' the crew said as one, all smiles and back-slapping.

'I'll not be forgetting any of you, on the way up. Okay, lock up before you go. I'm heading back to Belfast. Not a word of this to anyone. Understood?'

'Not a problem, Sean.'

Nolan exited, taking the pathway to the car, when something caught his attention. A movement somewhere in the thick overgrowth of weeds and bushes. He stopped. Walked hesitantly towards the thickets, wishing he had the gun with him.

A hare suddenly darted out, and ran for shelter, unnerving him. Then, just as he turned to continue his journey, he spotted something on the ground. He knelt on one knee. Examined the find.

* * *

Billy watched Nolan emerging from the back of the old church. He didn't look happy. Nolan never looked happy, but this time, he looked even less happy than usual.

'*Calm down. Calm down ...*' Billy whispered to himself in a nervous cadence. He tried blocking out the nightmare he had just witnessed, while sheltering in the long grass and deep weeds. His brain kept repeating the scene, over and over again, a young man being kicked backwards into a cesspool of death.

Like oil on leather, Nolan slid silently into the back of the car.

'Ready ... ready to go, Seamus?' Billy was working hard to control his breathing.

Nolan remained silent, staring at Billy via the rear-view mirror.

Taking the initiative, Billy started the engine, and manoeuvred the car out of the deserted grounds. If the long, silent journey to the old church was uncomfortable, he was certain the return journey home was going to be worse.

To add to Billy's woes, the sun had deserted him, and winter rain now commenced with a vengeance, making driving difficult in the dodgy and neck-breaking side roads. However, after a few minutes of driving, he was glad of the weather's sudden change. It helped him to focus better on his driving, rather than on Nolan, lurking behind him like a Machiavellian silent assassin.

'Treacherous ...' Nolan said.

Billy almost lost control of the wheel, as if he had just heard a dumb man speak for the first time.

'What ...? Did ... did you say something, Seamus?'

'Stop the car.'

'What?'

'*What?* Are you deaf?'

'No … sorry …' Billy eased down on the pedal, pulling over to the side of the road. The place was a jungle of overgrowth and withered trees. Not a soul in sight. Perfect killing and dumping ground.

Billy sneaked a peep at Nolan, whose hand was parked in the inside of his coat, as if searching for a packet of cigarettes. Billy knew Nolan didn't smoke, and surmised he was reaching for something a lot more lethal than a cig. He almost cried with relief when the item turned out to be a mobile.

'Treacherous,' Nolan repeated. 'This weather, it's treacherous.'

Billy nodded, then began giggling with nervous relief. 'It sure is. Hee-hee … heeeeeeeeeeeeeeeee!'

Nolan looked at Billy as if he had just grown an extra head. 'Are you on something?'

'What? No. God no, Seamus! Never touched drugs in my life.'

'Don't you think you should be driving a lot slower in this weather?'

'Oh! Yes … yes, you're right, Sean! I need to drive a lot slower. Hee-hee … heeeeeeeeeeeeeeeee. No problem. Bawwwwhahaha-hahaha!'

Nolan started hitting buttons on the mobile. A few seconds later, he was speaking into the device, so secretively Billy found it impossible to hear what he was saying, except for '… *this fucking clown driving the car. Something about him …*'

Because of the rain, it was almost two hours before Billy eventually stopped the car outside Nolan's house. For the longest time, Nolan remained in the car, staring at the back of Billy's head.

'Anything … anything else I can do for you, Seamus?'

Nolan leaned forward.

'I witnessed the strangest of things, back there in Dundalk. Did *you* witness anything strange, back there?'

'Back there in Dundalk? Strange? Me? No, I didn't witness anything back there at all.'

'A hare?'

'A hair? Like hair on your head – I mean *my* head?'

'The jumping kind.'

'Like a rabbit, you mean?'

Nolan eased closer, his breath crawling like an insect on Billy's neck.

'A hare that shits like a human. Must've been on steroids, the size of the shit it did. A miniature pyramid, with the steam coming off it like a fucking choo-choo train.'

Billy was felling faint, nervously eyeing the door, hoping Nolan didn't see him nervously eyeing the door.

'They … they say the hares down there can grow to the size of a dog, Seamus. Not a wolfhound, mind you, but … but a good-sized mongrel. They can kick the shit out of a Russell, those hares. That's what they say.'

'And so hygiene-conscious.'

'Hygiene-conscious?'

'Yes, this particular hare wiped its own arse.'

'A hare wiping its own hairy arse?'

'Can you believe that?'

'I heard about something like that, a couple of years ago. They say they can be trained to do almost anything, hares.'

'It gets weirder. It wiped its arse with what looked like a page from my *Andytown News*.'

Billy tried to respond, but his tongue refused to move.

Nolan eased closer. 'If I thought for one second you were nosing in my business, goat head, you'd be going for a swim in my private swimming pool.'

With that, Nolan left the car as silently as he had entered, leaving a sweating Billy to his thoughts and percolating stomach.

Chapter Twenty-Five

The world was getting dangerously crowded with crazy people.
John Dunning, *The Bookman's Wake*

It was late and pouring with heavy rain when Charlie and Rosie returned home from their stay at the hotel. A few seconds after parking their single suitcase in the living room and removing their coats, the doorbell chimed.

A frown appeared on Rosie's face. 'Who on earth would be calling at this time of night? Bet it's that Norton one. If it is that nuisance, tell him we're only in.'

Charlie suddenly seemed nervous.

The doorbell chimed again.

'Aren't you going to see who that is, Charlie?'

Charlie glanced hesitantly behind the curtains. Stared out into the street.

'You're right, love. It's only Tommy!'

'No need to sound so cheerful. Tell him you'll see him in the morning. We've just got in.'

'I'll only be a second. Stick the tea on.'

Charlie opened the door to his only neighbour. Tommy Norton was in his late seventies, but could pass for a springy sixty-five. He had a handsome, suntanned face from all his years travelling the world as a merchant seaman.

'We're only in, mate, having a cup of tea. I'll give you a wee shout in about an hour, and we'll go for a swallow. Okay?'

'Not a problem, Charlie, but just wanted to let you know, there's been a strange character sniffing about your house while you and Rosie were away.'

'What? What kind of strange character?'

'He's been in the street a couple of times. Always late at night. I was almost going to ask him what the hell he was up to, but he didn't look the type to take lip from the likes of me. There was something about him …'

'Will you stop talking in riddles?'

'It's hard to describe … just a feeling in my gut … then again, probably nothing. You know how suspicious I am of strangers.'

'I … sorry for snapping, Tommy. I'm just tired.'

Tommy laughed. 'That's why I never go on holidays. You need a holiday to get over it!'

'Thanks for looking after the place.'

'No problem, Charlie. That's what good neighbours do. See you in an hour, eh?'

'Yes … of course, mate. I owe you a few pints. I'll call up to your house, and we'll head over to the Rocktown.' Charlie quickly closed the door. Leaned against it. The hallway seemed to be spinning.

* * *

Robert Boyd waited until the last of the regular evening staff had left the station before heading upstairs to the second floor. Kerr was in an office on the same floor sorting through some files.

'Evening, Bob,' Kerr said, cheerfully.

Boyd nodded an acknowledgment, but otherwise ignored Kerr. He had a deep dislike for him, especially when seeing him master-classing in the art of arse-kissing the brass.

Across the corridor, Boyd headed into the communications office. A pretty young woman sat at one of the desks, her fingers working frantically on a computer keyboard.

'You're working late tonight, Julie.'

'Need the extra money,' she replied, without looking up.

'Don't we all? Any word yet on the owner of the car McCabe was driving?'

'Address and phone number came in about an hour ago. The computers were down since this afternoon. Hit by a virus.'

Boyd's heart did a little jerk. 'Was the information passed on?'

'Not yet. I was told to make sure it goes directly into the hands of Purvis, but he hasn't been in all day.'

'That's okay. I'll see he gets it.' Boyd held out his hand.

Julie stopped working the keyboard, and looked up at Boyd. 'Sorry, but McCafferty was quite adamant that it was to be given to Purvis. No one else.'

'You liked that Chanel perfume I got you for your birthday, last month?'

'Casting up? Have you forgotten what you got for it in return?'

'Just thought you might like a wee treat.'

'Some people might see that wee treat as a wee bribe.' Julie smiled.

'Others might see it as an appreciation of all the hard work you do, day in, day out.'

'Stop with the silver-tongue.'

'How does a hundred mil sound?'

'Two hundred sounds better.'

'You're an extortionist.'

'You like me smelling nice, don't you?'

'Now who's working the silver tongue?'

'Well, seeing you have a fondness for my tongue, I'm off work tomorrow. Fancy taking me somewhere nice?'

'Okay, somewhere nice and two hundred mil. Now, the info?'

Julie scribbled on a Post-it note, then handed it to Boyd. 'You've got three hours before I put it through the system. It has to be put in before midnight, if Purvis doesn't show up first.'

Boyd quickly left the office and headed downstairs, making his way across the road to the payphone in the Tesco supermarket. Dialled the number while feeding coins into the slot. Nothing. Just a repeated tone. He was about to hang up when a male voice said:

'Hello?'

'Yes, hello, this is Stevie Fitzpatrick calling from the office. Sorry for calling this late at night, but just wondering if I could speak to Albert about this morning's meeting at work.'

'Albert? You've … you've a wrong number, mate. No Albert lives here.'

'What? Oh! I'm so terribly sorry. I've hit the wrong button.'

Boyd quickly hung up, and hit another number. He tried inserting some coins into the phone's slot, but sweaty hands made the coins spill loudly onto the floor. A couple of late-night shoppers looked his way.

Bending down, he retrieved most of the coins, this time successfully inserting them. Listened to the monotonous dialling tone at the other end. It seemed to go on forever.

Easy … deep breath … nice and easy.

Finally, a voice at the other end.

'This better be good,' Nolan said.

'Charlie Madden … eighteen King's Court. He's home right now. I just spoke to him on the phone. You've less than an hour to get the job done, before the information is fed into the system. By then, officers will be crawling all over the place.'

'Less than an hour? That doesn't give me a lot of fucking time to –'

'You're wasting *fucking* time talking.' Boyd slammed the receiver down on Nolan's voice, feeling good; feeling like a man again, not a crawling dog. Not a golden goose.

Quickly making another call, he repeated the same information he had fed Nolan, only this time the recipient was Dennison, and a caveat added:

'Madden's not to be messed with. Our information says he's armed to the teeth, and highly dangerous. One of his mates could be with him. Be careful.'

'I'll make sure the right people know that.'

Task completed, Boyd crossed back over to the station, and went to where his car was parked, at the back. Quickly opened the boot. Checked inside the specially built compartment housing a SIG Sauer P226 and its silencer. Removing the two items, he married them as one long extension, then slammed the boot back down.

About to get into the car, something made him look up at the office with the lights on, the one Kerr had been working in. Had someone been staring out the window? He kept looking up for another few seconds. Nothing. His nerves and imagination playing tricks.

You fucked with the wrong man, Nolan. Big time, he thought as he drove on to the Antrim Road, heading north towards King's Court.

Chapter Twenty-Six

You tell 'em I'm comin', and hell's comin' with me, ya hear? Hell's
comin' with me!

Wyatt Earp, *Tombstone*

Charlie was in the pigeon coop, frantically pulling bricks
of money from the bird seed sacks, dropping them into
an old beaten-up duffle bag. He was sweating terribly despite the
night's coldness. The strange phone call twenty minutes ago call
had initially unnerved, then galvanized him.

'Charlie! Are you out there?' Rosie shouted from across the
yard. 'Tea's ready!'

Half a minute later, he walked into the living room, gripbag
in hand.

'What's wrong, Charlie? Why're you sweating? You look like
you're going to throw up.' Rosie looked puzzlingly at the bag in
his hand. 'What're you doing with that old bag?'

'We've got to leave, now, right this minute.'

'What … what are you talking about, leave? We just got back.
I'm not going anywhere until you explain what on earth you're
on about.'

'We've got to go *now*!'

'Don't you dare use that tone of voice with me, Charlie Madden!'

'I'm … I'm sorry, love, but we've got to get out of here. We've very little time. I'll explain on the way. I'll call a taxi.'

'I want to know what's going on, and no lying. You start your lying, I'll not move an inch from here. I mean it.'

Charlie sighed. 'Look, I should have told you this from the beginning, love, but I didn't want to worry you.'

'That'll be a first.'

'It's about Jim's murder.'

Rosie crossed herself. 'I wish you wouldn't bring that up. I still can't get those terrible pictures out of my head, what those evil people did to him, claiming he took their drugs.'

'It wasn't over drugs. It was money he stole from them.'

'Money? How would you know? You told me you hadn't seen Jim in months; that the two of you had fallen out, and that was why you didn't attend his funeral this morning.' A look of cold understanding spread across her face. 'That money … not horses. You lied to me! Is that what's in the bag?'

'This isn't the time for a tongue-lashing. Please … we need to start packing. I'll explain everything, once we get out of here. I promise, love.'

'You rotten dog, Charlie Madden. You dirty rotten dog …' She began sobbing.

* * *

Nolan, wearing a black baseball cap and dark clothing, parked the car out of clear view, before exiting, holding a small utility bag in his left hand. He walked beyond the Madden house, glancing to his right. Curtains were drawn, but not fully, allowing him a brief glimpse of two silhouetted figures, animated, possibly in argument.

He thought about forcing his way in through the front door, but the lights on in the end house at the bottom of the street made him hesitate. Someone could be inside, watching all comings and goings. He decided instead to check the back entrance, see how accessible it was.

Venturing down the almost-demolished alley, he stopped at the back door, '18' scrawled in paint on it. From the bag, he removed balaclava, gloves and gun. Jammed the gun down his waistband before removing his baseball cap, then slipping balaclava and gloves on.

Reaching his hand up above the wooden door frame, he unscrewed the back-entrance light bulb, bringing total darkness with the exception of the sickly yellow light coming from somewhere within the house.

From the bag, he produced a hunting knife and began harassing the door's lock until it sprang open with a dull *qwang*. He stepped silently into the yard, and began following the sickly light.

At the kitchen door, he tried the handle. It offered no resistance. He stepped inside. Loud voices could be heard quarrelling. He followed the sound down the darkened hallway, stopping at the living room.

The Maddens were arguing, tears running down the woman's face. He wished he could stand there forever, like a voyeuristic god spying on his subjects. Alas, there was little time for what had to be done. He would soon discover where the money was; equally important, the name of the smirking coward who hit him with the gun. He had something special planned for him; something oh-so-sweetly special.

Walking into the living room, gun aimed at Charlie's face, he smiled.

'Hello, Charlie …'

* * *

Behind a dilapidated snooker hall, Boyd had been spying from inside his car, watching Nolan disappearing down the alley.

He looked at his watch, then the SIG. Twenty minutes had slipped by, and there was no sign of Nolan's return. He lit a cig. It tasted good, bringing a nicotine kick all the way to a satisfying burn in his lungs. The nicotine helped settle his nerves, though he knew the respite would be short-lived.

I can do this. No problem. He won't know what fucking hit him. Two in the back of the nut. Bang-bang. Down he goes, to Hell or beyond.

He inhaled the nicotine again, visualising Nolan's head doing a watermelon explosion. But was that the way he wanted to kill him? Two in the head. Two seconds of satisfaction? Too quick.

Far too fucking quick for a scumbag like Nolan. No, something different. He could shoot him in the back, in the spine, watch him crawl, beg for his life like a worthless snail.

He flicked the finished cig out the window, and was about to exit the car when headlights from another car stopped him in his tracks.

* * *

The dark blue Audi slowed to a halt. The driver's door opened. Rasharkin stepped out into the streetlights' urine-coloured glare, armed with the information from a panicked-sounding Dennison, who had stressed the time factor and how dangerous Madden was.

Closing the car door behind him, he studied the street and beyond. Deserted. A soulless, barren wasteland.

Above, a sliver of movement on the edge of his peripheral caught his attention. A bird of some description, manoeuvring in and out of the night clouds like a kite cut loose. A seagull perhaps, though it looked small-scale for a gull. He watched until the bird disappeared into the darkness, leaving a wary feeling of foreboding in his gut.

Moving on along the street, he prepared for what was coming next. Madden's wife wouldn't be hurt, but she'd have to be tied up and gagged, in case nerves made her do something stupid and dangerous, like trying to save her husband from the inevitable.

As for Madden, it would be quick and semi-painless, providing he cooperated. He was determined not to allow this to turn into another melodrama, like McCabe's death.

He ventured down the alley, stopping at the designated number. Glanced up at the top of the wall. No barbed wire, but an army of broken bottles cemented in defence. If the back door proved too difficult he could go over the top, his coat covering the shards of glass. Checked the back door. Puzzlingly, it was ajar. Lock gutted. He gave the lock a long stare, hoping perhaps that it would tell a tale of why.

Removing a snub-nosed revolver holstered under his armpit, he proceeded cautiously into the yard. A large wooden structure dominated the middle, like a castle's medieval keep. It was a homemade shed, or something of that nature, roughly constructed from bastardised wooden scraps, sweating skin and blistered hands.

Silently bypassing it, he halted at the kitchen door. Ajar, also. Warily, he pushed the door wider with the toe of his boot, aiming the gun into the darkness, waiting for something to happen. It didn't. Now he stepped inside, cautiously making his way down the narrow hallway, towards the living room.

* * *

Two bags rested at Nolan's feet. The utility bag and the duffle bag. He was watching from within the shadows of the first-floor landing, gun aimed directly at Rasharkin's head. He didn't look like a cop, at least not one from Nolan's memory database, and that concerned him. If he wasn't a cop, then who the hell was he?

* * *

Rasharkin's nose captured the stench long before his eyes told the story. Two bodies, propped up in chairs. Like dummies stuffed with red sawdust. They sat facing each other, their suffering a dark mirror reflected back in each other's eyes. A man and a woman, naked, a garish blood-trail wash covering their aged skin. A pantomime of horror.

He speculated that the killer or killers worked on the woman first, her torment instrumental in facilitating the breaking down of Madden's resistance, as he watched, powerless to help her.

Looking beyond the dead, he studied the room. Money was scattered everywhere, all twenties and fifties. The same denominations as made up McCabe's share. All dotted in blood. On an oval-shaped table in the middle of the room, two untouched cups of tea and an uneaten chocolate éclair formed a macabre smiley face. A brochure, filled with photos of barges and river boats, hung aimlessly over the edge of the table, pages smudged with blood-lick blisters. Framed photos lay smashed, glass littering the area like a sea of scattered rhinestones.

Kneeling, he studied the carpet's nap. It was partially compressed by ghostly shoeprints. He studied their shape and direction, then stood and followed them as far as the yard. Looked around the grey concrete enclosure and the wooden structure centred there.

He cautiously approached the structure, now realising it to be a badly put-together pigeon coop. Strangely, it was silent. No cooing of birds, no percussion of nervous wings fluttering in the confined space. He speculated that someone had released the birds, and they had flown the coop, literally. Possibly Madden, in a mission of mercy, not intending to come back from whatever travels and new life he had planned.

From his coat pocket, Rasharkin removed a miniature LED flashlight. Pressed a button. The tiny utensil produced a sharp and wide beam.

He stepped inside. The stench of bird droppings and discarded feathers stifled the air. He turned in a slow pivot and the beam of light captured another slaughter. A bevy of homing pigeons in perfect-line formation, snapped necks forming macabre feathered question marks.

Madden would never have performed this grisly act, even if he had intended to abandon them. The work of a sadist, not a lover of birds. Perhaps used to loosen a tight tongue?

Two large sacks of bird seed had been toppled over, the spilt seeds forming pyramids almost identical in height and girth. He beamed the light inside the sacks. A cynical smile crawled onto his face. Whatever had rested within was gone, purchased by a thief-in-the-night.

Without warning, something came crashing through an open gap near the door. He instinctively dropped to one knee, pointing the gun, heart pounding furiously.

It was a pigeon. The same one he had seen in the sky earlier? Had it seen the light beaming in the coop, and followed it home? Its feathers carried a dusting of blood, liquid eyes watching him with silent curiosity.

His pulse slowed. Breathing became normal. He stepped out of the coop, quickly retracing his journey back into the living room housing the dead.

With the toe of his boot, he shifted through the broken glass. Prospecting. A photo emerged from the chaos. He bent and picked it up. A selfie of McCabe, Madden and Ross, in a pub, smiling, thinking of the future, not realising there would be none. McCabe seemed to be staring out at him. He crumpled the picture in his hand. Let it drop.

Rasharkin looked again at the bank notes spread across the floor. They weren't just randomly scattered, as he had first thought. There was a pattern to their chaos. Like a flower arrangement, waiting for visitors to sniff.

A faint noise sounded off from the hallway. He stopped all movement. Listened. Muffling the gun's cocking mechanism, he moved cautiously towards the hallway. The small, narrow space was filled with coats and shadows. They moved almost imperceptibly, in a breeze from the back door, now wide open. Someone gone. A ghost's ghost.

* * *

Boyd continued watching from inside the car, unable to decide what to do next. Who the hell was the second man? Someone connected to Dennison, perhaps?

'Fuck it all!' He banged his fists hard down on the steering wheel. There was no way he could take on two, even if he caught both by surprise. That would be madness.

He exited the car, lit another cig to calm his nerves. He needed to form some sort of plan, before it was too late and the opportunity was gone forever. Just then, something cold touched the back of his neck. He cursed himself for being rookie-careless.

'Both hands above your head, nice and slow,' Nolan said calmly, pressing a gun's muzzle tighter against Boyd's neck.

Boyd hesitated.

'I know what's going through your mind, Bob. Try it, you're dead.'

'You're going to kill me anyway.'

'It'll be a certainty if you *don't* raise both hands. I don't want to kill you. I still need you.'

Boyd's hands went slowly skywards.

'Good boy.' Nolan took Boyd's mobile and threw it on the ground. 'Now, with your left hand, reach into the car and *very* carefully, hook your index finger into the trigger-guard of that little beauty, and fish it out.'

Awkwardly, Boyd stretched his arm through the open window and hooked the Sig Sauer's trigger-guard with his finger.

'That's right. Bring it out, nice and *slooooooooow*.'

As soon as it was within reach, Nolan snatched it from Boyd's hand.

'A Sig Sauer? Now, *that's* what I call a gun.' Nolan whistled with admiration. '*And* a matching silencer as a bonus prize. Shit, you came to cause wilful damage, didn't you? Hope it wasn't against me?'

Nolan kicked Boyd hard in the balls. He collapsed to the ground. Despite the obvious pain, he did not cry out.

'You really thought I was just going to walk into your wee trap, Bob? How did you intend to do me? One in the head? Nice and clean? Or something a bit more bloody and drawn-out by your armed mate in the house?'

Boyd attempted to pull himself up, using the side of the car. Nolan kicked him in the face, sending him toppling backwards over the bonnet.

'No one gave you permission to get up.' He pointed the gun at Boyd's lower body, firing twice, shattering both kneecaps.

Boyd screamed, then went silent, hugging his bloody knees, face scrunched in agony.

'This really is a lovely gun. The balance is perfect.' Nolan fired again, this time in quick succession, taking out Boyd's elbows and ankles.

'*Argghhhhhhhhhhhhhhhhhhhhhhhhhhhhhhhhhhhhhhhhhhhhhhhhhh!*'
Boyd shook uncontrollably, blood seeping from the numerous wounds into the muck and grit.

'Agony, isn't it? If you were to receive *immediate* medical help, I'd say your chances of surviving, if this was a horse race, would be a photo finish. But seeing as you're out here in the arse of nowhere, by the time your mate in the house finds you, you'll be a dead docket.'

Boyd seemed to be trying to say something, through trembling lips. Nothing came.

Nolan reached into the duffle bag. Pulled out a fistful of money.

'Just to prove there's no hard feelings on my part, Bob, even though you tried to set me up, some money for you to spend the next time you go gambling with the wrong people.' He threw the notes haphazardly into Boyd's car, laughed, and walked off into the night carrying his booty, leaving a blood-soaked Boyd squirming and groaning in misery.

* * *

At home, Harry was on his way upstairs to join Elaine in bed when his mobile rang. He checked the number. It was the station.

'At this time of night? You've got to be bloody kidding me.' He hit the button. 'Yes?'

'Sorry for calling you at home, sir, and so late.'

'Kerr? What the hell? You better have a damn good reason.'

'I … it's about Bob Boyd, sir.'

'What about Boyd?'

'It's hard to explain, sir.'

'Stop dithering, man! *Explain!*'

'You told me to keep an eye on him, sir.'

'And?'

'He left the station almost an hour ago, and hasn't returned. I watched him taking a concealed weapon from the boot of his car.'

'A concealed weapon?'

'I've just found out from the dispatcher that the owner of the car McCabe was driving was a Mr Charles Madden. A call has just come in on the emergency line from Madden's neighbour. Madden and his wife have both been murdered.'

Harry felt suddenly cold. 'Address?'

'Eighteen King's Court.'

'Get McCauseland. Both of you, meet me there, ASAP.'

Chapter Twenty-Seven

Nothing goes so well with a hot fire and buttered crumpets
as a wet day without and a good dose of comfortable horrors
within. The heavier the lashing of the rain and the ghastlier
the details, the better the flavour seems to be.

Dorothy L Sayers, *Strong Poison*

Harry arrived at the Madden's just as the sky opened up and released torrential rain, black as ink and ice-cold, onto the scene.

The front door was wide open, enticing him in. Harry stood there, armed, hesitating. Experience told him to wait for back-up, but the cop in him was impatient. He stepped inside. All was eerily quiet. Began making his way from room to room, until the living room revealed its full horror.

'Dear God …'

The scene resembled a miniature abattoir. Despite the many bodies in the many crime scenes Harry had encountered over the years, nothing ever prepared him for the sight of a slaughter, especially if any of the victims were female; more so if they'd been tortured in such a brutal fashion as Rosie Madden obviously had been.

What kind of evil does this to a person without mercy or hesitation, especially to a woman?

He thought of Elaine, and a wave of apprehension swept over him as he realised he'd been holding his breath for the longest time, as if under water.

A hand touched his shoulder. He jerked at the electric touch.

'Harry, you okay?'

McCauseland was standing there, gun unholstered, looking uncertain at the uncertainty on Harry's face.

'Yes … any word on Boyd?'

'Nothing. Kerr filled me in on the way over here. You think he might be involved in this?'

'I don't know what to think any more about him. I called his mobile on my way here, but no answer.'

'What do you make of all that money, scattered about the floor?'

'Who the hell knows? Perhaps Madden was hiding it, when his mate in the robbery decided to have it. Could be a deliberate paper trail to send us in the wrong direction. If it was meant to cause confusion, then it's succeeding – for now.'

'The neighbour, Mr Norton, is outside, in the street. He's the one who called it in. You want to talk to him?'

'Where's Kerr?'

'Out in the alley, instructing a couple of uniforms in a search for clues.'

'The clueless looking for clues. I only hope he doesn't shoot himself or some other unfortunate.'

Harry followed McCauseland out into the street, where Tommy Norton stood looking lost, like a shipwrecked sailor.

'This is Mr Norton, sir, the neighbour who made the phone call,' McCauseland said by way of introduction. 'He lives at the end of the street. Mr Norton, this is Detective Inspector Harry Thompson.'

Harry put out his hand. 'Thank you for contacting us, Mister Norton.'

The old man's eyes were red, blotchy and wet. He shook Harry's hand.

'Tommy, Inspector. Just call me Tommy. Everyone does. I hope you get the animals who did this.'

'Animals wouldn't do this, Tommy. Only humans are capable of such evil. Can you tell me what you were doing at the Maddens' house?'

'Charlie and me are good friends. He and Rosie – his wife – just got back from a wee break. I was looking after the house for them, keeping an eye on things. Anyway, they arrived back earlier this evening –'

'What time would that have been?'

'Oh, about eight, or thereabouts. I rapped their door to tell Charlie about this dodgy character knocking about the street. He seemed very interested in Charlie's house.'

'How so?'

'Showing no interest, but interested, if you get my meaning?'

'Would you recognise this person if you saw him again?'

'I didn't get a real good look at him, but he was quite tall, a big fella. As I told Charlie, he looked the type you didn't want to mess with.'

'You were about to tell me what you were doing at the house.'

'Charlie said he'd call up to my house in an hour's time, and we'd go for a wee swallow, beer or something, nothing heavy. Well, an hour later and no sign of Charlie, which is unusual for him; he usually sticks to what he says. To cut a long story short, Inspector, I came to get Charlie. I was gasping for a beer. When I got here the front door was wide open. I shouted in a couple of times, but no answer. After a couple of minutes, I invited myself in …'

Tears began welling up in Tommy's eyes.

'Are you okay to proceed, Tommy?'

Tommy nodded.

'I … in the living room … horrible … horrible. I just staggered out of the house, backwards. Nightmare …'

'Do you remember touching or disturbing anything?'

'No … I touched nothing. I did hesitate for a second, just … just to see if they were alive … even though I knew they couldn't be … the state they were in.'

'Did they have any enemies, anyone you think may have wanted to harm either of them?'

Tommy shook his head, the tears now flowing down his face.

'No enemies. They … they were both well-liked. Great neighbours …'

'Okay, Tommy. Why don't you head home and get some sleep? We can get a full statement from you tomorrow when –'

Harry's mobile rang. Harry looked at the screen. *Boyd*. Harry answered it.

'This better be good, Boyd. You're on thin ice, with bricks in your pockets.'

Rushed breathing at the other end. No words.

'Boyd? You finding this funny? We'll see how funny it is when you're in front of my desk, first thing in the –'

'Hel … help … bleeding … badly … shot …'

'Are you trying to wind me up?'

'Snooker … hall …'

'Snooker hall? What snooker hall? Where the hell are you?'

No response, just night sounds embedded in heavy emptiness echoing from the phone.

Tommy pointed. 'There's an old deserted snooker hall over yonder, Inspector, top of the hill. It's behind where the trees start to form. Be careful. The hill's mucky and dangerous.'

'Come on!' With McCauseland in tandem, Harry ran in the direction of the hill. Upon reaching it, he realised how true Tommy's words were. Twice he reached the middle, before slipping and skidding back down on his arse.

When they finally reached the top, the dilapidated snooker hall emerged just beyond a family of trees.

'There's his car!' Harry shouted, knackered, staggering forward, slip-sliding on muck and rocks, almost stumbling over Boyd, the bloody mobile still gripped in his hand. 'Call an ambulance!'

Harry dropped to his knees, struggling to remove his overcoat. He placed it quickly over Boyd. 'Bob? Bob, can you hear me? It's Harry. Who did this?'

'I ... I ... I'm ... sorry ... fucked up big ...'

'Never mind that, who the hell did this?'

'No ...'

'No? Nolan? You mean Nolan? Was it Nolan?'

No response.

'Bob? Can you hear me?' Harry leaned closer, ear to Boyd's mouth. 'Bob? *Was* it Nolan?'

'Ambulance on its way, Harry,' McCauseland said. 'Tell Bob to hang in there.'

Harry looked up at McCauseland, then rose to his feet. 'You can tell them it's no longer an emergency.'

'Ah, shit.' McCauseland looked devastated. 'Was he able to say anything, who did this to him or to the Maddens?'

'It was barely a whisper. I wouldn't place my hand on the Bible, but ... I ... *think* he said Nolan.'

'We should've done Nolan when we had him in custody. Or some other way.'

'Some other way, it'll have to be.'

'No kid gloves?'

'Knuckledusters with spikes.' Harry looked towards a small gathering of trees, off to his left. A couple of night birds moved stealthily from branch to branch, making the leaves tremble.

'Wouldn't you just love to know what they know …?'

'You okay?'

A full moon came out from behind the darkness, washing over the bloody scene. Harry looked tired. Old. Feeling both.

'Okay? After two years, I just addressed a man in my squad by his first name for the first time, all because I disliked him. You tell me if I'm okay?'

'Boyd knew he was lucky to be under your command, especially after all the fuck-ups with his gambling. Told me that numerous times.'

'I treated him like shit, Bill. Let's not be gentle with words. I'm ashamed of myself now; now, when it's too late.' Harry looked into Boyd's car. 'More money conveniently left for us to find.'

'You think Bob knew something, all this time?'

'I don't want to think what I'm thinking.'

In the near distance, sirens could be heard.

'They were quick,' McCauseland said.

'Don't you know? Cops always get preferential treatment – *when they're dead.*'

* * *

Before heading back to the station, Harry did a quick detour, returning home, slipping in through the back door as quietly as possible, hoping to avoid Elaine. He got as far as the stairs in the hall before being spotted.

She looked pleasantly surprised to see him, until she eyed the state of his clothes, ripped and covered in muck.

'My God, Harry, what's happened?'

'I was hoping to get cleaned up before talking to you, love. There's no easy way to say this. Bob Boyd's dead, murdered.'

'Murdered …?'

'All a bit blurred at the moment, but a husband and wife called Madden were murdered, also. Boyd was found not far from the scene.'

She went to him, hugging him tightly.

'Careful. Your clothes are going to be covered in muck, love,' Harry said, gripping her tighter.

'I don't care. Muck can be washed away.'

Washed away. If only I could wash this night away, banish it from my memory, forever.

'Go up and have a lovely hot shower. I'll get a fresh set of clothes out for you. You'll feel a lot better afterwards.'

After showering, he did feel slightly better. Down in the living room, a hot cup of tea and Elaine waited.

'Better?' she asked.

He nodded. 'Have I ever told you how much I love you? Without you, I'm nothing.'

'Stop trying to sound romantic, when you're anything but.'

'I've put you through hell at times, with worry.'

'I knew what I was letting myself in for, the very first time I set eyes on you in bed!'

'And what a sight I was, blown to pieces! Terrible to say, if I hadn't been blown up, I'd never have met you. You really were my Florence Nightingale in the hospital, helping me get through the pain of all those skin grafts. You saved my life.'

'I know you don't like to be reminded of it, but I wasn't the one who administered first aid to you. *That's* what saved your life.'

'No, I don't like to be reminded of it, but it's something I have to live with.' He sounded bitter. 'The bloody irony of it, being helped by the man who was the intended target of the bomb. The angel and the devil, that's what I called the two of you.'

'Was I the devil?' She laughed, and it made him feel whole again.

He kissed her, gently, as if meeting for the first time.

'I wish my retirement day was now, instead of next month.'

'You're saying that now. Tomorrow, you'll be your old self. Right as rain.'

'It'll be a long time before I'm all right. I saw things tonight no one should ever see.'

* * *

In the station a few hours later, Harry bought a cup of his favourite hot brew from the coffee machine on the first floor, then entered his office. The moment he parked his arse at the desk, the door was flung open. Gordon Purvis stormed up to the desk, semi-running, finger wagging.

'Fuck you, Thompson! Wasn't it explained to you, that I was in charge of *all* to do with the robbery?'

'Not now, Purvis. Save your wounded-pride bullshit for some other time.'

'You and your circus shouldn't have been anywhere near the Madden house. Madden was a suspect in the robbery, and now he's dead, along with his wife.'

'So is Bob Boyd, in case that particular part of the news never reached you.'

'Yes, Boyd, who held on to vital information about Madden, before sharing it. Oh, I see from the look on your gob, *that* wee piece of the news never reached *you*.'

'What the hell are you on about?'

'Not much of a detective, are you? A bottle of perfume and a promised night on the town got Boyd the information from a dispatcher, prior to it being officially shared.'

'Which dispatcher?'

'See, that's what I mean about you not being a very good detective. You ask all the wrong questions. A more important question is, what the hell was Boyd doing withholding information, and hanging about at the Madden house?'

'I don't speak for the dead, but he probably thought he could arrest Madden on his own, get some credit for himself.'

'Now who's bullshitting?' Purvis smirked. 'You don't believe that any more than I do. Think that money in his car just flew into it?'

'For someone not there, you seem to know a lot about what happened.'

'It's my business to know these things. That's why I'm on the top rung, looking down on your miserable, pathetic attempts at police work. One of your own men, right under your nose, taking bribes and shit knows what the hell else?'

'Time for you to leave.'

'You've become a laughing stock. Lucky for you, you'll be leaving us soon. Perhaps some supermarket will hire you as a security guard. If you want a reference, come to me and kiss my arse.'

Purvis swept out of the office, leaving a seething Harry to his thoughts.

Chapter Twenty-Eight

'Keep in mind that I'm crazy, won't you?'
Stieg Larsson, *The Girl with the Dragon Tattoo*

Nolan sat contemplating, in a large yellow armchair shaped like Homer Simpson. He didn't feel entirely comfortable sitting in the cartoonish chair, but it was the only thing in the room able to contain his bulk. A small black book rested in his right hand.

It was four hours after his bloody visit to the Maddens and the slaying of Boyd. Now, having practically searched every inch of the apartment, he was boiling with anger. He had found no money worth talking about – unless he included the large collection of *Star Wars* and *Star Trek* money boxes, filled with plastic space currency. And there was no sign of the owner, Brian Ross. He really wanted to find Ross, almost as much as he wanted to find the rest of the money.

One thing he did find, however, was a small black book. It detailed all the items Ross had purchased over the last few years from a comic book shop in town called Heroes and Villains. A business card sandwiched between the pages named the owner as Kieran Kelly. One entry in the book stated: *George Reeves' SMC = 20G. Bought.*

'Twenty G. *Hmm.* Twenty thousand quid? Or just some strange coded language?'

Nolan was confused, and not a little unsettled by what he had witnessed while searching the apartment. It was like somewhere a child would live: superhero statues, sci-fi posters and thousands of comic books residing in boxes bordering on claustrophobic wall-to-wall madness. Was this fucker Ross a paedo? Had to be, living in a house full of kiddie toys and comics.

'God the night, what kind of fucked-up world are we living in?'

If Ross was a paedo, then he would take even more pleasure in torturing him when he eventually got his hands on him; and get his hands on him he would. It was only a matter of time. And timing.

Madden had given up his friend's address as well as the hospital he had been taken to after jumping out of a window in Heroes and Villains. But a contact at the hospital informed Nolan that Ross had checked out hastily. Apparently a shouting match with a visitor had unnerved Ross, and he left shortly after the visit.

Nolan had emailed a photo of Madden to the contact, and it was confirmed that, yes, that was the visitor. The contact also told Nolan that Ross had been accompanied in the ambulance by one Kieran Kelly, the shop owner.

The killing of McCabe had spooked the remainder of the gang, according to Madden. This was bad news for Nolan. He had been hoping that the killing had been brought on by infighting, making locating the rest of the money easier.

But no, not according to Madden. The gang had divvied up the spoils equally, but then someone had kidnapped McCabe, tortured and killed him, and taken his share. But who was the killer? Newspapers had speculated that it was Scarface Logan and his gang, but Nolan dismissed that immediately. Logan was squeamish about violence and the sight of blood.

Nolan's thoughts came back to the gunman in Madden's house. Could he be part of the mysterious gang responsible for McCabe's death, or was he a new player in the game entirely?

The thought of someone else getting to Ross before him was almost too much to contemplate. He had special plans for Mister-Tough-Guy Ross.

His hand went instinctively to his head, to the healing wound. It began throbbing. *I'm not gonna count to three. I'm not even gonna count to one. You will shut the fuck up or I'll sing you a lullaby!*

'When I find you, tough guy, you'll not be singing a lullaby, but you *will* be going for a little swim in my private swimming pool.'

Chapter Twenty-Nine

You ever get the feeling all hell's about to break loose
and there's nothing you can do about it?
Ali Vali, *The Devil Unleashed*

'**B**eautiful view from up here.' Conor O'Neill was sitting alongside Rasharkin on a bench in Belfast Castle's famous Cat Garden, looking over the night lights of the city. 'I always find this wee spot very calming, with the nine Guardian Cats watching over us. The legend say the Castle will always be safe as long as a cat is residing here. Do you like cats, yourself?'

'I've never owned pets,' Rasharkin said, diplomatically.

'Ah, that's a misconception. Cats are *not* pets, and they certainly aren't *owned*. They're individuals. My cats, Tiddles and Chairman Meow? They'll come home at mealtimes and naptime. In return for those comforts, they deal with any rodent foolish enough to venture into our street.'

A few seconds of silence was broken by Rasharkin's change of topic.

'I'm sorry how last night turned out. Madden's share of the money gone; sorry for Rosie Madden, also, what they did to her.'

'Completely out of your hands. Unfortunately, we lost Boyd as well. To say he was invaluable would be an understatement. Almost as big a loss as the money.'

'You trusted him?'

'Why would I trust anyone willing to sell his comrades? No, trust would not be the word I'd use. But I was more than grateful we had him working for us. In this business, betrayal is always practised and bought, by both sides. An informer is worth his weight in gold.' From his pocket, Conor produced his pipe. 'Mind if I smoke?'

'Feel free.'

Conor packed the pipe. Flamed it while sucking gently.

'Any explanation as to why Boyd was in the vicinity at the same time as I was?' Rasharkin said.

'That, my friend, is a mystery – as is the identity of his killer or killers. But it's something we're pursuing as a matter of urgency.'

'I have my own theory. Want to hear it?'

'I'm all ears.'

'You may not like it.'

'My chin is made of granite.'

'I think Boyd tried to set me up for the Maddens.'

Conor took a suck on the pipe; blew cobalt smoke into the air. The aroma spread everywhere. 'Why would he do that?'

'The money. As I already told you, someone was in the house while I was there.'

'You think it was Boyd?'

'Interested parties almost tripping over each other? It's a strong possibility. Plus, his body was found close by.'

'He didn't even know you existed.'

'We'll never know for sure if he did or not. I'm not a believer in coincidence. Perhaps it's just my suspicious nature, but something isn't sitting well on my shoulders.'

'If he was setting you up, why didn't he kill you when he had the chance in the house?'

'Running out of time, perhaps? Panicked. Had to make sure he got the money out of the house, before someone got too nosey.'

'If that's the case, *who* killed him?'

'If I'm right, he left the house with the money. Then he was shot while trying to make his escape in the car, probably by someone he had trusted to do the job with him.'

'You think Boyd killed the Maddens?'

'It looks that way.'

'Boyd was a lot of things, but killing a woman? I can't see it. And from what you've described, the way they were killed? Takes a special cold hand to administer the gutting of humans. No, that wasn't his *modus operandi*. Gambling. Any form of gambling, he lived and breathed it. You don't go from cards and horses to abattoir fanatic, overnight.'

'It wasn't overnight though. He was a cop for years. He was already a killer – or at least had the training to become one.'

'What about Ross? Could it have been him, waiting to ambush Boyd as he left the house? It makes sense that he'd want Madden's cut.'

'At the moment, he's in hiding for his life. I figure, when he left the hospital hastily, his first port of call was his apartment, perhaps to gather up his cut. I've been there. Searched it and found nothing. However, he left behind certain items that would be precious to him. I doubt very much he would show his face at the Maddens' house. Too scared.'

'You could be right. By now, he's probably down south, or even across the water.'

Rasharkin stood, preparing to leave. 'I think he's still in Belfast.'

'What makes you say that?'

'You're just going to have to trust me on this, but I'm getting to know a lot about Ross. He'll not want to lose those precious items he has stocked in the apartment. Our only problem is getting to him before someone else does. Whoever killed Boyd probably has their sights on Ross and his cut.'

'Hopefully we're not out of the game yet.'

Rasharkin started to move off. 'Want me to let your driver know you're ready to go?'

'No, not yet. I'm going to sit for a while. Tomorrow morning, I'll light a few candles to Saint Anthony for help.'

'Saint Anthony?'

'Patron saint of lost items.'

Chapter Twenty-Nine

Cast a cold eye. On life, on death. Horseman, pass by.

gravestone of WB Yeats

Milltown Cemetery, located in the west of the city, was practically deserted when Harry parked the car, the following afternoon, just beyond the entrance. A cold, greyish mist was materialising, knitting a gothic vignette into the tapestry of tombstones.

Opened in the nineteenth century, the graveyard's residents are principally Catholic – there is a single Protestant resting in this clay, against all odds. A section of the graveyard is held exclusively for socialists and republicans killed during the present-day conflict with Britain. Not far away is the City Cemetery, with its predominantly Protestant membership. Even in death, it would seem, Belfast's notorious sectarianism manages to live.

The last place on earth Harry wanted to be on this dreary afternoon was in another graveyard, witnessing another burial. However, paying his respects to the Maddens was only part of the reason for his appearance. On the off-chance that Ross would be foolish enough to turn up, Harry had ordered undercover police and photographers to be assigned throughout the area, watching and taking pictures of mourners and ghoulish onlookers. Plus, afterwards, there was an old friend to visit.

After the priest's prayers, neighbour Tommy Norton scattered fistfuls of dirt on top of the descending coffins in a final farewell, tears streaming down his lined face. He seemed too absorbed in his own grief to notice Harry standing nearby, watching.

The Maddens' sombre interment was in sharp contrast to this morning's hero's send-off for Robert Boyd in City Cemetery. The graveyard had more brass than grass, as rank-and-file stood shoulder-to-shoulder out of respect for their fallen comrade.

Harry had been given the task of saying the eulogy, fine words for the dead. The managed the job quite well, though he struggled to believe the words himself, with Purvis's accusatory barbs still lingering as a rotten taste in his mouth.

When the mourners at Milltown had left, and three gravediggers were bending to their work on the Maddens' final farewell, Harry made his way through the granite and marble maze of headstones and religious artefacts.

Some of the headstones had been smashed and toppled over by local vandals, graffiti scrawled on others. This sort of mindless thuggery always filled him with anger.

Eventually, he came to the designated spot. The grave of his old mentor, a man long gone but forever present in Harry's mind. The headstone told the tale:

In Loving Memory of my Dear Husband
Tommy Montgomery, Murdered by Evil Cowards
At Night, Under the Guise of Friends During the Day
Erected by Loving Wife Ann-Marie

Harry stood, contemplating the grave, saying nothing, having given up the charade of talking to the dead a long time ago. Eventually, he shifted his gaze from grave to graveyard. The mist was thickening, visibility waning. Time to be going.

As he made his way back, he saw a man enveloped in a heavy overcoat, standing in the shadows of two great oak trees, out in the unattended wilderness. He suspected the man was observing him. Something about him raised the hairs on the back of Harry's neck.

As he neared, Harry noticed the man's right hand sheltering inside the overcoat, causing a bulge to protrude from the material.

His training instinctively kicking in, Harry's hand reached for the gun hinged on the waistband clip on his trousers.

The man suddenly looked apprehensive. The hand inside the overcoat moved.

In a flash, Harry's revolver was levelled at the man's face. 'Don't even think about it! Hands up! *Now!*'

'Don't shoot! Don't shoot!' The man's hands popped straight out, clutching something.

'Drop whatever the hell you're holding! *Now!*'

The hand opened. The object fell to the ground. 'Don't shoot!'

'What the …?'

'Flowers. Just flowers. It's … only a bunch of flowers …'

'What the hell're you doing, sneaking about the place?'

'I … I wasn't sneaking about.'

'You can take your hands down.' The man looked vaguely familiar. 'Don't I know you?'

'I … I don't think so.'

'George Magee. Right?'

'Yes.'

'Lurking in a graveyard with a bunch of flowers hidden up your coat? Good way of getting shot.' Harry placed his gun back on its clip.

'I … wasn't "lurking", and … they weren't hidden,' Magee said defensively. 'I … I look after the graves.'

Harry scoffed. 'Graves? Is that where gangsters hide their money nowadays?'

'I … I wouldn't know.' Magee began picking the flowers up.

'I bet you wouldn't. Anyway, I suppose graves are a hell of a lot safer for keeping it in. Less chance of being robbed than banks.'

Harry continued his journey out of the graveyard, leaving a shattered-looking Magee sitting unsteadily down on a tombstone, clutching the flowers.

Chapter Thirty

A Psychopath: How does one become a Psychopath?
A Psychopath In Training, Michael Hodge

It was nearing closing time at Heroes and Villains, and despite the pissing rain battering against the windows outside, Kieran Kelly was in jubilant mood. It had been a long day at the shop, but he couldn't complain, having sold a large consignment of Batman silver-age comics to an international collector, earning him a nice profit.

Two customers remained, each browsing through multi-boxes of comics. As soon as he could get these two out of the shop, he'd close and make his way to the John Hewitt for a well-deserved swallow of their new gin, Jawbox, which was being given out as free samples.

One of the customers was an annoying, angry-faced teenager, dressed all in black like a Goth ninja, unable to make his mind up about purchasing a back issue of *Saga* or *Deadpool*. He'd been in the shop for a full three hours, debating intensely with himself on this life-or-death decision.

The other customer was a new face. *Always good for the longevity of the business*, thought Kieran, wondering if he could persuade him to sign up as a member and receive a generous twenty percent off first purchase, and a healthy ten off all other items.

'*Deadpool*,' Goth ninja finally announced to Kieran at the counter. 'Your *Saga* back issues are a rip-off. I can get them for half what you charge in Forbidden Planet.'

Fuck off to Forbidden Planet, if that's the case, you wee prick, Kieran thought, taking payment through gritted teeth. 'Thank you for your custom, little dude. Hope to see you again soon.'

'I won't be back!'

Good. 'Sorry to hear that, little dude. Hope you change your mind.'

Goth Ninja almost took the door off its hinges, slamming it so violently.

The last customer finally approached the counter, but, to Kieran's dismay, with nothing in his hands.

'If you don't see it in the boxes, I probably have it in the back with my extra stock.' Kieran smiled his smile-of-the-day smile.

'I'm looking for some information,' Seamus Nolan said, looking disdainfully at the Spiderman bow dangling from Kieran's hair.

'You've come to the right place. There's very little I don't know about any comic or –'

'A few days ago, I witnessed a terrible incident, a man jumping out of the upstairs window.'

'Jumping? God, no! A couple of people thought that at the time. No, Brian was … opening the window, and he slipped. Terrible accident.'

'I was just wondering if you've heard how he's doing? I haven't been able to get him out of my mind.'

'Oh, really doing great. It looked a lot worse than it actually was.'

'Brian a good friend of yours?'

A look of puzzlement appeared on Kieran's face. 'Why all the questions? You an insurance agent or something?'

'You accompanied him in the ambulance, if I remember correctly.'

'I don't remember seeing you outside the shop that day.'

'Well, you were very upset, of course. How would you remember another face in the crowd?'

'Look, I don't know what this is all about, but it's closing time. I'm sorry for rushing you, but you need to go. I open pretty early in the morning, so drop by and –'

Nolan reached over and bolted the door, before pulling the 'CLOSED' blind down.

'Hey! What the *hell* are you playing at?' Kieran came quickly from behind the counter, mobile in hand. 'Get out before I call the fuzz.'

Nolan grabbed Kieran's hand, removed the mobile, then started pushing him towards the back of the shop, into the office.

'When was the last time you two talked?'

'Look, I really don't know what business this is of yours, but –'

In a flash, Nolan slapped Kieran hard on each side of the face, almost knocking him off his feet.

'It starts gentlemanly at first, with a few taps to the gob, but can quickly deteriorate if honest answers aren't forthcoming.'

From the inside of his coat, Nolan produced a gun. Pointed it at Kieran's face.

'Shit!' Kieran put a hand over his face in defence. 'Is … that real, dude?'

'Want to find out? Now, when was the last time you talked to your friend?'

'I … he phoned me … from the hospital, but I haven't heard from him since.'

'See how easy that was?' Nolan handed back the mobile. 'Call him. Find out where he is. Say you want to get together. Tell him you have something very special to sell.'

'Special? Like what?'

'Something he can't resist. You can think of something. I saw his apartment. All the kiddie shit he buys from you. For your sake, he better want it bad.'

'Dude, can you point that somewhere else? I hate guns. They make me nervous.'

'Never worry about the gun; just the hand holding it. Now, call him. And remember: make it good. Your creepy life depends on how convincing you are. Put the speaker on, so I can listen in.'

Kieran, hands trembling, hit buttons on the mobile. After a few seconds, Brian's muffled voice could be heard.

'Kieran? What's up?'

'How … how are things, dude? Haven't heard from you since you left hospital. I was worried. You okay?'

'You don't want to know. Serious shit. I've lost good friends in the last couple of days. One of them was brutally murdered, as was his wife.'

Kieran's face paled. 'Shit … *they* were your friends? I … I heard about it on the news. So sorry to hear that, dude. Wasn't there a cop killed as well?'

'Yes.'

'What happened?'

'I don't really know, yet. The cops aren't saying too much, just that some cowardly scumbags broke into their home and murdered them.'

Kieran now looked at Nolan with an understanding of terror.

Nolan pressed the gun against Kieran's forehead, mouthing: 'Meet him.'

'How … how about I head over to your apartment. I just had some high-kicking coke delivered. We can share it, dude.'

'Coke?' A long pause. Then: 'I'm out of my apartment at the moment. Staying in a hotel. Things aren't cool at the moment.'

'Which hotel?' Nolan mouthed.

'Which … hotel? I can meet you in the lobby, bring the coke with me.'

'I don't want to say anything over the phone, mate. Not safe. What's up with your voice?'

'My voice? Oh, nothing … just finished a line of coke. Hit me the wrong way, dude, know what I'm saying?'

'Yeah, think so …'

Nolan pushed the gun's muzzle against Kieran's head. 'Get him to come here.'

Kieran held his hand over the mobile. *'How the hell am I supposed to do that?'*

The gun's hammer was pulled back. *'For your sake, you better figure something out.'*

Kieran swallowed hard, before speaking back into the mobile. 'I … I have something … I think you might be interested in, dude. You're not going to believe what it is. I promise you.'

'You've got my attention.'

'It's a … it's a George Reeves Superman cape, one of only five ever signed by the Man of Steel, before he was murdered.'

'Really …?'

'Yes … it's the only one in the whole of Europe, the rest are in American hands.'

'I'd … love to see that …'

'Got it sitting out for you.'

'I see …' Another long pause. Then: *'Okay … you've convinced me. That's something I really want for my collection, plus I need something to calm my nerves. The coke should help. Give me twenty to thirty minutes, and I'll be there. I'll give you a call when I get to the shop.'*

'Be careful … driving in that rain. It looks dangerous.'

'Yes … yes, of course. See you soon …'

Nolan took the phone. Set in on Kieran's makeshift desk.

'You did well. Let's hope for your sake you did well enough.'

Kieran reluctantly nodded.

'That name, George Reeves?' Nolan said, more to himself, looking puzzled. 'Where the hell have I heard it from?'

'Can I get you some tea?'

'Going all psychological on me, trying to sweeten me up with tea?'

'Just being courteous.'

'Tell you what, while you're being courteous, you can tell me what's in the safe.'

'Safe?'

'*That* safe.' Nolan indicated with the gun. 'The monstrosity in the far corner.'

'Oh, that old thing! I keep it for bills and things like that. Haven't a lot of use for it these days.'

'Open it.'

'Open it?'

Nolan stuck the muzzle of the gun against Kieran's ear.

'Your ears must be filled with wax. Want me to clear them?'

Kieran walked over to the safe. Hit the combo. Slowly pulled the heavy door open.

'Sit down on that armchair.' Nolan indicated with the gun. 'Don't try any stupid shit, and you get to open your shop tomorrow for all the little kiddies you love. Understood?'

'Yes.'

Nolan started pulling metal drawers out of the safe, spilling their contents onto the floor. Then he stopped. Removed a large pouch. Unzipped it. Held the contents in front of Kieran. 'So, you only keep the safe for bills?'

'And things like that …'

'How much is here? Lie, I'll blow your balls off.'

'Twenty thousand.'

'You know where this came from?'

'I didn't ask.'

'It was stolen from me, by your good friend Brian. Where's the rest of it?'

'The rest? That's all I have.'

'And I thought we were getting on so well. Why were you hiding only this amount?'

'I wasn't hiding it. It was from a purchase made.'

'A purchase! Fuck, Ross is very generous with my money. What did he buy that cost so much in this dump?'

'Numerous items. Some original comic book pages, but mostly golden-age comics.'

'Comics? I'm in the wrong fucking business if that's the kind of money they make.'

* * *

Brian was pacing the floor of his room in the Europa Hotel, pondering the phone call from Kieran. Everything about it was wrong, right down to the nervous twang in his friend's voice. Kieran had blamed it on coke, which Brian knew was a substance that Kieran detested. Also, his strange advice to drive carefully, when he knew well that Brian had never driven a car in his life.

Most tellingly of all, he already owned Reeves' cape. That was the operative word: telling. Kieran was telling him something; something so mind-blowingly awful, it was too dire to contemplate.

'Come on! Make a decision!' He stared at the gun resting atop yesterday's newspaper, a gift from Scarface Logan. It was a Glock 26, designed for concealed-carrying, but still retaining the killing power of its bigger brother, the 43.

He shoved the weapon down the waistband of his jeans, put on a heavy rain coat, and headed out.

Crossing the busy Great Victoria Street, he entered a local pub, hastily making a call on the public phone.

'Tenant Street Police Station. How can I help?' a male voice said at the other end of the receiver.

'I … I saw suspicious movement in a shop, a few minutes ago. The shop's supposed to be closed at this time of night, so it's possibly thieves. The owner's an old man. I'd hate to see any harm come to him. Can you hurry? I have a bad feeling about it.'

'Name and location of shop, sir?'

'Heroes and Villains, in Cornmarket.'

'Can I have your name, sir?'

'Just hurry the hell up!' He slammed the receiver down and headed in the direction of Kieran's shop.

* * *

'I just realised where I heard that name,' Nolan said, staring at Kieran.

'What name?'

'George Reeves.' Nolan slipped a hand inside his jacket, and removed the small black book. Leafed through it to the designated page.

'I found this in your friend's apartment. It details all the items he's been buying from you, over the years. Quite a lot. Here's one should interest you: *"George Reeves' SMC. Bought for twenty G."* I hadn't a clue who this George Reeves was, until I heard you talking about him on the mobile. More importantly, I hadn't a clue what these mysterious initials meant: *"SMC".*'

'And?' Kieran put on his best confused look.

'SMC. Super Man Cape. Bought for twenty thousand.' Nolan smiled a stiletto smile. 'Oh, I see you're no longer confused. Good. I must give you credit for telling the truth, and my apologies for not believing you. The money in the safe *was* from a purchase, after all.'

'That's what I've been trying to tell you.'

'What puzzles me is, if you've already sold him this cape, how come you're trying to sell him it all over again?'

'What? Well … I …'

Nolan glanced at his watch, then back over at Kieran.

'The cape was a warning to him. He's not coming, is he?'

Kieran thought for a second before answering. He smiled. Nervous but defiant. 'I hope not.'

* * *

Brian turned the corner running, his shoes finding it difficult to gain traction on the slick cobblestones. Twice he slipped on the rainy surface and lost his balance, but he continued running, gathering pace as Heroes and Villains came within sight at the far end of the street.

He hoped his negative thoughts were a million miles wrong, and Kieran would be pissing himself laughing once he shared them. He hoped, but he wasn't optimistic.

He stopped running when he reached the shop's shadow. Ominously, the shutters were still up. He leaned his back against the wall, tried to calm his breathing.

A few seconds later, he stole a quick peek in the window. No movement. Everything immersed in darkness. Removed the Glock from the waistband of his jeans, took a few deep breaths and was about to make a move for the door when an explosion lifted him off his feet, showering him in glass, fragmented wood and metal.

The last he remembered was Kieran staring up at him from the pavement, a grisly grin on his decapitated head.

Chapter Thirty-One

'The treacherous are ever distrustful.'
JRR Tolkien, *The Two Towers*

Arare ray of morning sun was shining through the windows of Harry's office. He sat at his desk, sipping coffee from a styrofoam cup, listening to Brahms playing softly in the background, and glancing through the pages of the morning newspaper.

There was very little of interest in the paper, with the exception of an incident at a comic shop in the city centre the previous night – a deadly explosion, followed by a fire. Officials had yet to confirm the genesis of it, but the newspaper was hinting at a gas leak, as the owner, a Mr Kieran Kelly, made tea on an old gas stove.

However, Harry knew it was a lot more sinister than a cup of bloody tea. Detectives were working on a theory of petty larceny gone deadly wrong.

Shortly before the explosion, an anonymous caller to police had claimed to have witnessed suspicious movements in the shop. In the middle of the road, covered in debris, a nasty piece of hardware had been recovered, possibly dropped by one of the perpetrators in their haste to flee. Not just any old piece of hardware, but a Glock 26, of all things. It would seem that

Belfast's petty thieves were signing up for the major league, and the days of a cudgel on the head were now passé.

Apart from the owner taking the full blast of the explosion, literally losing his head in the process, two other people were on the casualty list: a homeless man sleeping in the hallway of an abandoned shoe shop next door, and a passerby. Both were knocked unconscious and rushed to hospital for observation.

Harry put the paper down and made his way to the window. Looked out at the car park down below, paying special attention to Purvis's impressive black Jaguar F-Type convertible parked in its own private section, loudly advertising his status. Harry also had a private section for his modest Suzuki Celerio, but he never used it, knowing that small touches of humility prevented big knives of resentment in the ranks.

He sipped on the coffee again. Made a face. The liquid had gone tepid. Glanced at his watch. Almost time to get some real work done. He was about to turn back to the desk when he spotted Purvis's heavy, Carson McComb, getting into the Jag, then speeding out of the parking area like a hound from hell.

'I hope you crash into a wall, scumbag.'

Instead of returning to the desk, Harry walked quickly out of the office. Taking the lift, he emerged outside Purvis's newly acquired office on the fifth floor.

He glanced left, then right, before knocking silently on the door. No answer. Turned the handle slowly. Eased the door open a few inches, then peeped inside.

Purvis wasn't in the main part of the office, but a door to an adjacent room was ajar and Harry could see enough of Purvis' lower body, in a kneeling position, beside an open safe.

Harry stepped inside, quietly closing the door behind him.

'You're either praying or giving that safe a blowjob, Purvis.'

Purvis jerked upright, almost banging his head on the safe. 'What the hell're you doing here?'

Harry held out the half-filled styrofoam cup. 'I brought you some early-morning coffee.'

'Get out.'

'You were conspicuous by your absence at Detective Boyd's funeral, yesterday – not that you were missed, mind you.'

'The so-called fallen hero? Don't make me laugh.' Purvis smirked, then stood. 'I note you still haven't followed up on what I told you about him. Are you hiding something, Thompson? Perhaps someone ought to be investigating your entire squad – investigating you? Perhaps that someone ought to be me?'

'I attended the Maddens' funeral too. Coincidently, Tommy Montgomery is buried in the same graveyard as the Maddens. Tommy was asking me if you're still up to your greasy neck in dirty deeds. I told him yes, indeed you are.' Harry rested the cup on top of the desk. 'What's wrong? You look slightly off-colour. I told Tommy time is catching up with you, that Justice is about to put its coat on and come visiting you.'

'Time you faced the truth about your Catholic mate and mentor. He was passing information on to the Brotherhood.'

'Sectarian drivel and bullshit. Is that how you try to justify murdering him like the coward you are?'

Without warning, Purvis made a clumsy grab for Harry's throat. Harry, calmly sidestepping the move, grabbed Purvis's right hand, twisting it, forcing Purvis to a semi-kneeling position.

'You've crossed the line, Thompson!' Purvis hissed through clenched teeth. *'I'll have you up on assault. You're finished in the Force.'*

'Finished? I haven't even started.' Harry's mouth came close to Purvis' ear. 'I note *you* never reported Boyd to McCafferty. Why? Something to hide? For your information, someone is investigating *your* entire squad – especially *you*. That someone is me. And this time, I won't let you get away like you did in the past. That's a promise I made to Tommy. One way or another, I'll have you.'

'Let fucking go!'

Harry shoved Purvis towards the far corner, landing him on his arse. 'Stay there until I leave. It'll be safer for you.'

Purvis mumbled something incomprehensible, just as the door opened, revealing Carson McComb.

McComb moved towards Harry. 'Want me to throw him out on his ear, boss?'

Before Purvis could answer, Harry stood face-to-face with the heavy.

'You look stupid, McComb. Don't prove it beyond a doubt. Now, move out of the way before you join your boss on the canvas.'

'Let him go, Carson,' Purvis instructed. 'His days are numbered anyway.'

Chapter Thirty-Two

'I hate to say this, but this place is getting to me.
I think I'm getting the fear.'
Dr Gonzo, *Fear and Loathing in Las Vegas*

Brian awoke in a claustrophobic world of darkness. A ghostly apparition floated above him, barely a tooth or hair to its name, eyes sunken tunnels of darkness. The Ancient Mariner wearing a withered gown of cobwebs.

It was whispering something through its gummy mouth, but he was finding it difficult to decipher exactly what, because his cognitive functions felt out of kilter. An intravenous drip attached to his left arm kept sending liquid thought-patterns of *déjà vu* to his brain, but those also confused him.

'Where …?' *What comes after where?* Too confused to think, he wanted to fall back into deep sleep again, but his watered-down intuition was sending out feeble warnings not to.

'In the hospital, lad.' Ancient Mariner said.

'*Hospital* …?' A sharp smell of fresh linen suddenly lined his nostrils like smelling salts. The last thing he remembered was throwing bananas at Charlie; or had he pointed a gun, threatened to shoot him? Something about a gun. *Think!*

Something about Kieran. *What?* 'How … how long … I … been here?'

'They brought you in last night. You look a hell of a lot smarter now than what you did then, I can tell you. Thank those lovely wee nurses for that. I heard them saying you'd been in an explosion.'

'An explosion …?'

'That's what they said. Some poor fella was killed in a shop. The cops were here this morning, they wanted to talk to you, but the nurses chased them away. They told them you're in no condition to talk.'

'I … need to leave …' He pulled the drip out.

'Wait, lad! Take it easy!'

Brian was edging slowly to the side of the bed. He was practically naked, with a mishmash of bandages mummifying his upper torso. Tried standing. The room began spinning. He wanted to vomit, but nothing came except sour retching.

Ancient Mariner quickly grabbed him by the shoulders, steadying him back onto the bed. 'Trying to kill yourself? You're going the right way about it.'

'I … I've got to leave … now.'

'That explosion must've melted your brain. Have you seen the state of yourself? Hold on a wee sec.' Ancient Mariner shuffled over to a tiny cabinet at the side of his bed. Retrieved a mirror. Shuffling back, he held the mirror at arm's length. 'Go on. Have a good look at the state of yourself.'

Reluctantly, Brian brought his face in line with the mirror. *Shit …*

He barely recognised what stared back. Skin had turned a horrible deep purple. The hair on his head had been singed into black clumps of stubble. Eyebrows and lashes gone. Fragments of wood, dirt and glass were still embedded in his face. He looked like a battered mannequin discarded in a dumpster.

'Where … my clothes …?'

'Clothes? You're having a laugh. They brought you in naked as the day you were born. They were blown clean off you. Do you know how lucky you are?'

'Lucky's my second name. I … I have to get out of here … now …' He stood again, unsteadily. However, the spinning in his head was calming. Slightly.

'You can't walk out looking like that.' Ancient Mariner did a return shuffle. Opened his cabinet. Retrieved some clothes, along with a bottle of Lucozade. He placed the clothes on Brian's bed. 'They're old, but clean. The nurses washed them for me yesterday. Sorry I can't offer you footwear. I never wear the things!'

Brian looked at the battered clothing, more holes than cloth, then at the man offering everything he probably owned. 'Why … you doing … this?'

'I hate cops. Anyone wanted for questioning by them, must be okay.' Ancient Mariner smiled a toothless grin. 'Here. Take these painkillers and Lucozade. They should do the job.'

'Thank ... thanks ...' Brian took the tablets, and washed them down with the liquid. He felt like puking again, but nothing came. 'I don't even know your name.'

'Phil.'

'Brian.' He offered his hand and Phil shook it.

'Well, the sooner you slip into those clothes and get heading, Brian, the better it'll be. Once you're gone, I'll make a dummy for your bed. That'll buy you some time.'

Helped by Phil, it still took Brian five minutes to struggled into the clothes.

'I appreciate all you're doing for me, Phil. Where can I reach you, to repay your kindness?'

'It's no big deal. That's what friends are for. But you'll find me on the streets, near City Hall. That's where I live. If you're ever passing, be sure to drop in for a chat. Just ask for the Mayor.'

* * *

Brian kept his head low as he negotiated the night streets, grateful for the darkness and heavy rain, and for Phil's miraculous painkillers. People moved quickly out of the way of the ragged, bare-footed figure, drunkenly swaying from side to side, lurching in their direction, as if fearful of contamination.

Nowhere else to go, he reached his apartment building almost forty minutes later, exhausted mentally and physically, but overjoyed to be home. He wouldn't stay long, just an hour or so for a much-needed shower, a change of clothes and a quick stock-up on enough money to tide him over.

Outside his apartment, he entered the password into his Isecure system. The door opened. He stepped inside, closing the door behind him, resting his back against it for a breather. Dearly desiring to head into the bedroom for the sleep of his life, he knew he couldn't risk it, so he moved towards the shower instead.

* * *

'*Man …* ' It was the most heavenly shower he could remember having, ever, even though the water stung like hell in a hundred raw wounds. The warmth seemed to be seeping into every ache in his body, revitalising him, adding something almost positive to the clusterfuck of the last twenty-four hours.

He wanted to stay under the water's heavenly propulsion forever, luxuriating in it, but he knew he had to get moving, sooner rather than later. He was top of the cops' and IRA's menu, and he didn't want to offer himself up on a plate.

At least it can't get any worse, he was thinking, stepping out of the shower and walking towards the living room, his naked body glistening like a newly-formed skin graft.

'Hello, Brian,' Rasharkin said, cloaked in semi-darkness, sitting in the Homer Simpson chair, gun in hand.

Brian's entire body constricted with fear. Couldn't speak.

Couldn't think. Couldn't breathe. Everything was swallowed up in a blue haze of terror and cruel certainty.

'Sit down, on that.' Rasharkin pointed the gun at a novelty chair of The Joker.

Brian collapsed into it, his breathing laboured, like the final throes of the dying.

'I need you to start breathing, Brian, calmly, otherwise you'll faint. You really don't want to faint. I have ways of reviving you. Not very nice ways. Now, take controlled, deep breaths.'

Brian began inhaling.

'Now, exhale slowly. One … two … three …'

Robotically, Brian exhaled.

'You're doing great … that's it. Once more.'

Brian repeated the performance.

'Feeling better?'

Brain wanted to laugh at the terrible irony of such a question. He nodded without saying a word.

'You look like you've been in the wars, but that's the least of your worries. Know who I am?'

'Seamus Nolan.'

'Seamus …?' Rasharkin smiled. 'Know why I'm here?'

'I don't give a shit any more. I'm drained mentally and physically. Too finished.'

'The money you and your friends stole. Other than that, I've no interest in you.'

'Except to kill me? Right?'

'That also, but there are many ways to be killed. I hope you'll be smart and take the less painful route. If you do, I promise it'll be done mercifully, in the blink of an eye.'

'How'd you know I'd come back?'

'You're an addict. You need your fix.'

'I'm no addict. I've never taken drugs in my life … except a little blow.'

'Not all addictions are to drugs.' A wry smile appeared on Rasharkin's face as he glanced about the room. 'I knew you couldn't leave your collection of comic books and merchandise. Too much time and money invested. Too many years of searching for that special item. Too much love. They're a part of you. Now, where's the money?'

'You're sitting on it.'

'Sitting …?' Rasharkin looked puzzled. Stood. 'Where?'

'Push the middle button on Homer's shirt.'

'I've a better idea. Stand up.'

Brian stood.

Rasharkin pointed the gun at Homer. '*You* push the button.'

The moment Brian reached over and pushed the button, Homer's legs parted, revealing a hidden alcove of darkness. 'Want me to reach in and get it for you?'

'No, I'll do that, just in case you have something more lethal than money hidden in there. Stand over to the side. Don't be foolish and try anything. You haven't died in a nice way, yet.'

With one hand, Rasharkin kept the gun aimed at Brian, while the other searched inside the alcove. A quick rummage, and a large Batman gripbag was pulled out. Rasharkin threw it at Brian's feet.

'Open it.'

Brian complied, allowing the remaining money to spill open. 'I've spent quite a bit of it.'

'As one does with other people's money. Hope it was worth it? It'll be the last you ever spend.' Rasharkin pushed the button, and Homer's legs returned to their original position. 'Park yourself.'

'Can I put some clothes on first?'

'Do you realise how ridiculous that sounds? Sit the hell down!'

'You're going to shoot me anyway, so I'd rather stand like a man.'

'*Sit down,* Don't make me shoot your dick off, then you'll not be so concerned about being a man.'

Brian walked towards the chair, and was just about to sit down.

'Stop …' Rasharkin's voice had a slight hesitancy in it. 'Turn … turn around.'

Brian turned.

'Sit down …' Rasharkin said, suddenly looking very weary. He waited until Brian sat before continuing. 'I want you to tell me everything there is to know about that tattoo on your back. Leave nothing out, if you value your life.'

Chapter Thirty-Three

This is what you know about someone you have to hate: he charges
you with his crime and castigates himself in you.

Philip Roth, *The Anatomy Lesson*

'Tell me all you know about the winged horse.' Rasharkin
sat opposite Brian, who was no longer naked, having
been given a large towel. Rasharkin still held the gun, but not
directly at Brian.

'His name is Mercury. He was created by a man called Harmenszoon – a genius, to me the greatest artist of all time. He saved my life.'

Rasharkin leaned forward, voice almost an undertone. 'Saved
your life? How?'

'When I was thirteen, my parents were murdered. I was with
them, when it happened. The gunman tried to shoot me too, but
his gun jammed ...' Brian's eyes seem to glaze over. 'Afterwards,
had I not been able to escape into the wonderful worlds created
by Harmenszoon, I would have gone insane, perhaps even committed suicide.'

'Who murdered your parents?'

'We were on a bus, returning home from the movies. It was my
birthday. As a treat, my parents had brought me to watch *Bedknobs*

and Broomsticks. On the way home, the bus went past Saint Patrick's chapel on Donegall Street. Being Catholics, my parents made a sign of the cross. The sectarian killer, who had been on the bus from the beginning of its journey, had been waiting for someone, *anyone*, to do this, indicating their religion.'

'Did they ever find him?'

'No.'

'If you had him, now, captured, would you kill him?'

'I couldn't kill.'

'Even to avenge your parents?'

Brian shook his head. 'It's just not in me.'

'What if you had had a gun, that day on the bus? If it meant saving your parents, would you have shot the killer?'

'I can't answer a hypothetical question.'

'You won't, you mean. Don't want to portray yourself as something less than human, something like me.'

'I don't want to talk about it any more. Do what you're going to do. Just get it over with.'

'You're in a terrible hurry to die. Tell me all you know about Harmenszoon.'

Brian sighed. 'He was an American. Born in New York. He met a woman in London, when he was doing a European signing tour of his works. They married and had one kid, a wee boy. A few years later, Harmenszoon was dead, his body discovered in a car, at his garage, carbon monoxide fumes the culprit. They said he committed suicide, but I've never believed that.'

'What *do* you believe?'

'I think it was an accident, that he was exhausted and fell asleep in the car, the engine running. He had too much to give to the world to commit suicide – too many people loved him. I was devastated.'

Seemingly hypnotised by Brian's explanation, Rasharkin hadn't moved. Only his eyes seemed to be alive, renewed.

Brain continued. 'After his death, tragedy seem to follow his family. His wife remarried. To a cop. Tragically, they were both shot dead by the son, using the cop's gun. He was only about eleven or twelve at the time. He ended up in an orphanage, after being found not guilty of murder but guilty of manslaughter. Most people believed the boy was just fooling around with the gun when it went off accidently. He was never heard from again, after being given a new identity to shield him from public scrutiny.'

'You got it right. Almost.'

'Almost? I doubt that. I've read everything there is to read on Harmenszoon.'

'It wasn't an accident when the boy shot them. It was deliberate. Want to know why he shot them?'

'If you have another version, then go ahead. I'd like to hear it before you shoot me.'

'You were right when you said Harmenszoon didn't commit suicide. He was murdered.'

'Well … I have heard that over the years, but usually from conspiracy buffs. I don't think we'll ever know the truth.'

'The cop, assisted by Harmenszoon's wife, murdered him. They were having an affair.' Rasharkin's calm voice suddenly filled with anger. 'They overdosed him with sleeping pills, the same pills she used to swallow every night to take her "damn headaches" away, the ones she washed down with rum, Havana Club, her favourite.'

'How … how would you know something like that?'

'Just pay attention!' Rasharkin pointed the gun at Brian's face.

'Okay …'

'Just … pay attention … *please*.' The last word was a whisper. The gun rested back in Rasharkin's lap. 'They placed him in the car, like he was a piece of garbage, an afterthought, then turned the engine on, and watched the exhaust fumes consume him in a fog of death. The perfect crime. Almost. They would have got away with it … if not for the boy … the boy. He saw everything. Knew everything. All their dirty little secrets.'

Outside, the night sounds were settling down to a faint nothing, a nocturnal hush finally spent like a dying star. Inside, not a word, yet a million questions. Brian was aware of his own breathing, slightly laboured. Rasharkin hadn't moved. He sat, lifeless, staring into nothingness.

Then Rasharkin stood, disturbing the bizarre vignette. He reached down and took the gripbag. Walked towards the door. Turned and stared at Brian for the longest time, then at the gun in his hand, as if contemplating a reluctant decision. He pointed the gun at Brian.

'The boy wasn't placed in an orphanage. He was imprisoned in high-security Broadmoor, a psychiatric so-called hospital, for ten years. Try to imagine what that would do to a young boy.'

He tucked the gun away. Opened the door, closing it gently behind him.

Chapter Thirty-Four

The criminal is the creative artist; the detective only the critic.
GK Chesterton, *The Blue Cross: A Father Brown Mystery*

As one door closed, another was opening, this time in the north of town. Two other characters on opposite sides of life were about to become a little better acquainted than either would have anticipated, or sought.

Harry entered the premises of the Old Dander Inn on the Antrim Road, like a sheriff searching for the town's last outlaw. Moseying up to the dimly lit bar, his eyes scrutinised the motley crew of evening patrons drinking and drooling over dodgy deadman's droplets.

'You!' Harry pointed at a crouching figure at the end of the bar. The man was semi-balancing on a metal stool, and appeared to be trying to will himself into invisibility. 'Flanagan, outside – now!'

Frankie slumped down from the counter, and walked obediently towards Harry.

'Aren't you forgetting something?' Harry asked.

'Oh …' Frankie walked back to his stool, retrieving his bag of tricks from beneath it.

Outside, Harry took the bag, and placed it in the back of his car. 'Evidence.'

'Evidence? I swear, Mr Thompson, I had nothing to do with it. I swear!' Frankie looked on the verge of crying. 'I've an alibi.'

'So had OJ Simpson. Just get in the bloody car.'

Inside, Harry started the engine, but not before addressing Frankie's protestations.

'I'll check out your so-called alibi when we get to the station, *and* your nocturnal shenanigans.'

* * *

From his office window, Harry watched Purvis get into the Jag. He waited until it had completely vanished into the night's darkness before making his way down to the cells.

'How's our guest, Bill?'

'Looking *very* guilty.' McCauseland smiled.

Harry looked in through the security flap. Frankie was pacing up and down, mumbling to himself.

McCauseland opened the cell door. Harry entered.

'Mr Thompson!' Frankie practically threw himself at Harry. 'Please, you've got to help me. I can't stand being locked up in such a small room. I can hardly breathe. I suffer from claustrophobia. I take medicine for it.'

'A burglar suffering from claustrophobia? A bit like a surgeon suffering from hemophobia.'

'Hemo-what?'

'Don't concern yourself with what it means. What you *should* be concerned about is that I've checked out the retired judge whose house you burgled, and it's not looking good for you.'

'But I keep telling you, I had nothing to do with that. Check out my alibi. You'll see.'

'I just did. Paul the barman says he never saw you in the Inn last night.'

'Paul? Did I tell you it was Paul? I meant his brother, the other one, with the glass eye. I can't remember his name at the moment. I'm still in a state of shock at being wrongfully arrested.'

'The only name you should be concerned about is the retired judge's. Wilfred Braithwaite the Third. Once gave a man five years for stealing coal from the business of one of his friends, also a judge.'

'I know all about the bastard – I mean his honour.'

'They stick together, these judges. Can you imagine being up in court in front of Braithwaite's mates? You'll be made an example of, a warning to anyone foolish enough to contemplate burgling another judge's home. The keys to your cell will be dropped down the Well Of No Return.'

Frankie seemed to collapse into himself, sinking onto the concrete seat attached to the wall, head in hands. His pallor became as grey as the seat itself.

'I'm finished, Mr Thompson. I'll die in prison.'

'Maybe. Maybe not.'

Frankie slowly raised his head, and looked up at Harry. 'You mean you'd give me a second chance, Mr Thompson? Me, a nobody, but a bloody menace to society?'

'Depends.'

A ray of hope seemed to suddenly shine in Frankie's eyes. He stood.

'Anything, Mr Thompson. You name it, it's done. Just name it. Please, I beg you.'

'Follow me.'

Harry left the cell, quickly followed by Frankie. He was almost tripping over himself, now looking like a condemned man granted a miraculous lifesaving stay of execution. McCauseland lurked silently behind.

Harry and Frankie took the back stairs normally used by contractors, or civilians on propaganda tours. However, due to lack of funds, dust and cobwebs were all that now occupied the stairways. McCauseland departed in the opposite direction, not saying a word.

'Listen carefully, Frankie. Screw this up, and it's back to the Well Of No Return. You got that?' Harry was squeezing a pair of disposable gloves on.

'Thank you Mr Thompson, for giving me this chance. I won't screw up. That's a promise.'

'You're going to be needing that.' Harry pointed to a barely visible lump in a darkened corner.

Frankie looked more confused than ever. It was his bag of tricks. He quickly picked the bag up. Hugged it like a first-born. 'What's my bag doing here?'

Harry didn't answer, but led the way through a formidable-looking red door, out to the fifth-floor corridor. An office to the left became the focus of his attention.

'I need this opened as quickly as possible. We don't have a lot of time.'

Frankie looked confused. 'You want me to break in?'

'Let's just say I forgot my keys. I want no damage done, or signs showing it's been opened. Here, put these on. No prints.' Harry handed Frankie a pair of the disposable gloves.

Frankie put them on. Opened his bag. Produced a small, metal device, shaped like a drill bit. Inserted it in the lock. Three minutes later, with a bit of manoeuvring and twists of the wrist, the door popped open. Frankie smiled triumphantly. 'Easy peasy.'

Harry pushed Frankie into the room. 'Don't get too cocky. That's only the start. I need that door opened.' Harry pointed at an inner door. 'Inside, there's a safe. I need that opened too. If you can do that, you're on your way home, with a few extra quid in your pocket.'

'There's not a safe built I can't open.'

'You better be able to stand by that boast. And remember: no sign of a break in. Understand?'

'Loud and clear.' Frankie smiled. The smile quickly faded, as he scrutinised the lock on the door.

'Holy … shit …'

'What is it now?'

'A Diamond Cylinder King.'

'And?'

'This isn't your average lock. It's one of the best on the market, if not *the* best. It's like a miniature computer, containing a defensive device to fend off attacks. Very smart. Very cunning. Very –'

'I don't want to buy the bloody thing!' Harry was becoming agitated, glancing around him. It was all irritating his irritable bowel syndrome. 'Can you open the damn door or not?'

'Yes.'

'Then bloody do it! Just get a move on. We haven't got all night.'

Frankie kneeled down, chose two tools from the bag, and set about making Harry's command a reality. It took all of three minutes.

'There you go.' Frankie stood back, a proud smile on his face.

'Very good. Now, one last task, and you go home.' Harry opened the door, and pointed at the safe.

Frankie whistled. 'A Bulldog Redden. That's heavy-duty shit. Government issue. I've only ever come across one before. Most safes have a combination-style spinning tumbler – you have to make the correct clockwise and counter-clockwise turns to disengage the lock. But the Bulldog operates on individual niches on each rod.'

'I don't want its history. Can you open it?'

'I couldn't open the one I tried a few years back. It was the first time in my career I had to give up on a safe.'

Harry looked as if he had just been punched in the irritable bowels.

'What happened to "there's not a safe built I can't open"?'

'That was a slight exaggeration. Jesus, it's haunted me ever since, that safe, laughing at me every time I shut my eyes. It damaged my reputation amongst the burglary fraternity too.'

'Tell your sob story some other time. All right, pack up and let's get the hell out of here.'

'I'm not going anywhere, Mr Thompson.'

'What?'

'This night was meant to be, don't you see?'

'What're you talking about?'

Frankie's face lit up in rapture, like a pilgrim finally arriving at his holy destination. 'I think you've just given me a chance of redemption, to get my reputation back. Hand me my bag of tricks.'

* * *

Purvis arrived home in Hazlebank, almost five miles from the station. He was exhausted, trudging up the path to his heavily fortified house, briefcase in hand.

Four spotlights automatically lit up the entire area, and a family of motion-detector security cameras clicked and whirred smoothly. A metal door opened, allowing him into the front of the house. No sooner had he hit the combo on the front door, than he released a silent curse.

'*I don't believe this!*' His hand went into the briefcase. Mobile missing.

He returned to the car, and headed back in the direction of the station.

* * *

Frankie made himself comfy on the floor, arranging an impressive array of tools, all shapes and sizes, around him. He looked like a medieval medic, about to perform major surgery on a fallen knight.

'Take your bloody time, won't you?' Harry said sarcastically, looking at his watch. 'Want me to get you a sandwich and a cup of coffee, while you're sitting on your arse? Some cake, perhaps?'

'Worrying and trying to put me under pressure won't help, Mr Thompson. Breaking into a safe of this calibre is very delicate. It has to be treated with respect.' Frankie picked a slender instrument, and began worrying the safe's dial.

Harry continually glanced at his watch, though he knew Purvis wouldn't be back until morning. His stomach kept making strange bubbling sounds, testing what little nerve he had left.

Ten minutes slipped by. To Harry, they stretched like hours. He watched, fascinated by Frankie's surprisingly delicate fingers manoeuvring small metal rods into the lock's now hollowed-out dial.

Soaked in sweat, Frankie stood.

'Well?' Harry asked.

'I beat the devil. The privilege is all yours.'

Relief flooded over Harry's face as he pulled open the safe's door. Inside, neat little rows of papers were indexed and segregated in colour-codes and metal spines. *Thank God Purvis is a dinosaur like me. No USB sticks or discs.*

He reached in, and began scrutinising the pages, uncertain what exactly he was looking for, but believing the moment he saw it, he would know.

Suddenly, footsteps came scurrying along the corridor. Harry and Frankie stopped all movement. The door flew open.

'The Jag has returned, Harry,' McCauseland said, alarm in his voice.

'I need time, Bill.'

McCauseland slammed the door, his footsteps echoing back down the corridor.

Harry turned on a copier in the corner, and began scanning page after page, spilling some onto the floor in his haste to return them safely to the safe.

* * *

Purvis walked briskly from the car towards the station entrance, taking the concrete steps two at a time. When McCauseland side-bumped him, he went tumbling down the stairs, arms flailing wildly as he tried to keep his balance. He landed flat on his back.

'Sorry, mate!' McCauseland exclaimed, bending over Purvis, hands out in a gesture of help. 'I wasn't looking where I was – oh, Mr Purvis. Sorry about that.'

'You bloody fool! What the hell's wrong with you?' Purvis brushed away McCauseland's offer of help. Purvis pulled himself up using the safety rail, then continued on his way into the station, glancing back towards where McCauseland stood.

Inside the station, he pressed the lift's button. The lift stopped on every floor, in a slow-motion ritual.

'What the –? Some clown has pressed all the buttons!'

The lift finally opened at the fifth floor, and he made his way along the corridor. Opened the door to his office, immediately spotting his mobile on top of the desk. Secured it and was just about to step back out when he stopped, dead in his tracks.

Something. What? He looked about the office. Nothing seemed out of place. Yet … what? Something *was* out of place, but he couldn't quite put his finger on it. He considered the air, sniffing like a wolf hunting prey. The ambience had been disturbed somehow. He eyeballed the printer. *What?* Walked over to it, resting his palm on top. His face tightened.

Warm …?

Chapter Thirty-Five

Joining the church felt like joining a secret club; and you learned the rules after you joined. The first rule of the church was: Never question what it is that you have joined.
Stephen White, *Higher Authority*

Whispering. A chant, rising, falling. Hypnotic. Not Gregorian. Belfastian. Old men. Old women. Old souls. Heads bowed in humility. All one. Seeking redemption, forgiveness, assurances, answers. A blank cheque in return for their unwavering faith in the unknown.

Two days after breaking into his own police station, Harry stood at the back of the church, camouflaged by the shadows of ancient marble pillars. He wasn't there seeking forgiveness for his peccadilloes, more of a business meeting without the lunch. A thick cardboard folder, secured with a black ribbon, rested under his arm.

An out-of-place Presbyterian, comfortable in his own shoes on Catholic sacred tiles, he'd been here many times, with many different reasons for his visitations – sometimes loose ends that needed tying up, sometimes secretly seeking something other than the person he watched clandestinely.

He was studying a kneeling Conor O'Neill, a few pews down near the far aisle, seemingly lost in prayer or contemplation, when suddenly the entire congregation stood as one. Within seconds, they disassembled, some sitting, some making their slow journey towards the priest dispensing the wafers of Holy Communion.

A young woman, very pretty, conservatively dressed, stood close to Harry, head bowed, hands steepled respectfully in prayer. She wore black silk gloves from a bygone era, and carried a small, matching handbag.

Harry could pick up the slightest aroma of her perfume, and for some reason it made him feel uncomfortable, as though he had broken some arcane canon of religious sanctity.

A few minutes later, the priest gave his final blessing, and the congregation quietly began ushering themselves out into the cold morning rain.

Harry tried keeping track on Conor, but the crowd's swelling movement made it near impossible. He attempted to join the flow.

'I think it best you stay where you are,' the young woman suggested in a calm but firm voice, blocking Harry from progressing onwards.

'Don't be silly. Move out of the way before you get yourself into trouble,' Harry said, annoyed but not wanting to make a scene in front of so many people.

The young woman stood firm.

'Do you know who I am?' Harry could feel his face becoming warm.

'Yes I do. That's why I'm asking nicely – but just the once.' The tiny gun in her hand was as black as the gloves she wore, rendering it almost invisible. 'Don't be under any illusions – I'll use it if I have to, church or no church.'

'I bet you damn well would.' Harry stood still and waited while she frisked him – *very* professionally, causing his already warm face to heat even more.

'You've got the delicate touch of a policewoman,' Harry said sarcastically.

'You'd know all about that, I bet.' Finished, the young woman pointed over at the pews. 'Conor's waiting for you.'

A flustered Harry made his way over, moving to sit directly behind O'Neill, until the young woman shook her head and pointed to the row in front. A not too happy Harry repositioned his bulk as directed, and sat down.

'Now you're the driver on the big bus, Thompson!' Conor was grinning.

'A bit like getting an audience with the Pope, trying to bloody see you.'

'Language, please.' Conor's grin widened. 'Show a bit of respect.'

'A gun in church? Is *that* respectful?'

'I call that a precaution. Anyway, it's been blessed by that wee priest you saw saying Mass.'

'He sure knows how to prolong a sermon. I thought it was never going to end.'

'Brevity's never been his forte, and he tends to go overboard on the incense, but you can accumulate extra brownie points for Purgatory when he's saying Mass.'

'Actually, the smell of that incense he was releasing into the air, made the waiting more pleasant. Calming, almost. I think if they dropped a ton of it over Belfast, it would be beneficial to everyone.'

'Incense to Catholics is like catnip to cats. I could tell you a story or two about an American Jesuit we once had here. One of the flower people, in his time. Wasn't above dropping a little marijuana into the censer, spreading the good news everywhere, so to speak. The congregation thought they had died and gone to Heaven, the elderly standing without canes or Zimmer frames.'

Conor left his pew, and sat beside Harry.

'I'm sure you didn't come here to discuss the mysteries of incense. The go-between said it was urgent. The last time he used that word was four years ago, if my memory serves me well.'

'I've come to finally pay off my debt to you,' said Harry.

'You owe me nothing. I've told you that before. I was only doing my duty as a member of Saint John Ambulance. Get over it.'

'I don't like being beholden to *anyone*. I've told *you* that before, though I will be keeping your Saint Christopher.' Harry handed Conor the folder he had been carrying. 'You saved my life. For that, I'll always be grateful, but this ends it. The slate's now clean. Payment in full.'

'Should I open it here?'

'Best done somewhere a bit more private. You'd be surprised where they have bugs and double-agents nowadays.' It was Harry's turn to grin a knowing grin. He stood. Eased out of the pew. 'One thing I've always wanted to ask you, O'Neill, and didn't. Had you known I was an undercover cop that day, spying on you, would you have saved my life?'

For the longest time Conor stared at Harry, before answering.

'The truth is, I've asked myself that very question.' Conor pointed at the door. 'Now, I think this meeting is over, Thompson. Have a good day.'

Chapter Thirty-Six

'You wouldn't kill me in cold blood, would ya?' Roy Parker
'No, I'll let ya warm up a little.' Cody Jarrett
White Heat

Almost a week later, Seamus Nolan zipped an overnight
bag closed, then took a last look about the small abode
he had called home for the last little while. It belonged to a sym-
pathiser, who allowed him to billet there until the heat from the
Madden killings cooled down a notch.

He was on a euphoric high. After years of being in the shadow
of Conor O'Neill, his time had finally come. He was to be promoted to the Brotherhood's elite hierarchy at GHQ, down in
Dublin, tomorrow afternoon.

The cryptic message had come to him only yesterday, but it
was a message he had been anticipating for months. He couldn't
wait to see the look on O'Neill's face when he came back to Belfast to tell him his days were over as leader. And down the line,
he had further plans for O'Neill. Payback plans.

A car's horn beeped. Nolan parted the curtain. It was pitch
black outside, with heavy night rain. He raised a finger, indicating
one minute, then opened his wallet to check his new ID for the

umpteenth time. It looked perfect. He hoped he wouldn't have to use it, but better safe than sorry. Sliding it back into the wallet, he opened the front door, then stepped out into the pounding rain.

He didn't usually like rain. It depressed him. But not tonight. Tonight, he decided, nothing could bother him. Then he opened the door to the car, and proved himself wrong.

'Okay, Sean? What an atrocious night, eh?' Billy Butler said eagerly, a half-smile on his less-than-eager face.

Nolan made a grunting sound before squeezing his bulk inside.

'I've got the heat up full blast, Seamus. Anything else, just let me know.' Billy's hand reached over to turn the radio on.

'How about silence until we get to Dublin?'

Billy's hand stopped in midair, then returned to the steering wheel, as he guided the car out onto the road.

The normally less than two-hour trip would take longer, using carved-out side roads and clandestine routes instead of the motorway, but getting to Dublin safely was paramount to Nolan, especially now at this stage of the game, when he was within touching distance of his destiny.

Halfway through the journey, his euphoria was beginning to wane. The chaotic driving was grinding on his nerves. This clown of a driver seemed to be hitting every pothole and bump he could find, as if they were points in an arcade game.

'For fuck sake!' The latest bump sent Nolan springing up and down like a puppet with tangled strings. 'Where the hell did you learn to drive?'

'Sorry ... sorry, Seamus. Doing my best on these so-called roads. The rain isn't helping. I tried putting the gears into –'

'Just get us there – *in one piece.*'

'Yes, Seamus, I'll make sure I –'

Without warning, Billy hit the brakes, and the car went into a mucky sideways skid, slamming to a stop among a cluster of thorn bushes and uprooted tree stumps. A tree branch came crashing through the window, narrowly missing Nolan's face.

'You crazy fucking bastard! I'll make sure you never –'

'*Up ahead, Seamus.*' Billy said in a terrified whisper.

In the ghostly distance, three dreaded words appeared:

HALT!
POLICE CHECKPOINT

'What should we do, Seamus?'

Survival mode kicked in. Without answering Billy, Nolan reached for the door. It was blocked by an enormous tree stump. He slithered across the leather seat, and opened the other door. A sheet of rain hit him up the face, taking his breath away.

'Split up. Cause confusion. Head you that way.' Nolan pointed. 'Remember, if they catch you, say fucking nothing. Get that into your thick skull. Understood?'

A petrified-looking Billy nodded before quickly exiting the car, heading in the indicated direction.

Disorientated in the heavy darkness and claustrophobic rain, Nolan's human compass guided him downwards towards where distant lights glowed, of night homes and premises.

Behind him, voices were shouting to halt, but he kept going. A shot rang out. Then another. He moved faster.

The lights below became bigger. Car headlights. A small road. He was feeling lightheaded, needing to stop and catch his breath. But his survival instinct kept him pushing ahead. To stop now would be disastrous.

It was twenty long and tension-filled minutes before he finally landed on terra firma, near the back of an old, dilapidated house. He was a mess, covered in muck and all sorts of shit. He felt as bad as he looked. If he could get his hands on transport, he would have a chance of escaping.

'Go on. Make a move and join your mate,' a rain-drenched cop hissed, pressing a gun against the side of Nolan's head.

Other cops quickly emerged, forcefully toppling Nolan to the ground, pushing his face into a river of gravelly water. Handcuffs snapped shut, cutting into his skin. Boots began kicking all over.

'We wanted you to enjoy your wee journey down the hillside before apprehending you,' the cop smirked. He had an enormous moustache, and the smirk made him look like the Cheshire Cat. 'Right, stand the bastard up!'

Nolan was pulled up to standing, then slapped across the face a few times.

'What was all that about, fleeing from police?' Moustache was searching him. Found the wallet. Removed the fake driving licence. Read the details. 'Peter Johnson? Well, Johnson? Why were you running?'

Nolan stared into Moustache's face, defiantly remaining silent.

'Hard man, eh? We'll see how hard you are in a few minutes.'

The cops manhandled him into the back of a waiting police car.

Despite the overwhelming odds, Nolan was quickly regaining his composure. He wasn't beaten yet, at least not mentally, and that's what counted when it came to interrogations: mental stamina. He still had a card up his sleeve. A wildcard, yes, but it could still win him the game, if played correctly.

The car took sharp swerves as it climbed the steep hill. He could hear the two cops in the front talking in whispers, something about being *shot in the back, dead.*

'Hit the talking on the head, you two,' Moustache said, sitting beside Nolan. 'I can hear every word coming out of your mouths.'

'Sorry, sir,' the driver mumbled. Silence descended upon the vehicle.

They passed Billy's car, skewed sideways on the hill. Flashing lights surrounded the area. There was a scene up ahead. Cops huddled around a covered shape.

The car came to a halt, and Nolan was dragged out, thrown onto the mucky ground.

'Your mate was lucky,' Moustache said, pointing at the covered body. 'It's all over for him, but not for you, Mister Nolan. Oh, that surprised you, hard man? We were tipped off about your little journey; we've been watching you all the way from Belfast.'

Nolan's face tightened slightly, then relaxed into indifference.

'Does the name Sandy Martin ring a bell to you?' Moustache asked.

Nolan said nothing, but his eyes seem to look elsewhere, if only for a split second.

'Let me remind you. He was a cop, just like me. Had his faults, just like all of us, but he was a good man. A family man. He was shot dead ten years ago, along with three other constables. Shot in the back of the head, execution style, in a desolate place at night – not unlike this place – while his wife and three kids waited for him to come home.' Emotion was building up in Moustache's voice. 'You see, it was a special day for Sandy. It was his birthday. I was there with his family, also, that night, waiting for him to come home. Sandy was my big brother. He always took care of me when I was a kid. You murdered him, shot him like a dog in the gutter.'

Nolan's features changed from certainty to a picture of inner horror; horror about to be visited upon him for the first time in his life.

The other cops watched from afar, uncertain, not wanting to be involved in whatever scene might play itself out in the freezing rain.

From his holster, Moustache removed his gun, aimed it at Nolan.

'Kneel, the way you made all four kneel that night.'

Nolan slowly knelt. Transfixed. His mouth opened. He was struggling to form words. 'If you kill me, you … you'll be making … the biggest mistake of … your life …'

'Ten years of patiently waiting rules out mistakes. A chicken farm is going to be built over the hole I'm going to dump you in. Poetic justice or what, eh?' He cocked the gun. Pressed the muzzle against the back of Nolan's head. 'Go to Hell, where you belong.'

'I work for MI5! I'm their … number one agent. Years and millions of pounds have been invested in me. Think, man. For God's sake, *think*!'

'Think? I think I don't give a fuck. Fuck you, and MI5. This is for Sandy and the other lads.'

'Gordon Purvis! He's my handler. You kill me … he … he'll hunt you down until he finds you.'

Moustache seemed to hesitate at Purvis's dreaded name being mentioned. The other cops, looking even more uncertain now, began talking among themselves.

'You think you can hide from Purvis?' Nolan quickly continued, sensing the uncertainty among the ranks. 'No one hides from Purvis! You all know his reputation. Someone will eventually talk. He'll kill you – he'll kill you all!'

Suddenly, one of the other cops grabbed Moustache by the arm. 'Let's think this out, Ian.'

'What's to think out? All the murders he's got away with! Should we think those out too? What about Sandy and the lads? You want me to just forget them?'

'We all want justice, Ian, but what if he's telling the truth about Purvis? None of us want any involvement with that psycho.'

'Call Purvis!' Nolan screamed. 'I've got his private number. Don't do something you'll all regret!'

'Can't do any harm, Ian. Let's call the number. Keep ourselves right. If this bastard is lying, I swear to you, *I'll* dig his grave.'

Chapter Thirty-Seven

There's only room for one hero in this story —
and everyone knows the devil doesn't get to be the good guy.
Joe Hill, *Horns*

The darkness rested on Nolan like a tight-fitting garment. Not a suit or a coat – more like a straightjacket.

The last thing he remembered was being smacked viciously over the head by Moustache, until darkness came and floated him out on a flying carpet of blissful oblivion.

The old head wound had been ripped open, but he couldn't really complain. It was a small price to pay, having shot Moustache's brother all those years ago.

He reached to touch the wound, but his right hand would not obey. He tried using the left hand. Same result. He tried to speak, but nothing came. Bizarrely, he could feel no pain, even though he knew the busted wound should be throbbing like hell.

Without warning, sharp lights chased the darkness. It felt like someone throwing bleach into his eyes. He instinctively shut his eyelids.

'I'll give you a few seconds to orientate and acclimatise yourself, then we can begin,' Rasharkin said. 'I've given you some Ketamine to dull your pain. It will help to keep you calm, until I no longer need your calmness …'

Chapter Thirty-Eight

The devil's agents may be of flesh and blood, may they not?
Arthur Conan Doyle, *The Hound of the Baskervilles*

The sun was out, shining down on Conor and Rasharkin as they sat on a bench in the Cat Garden. In the curved distance, luxury liners were sliding into Belfast harbour. Nearby, kids were out in force on bikes and skateboards, not a care in the world on a school-free Saturday morning.

'I've written down all of the actions Nolan confessed to, including a list of his victims,' Rasharkin said matter-of-factly, handing Conor a thick envelope. 'Also included are the names of people he intended to *deal with* when opportunity presented itself in the future. Your name is top of the list.'

Conor nodded nonchalantly, then took a puff on his pipe. He let the smoke gather over his face, before brushing it away with his hand.

'How long before he broke under?'

'Surprisingly, for a man of his reputation, it was pretty quick. He was no Jim McCabe. I think he was resigned to what was coming.'

'He deserved everything that *was* coming – and more.'

'There was a comedic moment of vanity from him, when I called him an informer. He took umbrage at that, saying he was no common informer, but an "agent of influence".'

Conor scoffed. 'Grand-sounding title for a traitor. My grandfather always said that a rat is a rat, even when it wears silk socks and a fancy hat!'

'His handler was a cop by the name of Gordon Purvis. He was up to his neck in all this, along with Nolan. You know Purvis?'

'Demented scumbag. Not unlike Nolan, he'd kill anyone who got in his way. Purvis was a leading member of a loyalist murder gang, the Glenanne Gang. Its members consisted of RUC, UDR, and a fair scattering of violent paedophiles. Many years ago, Purvis was suspected in the killing of an old cop called Tommy Montgomery, simply because he was a Catholic. The Brotherhood were blamed for the killing, of course, as we looked upon cops as legitimate targets. It was never fully investigated by other cops; there was only one who was interested – Harry Thompson.'

'Perhaps I should pay a visit to Mr Purvis? He sounds the type of person I need to sit down and get acquainted with.'

'I'd be tempted to give the go-ahead, but I have a feeling Thompson has other ideas for Purvis. I don't think he'd appreciate us getting involved. At least not at the moment …'

'As instructed, Nolan's body was cremated, ashes scattered to the wind.'

'Did … he say anything about Michael Harrison?'

Rasharkin nodded. 'I'm sorry, he was on the list of victims.'

For a second, Conor lost his composure. His face seemed to sink inwards.

'You okay, Conor?'

'Yes …'

'I've also included all the places Nolan bugged, under instruction from Purvis, including the restaurant where you have your meetings. That was where he discovered the name Doc Holliday, Boyd's alias.'

O'Neill looked crestfallen. 'The blame for that falls squarely on my shoulders. I of all people should have known better than to discuss business in confined places, even in a whisper. I'm disgusted with myself, not practising what I preach habitually to others.'

'On a brighter note, I was able to retrieve the money he stole when he killed the Maddens. That means most of it is now accounted for, with the exception of earlier losses noted, and my fee.'

'I can't thank you enough, Rasharkin, for what you've done.'

'You already have, plus I appreciate the bonus you gave me.'

'Well earned, my friend. Well earned.'

Rasharkin stood. Offered his hand. Conor shook it. Smiled.

'Stay safe.'

'I always do, Conor. Take care.'

Conor watched Rasharkin walk up the old stone steps leading to the car park, never looking back.

For the longest time, Conor sat, smoking and contemplating, with his eyes closed. He could smell Saturday morning cooking in the Cellar restaurant, directly behind him. Any other time, he would have popped in for tea and toast with marmalade, but he had no stomach for it this morning. He had things to do. Unpleasant things he was not looking forward to, especially having to tell Fiona Harrison that he had let her down when she needed him so badly, when her son needed him.

'You okay, Conor?' A voice asked.

Conor opened his eyes. Billy Butler was looking at him with concern on his face.

'I mustn't be, as you're the second person to ask me that in the last five minutes.' Conor forced a smile. 'I'm fine, Billy. Take the weight off your feet.'

'Lovely wee morning, isn't it?' Billy said, sitting down and answering his own question, as Belfastians tend to do.

Conor took a long draw on the pipe. Released the smoke through the side of his mouth. 'You did a great job on the road to Dublin.'

'Thank you, Conor.' Billy beamed with pride. 'Means a lot, coming from you. Thank you for having faith in me, even if I was playing dead for most of it!'

'I was never in any doubt about your capabilities, or your loyalty to the movement. The other lads did a stellar job as well.'

'They were all very convincing as peelers. I bet they never thought they'd see the day they'd be wearing the uniform of the PSNI! To be honest with you, I hated and feared Nolan, but I never would have suspected he was an informer.'

'That's what made him such a good one. *No one* suspected. Unfortunately, I doubt very much he'll be the last one we have to deal with, judging by what was gleaned from his interrogation.' Conor tapped the pipe on the side of the bench, clearing out the chamber. He stood. 'Time to go. I need you to drop me off at Fiona Harrison's house …'

Chapter Thirty-Nine

I have a secret passion for mercy. But justice is
what keeps happening to people.
Ross Macdonald, *The Goodbye Look*

The old canteen in the station's basement, long vacant due to cuts, had been given a quick revamp, with a lick of paint and a rub to the grubby windows. In the middle of the floor, two long wooden tables displayed a mixture of beverages, some limp sandwiches and a cake long past its sell-by date.

A motley crew of banners proclaiming 'Happy Retirement Harry' dangled precariously from the ceiling, alongside 'Wanted' posters showing Harry with various facial hair changes over the years. A small clique of friends and associates had gathered to say their farewells.

'Sure I can't get you a drink, Harry?' McCauseland said, voice slightly slurred, a full glass of whiskey in one hand, half-eaten sandwich in the other. He wasn't drunk exactly, but wasn't too far from the tipping point.

'No thanks, Bill. I'm driving home in one piece.' Harry indicated his glass of orange juice, resting atop the table beside him. 'I'm hoping to be out of here within the hour, or even less if I can slip out unnoticed. Elaine's taking me out for dinner to celebrate the beginning of civilian life.'

'I don't think it'll be too long before I follow you, literally and figuratively. My days are numbered once you go.' He sounded despondent. Downed the whiskey in one swallow.

'Don't be so pessimistic, Bill. You're a damned good detective. They need good detectives with plenty of experience. They'll always need good detectives.'

'Don't make me laugh. What they need and what they want are two different animals. You know yourself, it's all PR now. They want arse-kissers and poster boys, like that useless prat over there. Thinks he's a real cop. Look at the way he's standing there, like Clint Eastwood.' With his chin, McCauseland indicated Jeffrey Kerr, standing near the far door, arms akimbo, look of smug contentment on face. 'Fuck, if he was chocolate, he'd lick himself to death when he's not licking McCafferty's hairy arse. Speaking of that prick McCafferty, looks like he's a no-show.'

'Thank God for small mercies. He's in London, some sort of police convention, high-profiling his plusses and hiding his minuses. Did I show you what he got me as a retirement *gift*?'

'That cheap prick actually bought you something?'

Harry reached behind to a bin half-filled with discarded cake, soggy sandwiches and paper napkins. Pulled out a framed official photo of McCafferty, grinning like an undertaker at a massacre, his shoulders lined in brass. 'He even had the audacity to sign it to "*my good friend, Harry*". And there's me thinking all these years he never had a sense of humour!'

Harry turned to throw it back into the bin.

'No, don't do that! I'll take it home for practice at the dart board. Just leave it on the table. I'll grab it before I go.'

Harry left it on the table. Glanced at his watch, then sneezed loudly. Removed a handkerchief from his pocket. 'I hope this isn't the start of a bloody head cold. Been sneezing all evening.'

'A hot whiskey will fix that.'

'Stop trying to tempt me.'

'Well, I sure as hell want one, and I don't care if it's hot or cold, so long as it's wet!'

'Go and enjoy yourself before the booze is all gone.'

'You sure?'

'Sure I'm sure.'

'The best way to drink whiskey?'

'Tell me.'

'Put in glass. Drink!'

They both laughed.

'Look, if I don't see you before you sneak off, Harry, I'll call you tomorrow.' McCauseland threw his arms around Harry, hugging him, before kissing him on the left cheek. 'I was lucky to have you as my best mate and boss.'

'What do you mean *was*? You'll still have me tomorrow as your best mate, provided you disentangle yourself from me immediately!'

'Sorry, mate ...' McCauseland pushed himself away, looking slightly embarrassed, and to Harry's surprise the tough-as-nails cop was teary-eyed. He walked away, in the direction of the booze table.

Harry glanced at his watch, then about the room, trying to figure the best escape route.

'Sir?' a voice behind him said.

Harry turned. It was Kerr.

Oh, God, no. Not this late in the game. 'Hello, Kerr. Everything okay?'

'Yes, sir.'

'Not having a drink?'

'I don't drink, sir. Besides, I'm the only one on duty.' He pulled his coat back slightly, exposing a holstered gun. 'I'm looking after the fort, so to speak.'

God help us. 'That's great. Good man.'

'I just want to say, it's been an honour serving under you, sir.'

'Well ... thank you. I really appreciated ... your enthusiasm, and work.'

'I learned so much under your command.'

Harry didn't know if Kerr was being condescending, or sincere. He chose the latter. 'You'll make an excellent detective. Just give it time, don't try to rush it.'

'Thank you, sir! I'll take your words of encouragement on board.'

Harry sneezed again. Took out the handkerchief. Blew his nose, surreptitiously looking at his watch. *Shit! Got to be getting going!*

'If it's not too presumptuous of me, sir, have you ever thought about writing a book? So many people would be fascinated by your life in the Force.'

Again, Harry didn't know if Kerr was being sincere. This time, he suspected not.

'Blowing smoke up my arse, lad, the way I'm blowing snot into this hanky? Keep that bullshit for McCafferty.' Without another word or a look back, Harry stormed off. He headed quickly towards the toilets, only to do a sharp left turn, up the stairs to freedom.

Outside, he let the cold, refreshing night air gather on his face, chasing the canteen's stuffiness from his nostrils.

'Ah, that's nice ...' He walked around the corner towards the back of the station, where his car waited like a loyal steed.

Upon reaching it, he took one last, nostalgic look back at the old place, nestling in its own shadows and secrets. It had become part of his life and soul. Shit, he'd spent more hours in there than at home. 'I hate to admit it, old girl, but I'm going to miss you, despite all the bullshit.'

He settled into his car seat. Got comfortable. Pressed the CD button. Brahms's sorrowful 'Intermezzo, Op. 118, No. 2 in A major' began. A suffocating feeling of melancholy suddenly welled up in him. He sighed. Thought of Elaine. It brought a plaintive smile back to his face. Thought about phoning her, but decided he'd be home soon enough.

The barrel of the gun touched his neck gently, then moved

slowly to the back of his ear. He looked in the rear-view mirror at the eyes of a shark, regarding him like prey soon to be consumed.

'Didn't know you liked classical music, Thompson. Always took you for a country-and-western listener,' Purvis said. 'Sorry I missed your wee going away, but I thought I'd make it more personal by surprising you in your own car.'

Harry continued staring at the eyes. He said nothing. He felt strangely detached. Brahms's composition was everywhere in the car. It seemed to calm him.

'Don't be stupid, Purvis. You'd never get away with murdering me.'

'Won't I? You got away with murdering Seamus Nolan, or at least you thought you had.'

'What? I don't know what you're talking about.'

'Of course you don't.' Purvis smirked menacingly. 'You may not have pulled the trigger, but you killed him as surely as if you had. Think I don't know you broke into my office, and raided the safe? You even had the balls to use my copier! Unfortunately for you, it was still warm when I went back in to get my phone. Ah, there it is, a little twitch in your cheek, an admission of guilt!'

'You've lost the plot. Get out of the car now, and that's the end of it. You're drunk.'

'And the clumsy attempt by your best mate, McCauseland, to stall me for time. A pity you didn't wipe your fingerprints from the scene of the crime. You might just have got away with it. The irony of it – even though you *were* wearing gloves, they still left a blank imprint, an imprint of three fingers.'

Purvis started laughing, as if he had just told the best joke in the world. 'Caught by your own hand, or I should say, fingers!'

'You're mad, Purvis. Sick. You don't know what you're talking about. Listen, you don't have to do this. You can still pull back from the brink.'

'Before you go to wherever the hell the devil takes you, I just want you to know that I did kill Montgomery. Probably one of the most enjoyable killings I ever carried out. He begged like a Fenian dog, cried his eyes out. I shot him first in the mouth just to shut him up. Then in the eyes – those sneaky Catholic eyes.'

Harry hadn't moved. He thought of Elaine; felt his breathing slowing to an almost numb nothingness of acquiescence. A Genesis-to-Omega moment in his life had arrived.

'See, that's the difference between Prods and Taigs, Thompson. We don't beg or cry when faced with death. You've done yourself proud.'

'Put the gun down, Purvis.'

Harry didn't know where the words were coming from, but he kept repeating them, over and over in his head, as if words could defeat evil.

Put the gun down! Put the gun down!

An explosion, then blood. So much of it, blinding Harry, stinging his eyes. He could no longer hear Brahms; could no longer hear a thing, the side of his face a goulash of brain tissue and bone matter. Everything so sudden. So violently sudden.

Okay ... okay ... are ... you ... you ... you ...

'Sir? Are you okay?'

Kerr was staring at him, gun in hand, still pointed at Purvis, slumped against the back seat, half of his head missing.

'What … what happened? Where …?' Harry felt a tingling of pins and needles covering his skin. Something terrible had happened. Followed by something wonderful. Tears were forming in his eyes. He brushed them away, smudging Purvis's blood across his face.

'It's okay, sir. It's me. Kerr. I shouted at Purvis to put the gun down, but he wouldn't. I feared you were about to be shot, so I fired first. Purvis left me no option. You're a witness to that, sir.'

Harry looked at the face. Young, enthusiastic, determined. Looked at the hand holding the gun. Not a shake. Not a doubt.

'I … thank you, Kerr. You saved my life … thank you.'

'I wish he had put the gun down. I didn't want to shoot him.'

Harry could detect regret in the young voice, but also resolve. *'Thank God he didn't. Thank God you did,'* he whispered to himself.

Harry eased out of the car. He was shaking terribly. People were pouing out of the station, running in his direction. Some shouting his name. He leaned against the car for support. 'How … what were you doing here, at my car?'

Kerr reached into his pocket and retrieved an item. 'This fell from your pocket when you pulled out your hanky to blow your nose, sir. I came looking for you, to give it back. Strange … had it not fallen out, I wouldn't be here talking to you.'

Harry took the item. Shook his head in disbelief, wry smile on face. O'Neill's Saint Christopher. 'The bloody irony of it. Now I'm indebted to him again!'

'Pardon, sir?'

'Nothing. Just talking to myself.' Harry put out his hand. 'Thank you, Kerr.'

Kerr reached and shook the hand, firmly. 'You're welcome, sir. Just doing my duty.'

'You're going to make one hell of a cop, Kerr. One hell of a cop, definitely.'

In the distance, an ambulance's siren screamed in the dark. He gripped the medal so tightly it pierced his skin. He thought of Elaine.

Epilogue

'To be a successful assassin, you have to operate alone.
Once someone else is introduced, your problems
multiply exponentially.

Rasharkin

'**Y**ou sure you don't want me to stay overnight?' Alice purred, smiling seductively, her left hand inside Rasharkin's Hermes Woven boxers, as her right hand accepted an envelope.

'Best we keep it like this. Once a week. That way, we won't get bored of each other's company.'

'Speak for yourself when you say that. I never tire of your company, standing there like Tarzan, teasing.' She kissed him long and hard, and began fondling his balls. She felt him go rock hard again. 'Looks like someone else is in full agreement with me!'

He laughed. Removed her hand, then guided her out into the corridor.

'Next Tuesday?' She asked.

'Unless something comes up.'

'Looks like it already has.'

She kissed him quickly, and made her way down the corridor towards the lift. She waved to him, then disappeared inside.

Closing the door, he made his way to the drinks cabinet, and prepared a small whisky, more from habit than need. He smiled, thinking of Alice's antics in the bed earlier, void of all sexual inhibition. She made him feel good, knew how to take the darkness from him, if only for a small measure of time. Still, he had to be careful not to think it was anything other than business.

The blue phone began ringing, breaking his thoughts.

Brrrrlllllllll … Brrrrlllllllll … Brrrrlllllllll …

He watched the little trail of dotted silver lights leapfrogging to the red security descrambler, journeying all the way to the cordless white phone.

Brrrrlllllllll … Brrrrlllllllll … Brrrrlllllllll …

He picked up the receiver. 'Hello.' Listened to the voice at the other end. Nodded a few times, then said: 'Send me the details the usual way. In the meantime, I'll start making preparations …'

Other books by Sam Millar

'Mesmerizing and fascinating, *On The Brinks* is one of the most revealing and powerful memoirs you will ever read.'

New York Journal of Books

In 1993, $7.4 million was stolen from the Brinks Armored Car Depot in Rochester, New York, the fifth-largest robbery in US history. Sam Millar was a member of the gang who carried out the robbery. He was caught, found guilty and incarcerated, before being set free by Bill Clinton's government as an essential part of the Northern Ireland Peace Process.

This remarkable book is Sam's story, from his childhood in Belfast, membership of the IRA, time spent in Long Kesh internment camp and the Brinks heist and its aftermath. Unputdownable.

Karl Kane

'Crime noir doesn't get much darker or grittier'
Booklist

Karl Kane is a private investigator with a dark past, his mother murdered when he was a child. Years later, Karl has a chance to avenge his mother's murder, but allows the opportunity to slip through his hands. When two young girls are sexually molested and then brutally murdered, Karl holds himself responsible.

Young homeless women and drug addicts are being abducted before being brutally mutilated and murdered, and a city is held in the grip of unspeakable terror. By abducting Katie, the young daughter of private investigator Karl Kane, the killer has just made his first mistake, which could well turn out to be his last.

Private investigator Karl Kane returns to the streets of Belfast, investigating the discovery of a severed hand. Believing it's the work of an elusive serial killer, Karl embarks on a nightmarish journey as he attempts to solve the mystery. As the winter days become darker, Karl has to battle to keep from becoming the next victim.

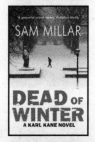

A young girl disappears after escaping from a religious orphanage, and another is caught on grainy film being abducted as her family home burns down. Investigating the missing girls, Karl Kane catches a glimpse of a demon from his past – could it be that Walter Arnold, the monster who raped and murdered his mother, is walking the streets again?

A tense tale of murder, betrayal, sexual abuse and revenge, and the corruption at the heart of the respectable establishment.

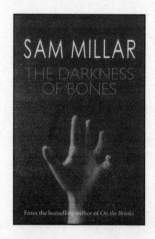

In a wood at night, a young woman witnesses the murder of a whistle-blower by a corrupt businessman, owner of an abattoir. Paul Goodman, a would-be snooker champion who works at the abattoir, has never known his father and believes that he deserted him when young. But he is befriended by the one man who holds the key to the mystery of his disappearance, the man responsible for his death.

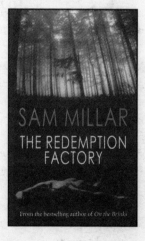

BRANDON